RESTITUTION

Books by Stephen H. Moriarty

Bill Duncan series
Restitution

Coming Soon!
Reckoning at Paradise Lake
A Bill Duncan mystery

RESTITUTION

Stephen H. Moriarty

SPEAKING VOLUMES, LLC
NAPLES, FLORIDA
2022

Restitution

Cover design by Hannah Linder

ISBN 978-1-64540-697-6

For Marie Louise
My Steady and Guiding Light

Acknowledgments

I am fortunate to have had the benefit of several friends and fellow authors to assist me in the preparation of Restitution. Whether it was catching mistakes or offering guidance, I am indebted to Nick Bruner and Angela Glasscock of the Writers of Chantilly, along with Trish Harman, a writer and former detective. The insights of Molly Moore, an accomplished journalist and author as well as a dear friend, were invaluable.

Ginger Moran showed me how to begin and complete a novel, and David Tabatsky did a masterful job of editing. The efforts of Nancy Rosenfeld, my agent, made this book possible.

The story is a work of fiction but without question some of my colleagues over the years contributed to it, albeit unwittingly. I have drawn heavily from watching and learning from Robert F. Horan and Rodney G. Leffler, two of the finest trial lawyers I ever saw, and the many police officers and detectives with whom I had the pleasure and privilege of working.

As a final note I must credit Sr. Laurence Bucher, O.S.B., a teacher and mentor, for inspiring me to write at all. She never heard an excuse worth accepting.

Chapter One

Lawyer Needs a Lawyer

"My lawyer."

I never thought I would use these two words together. I must now get accustomed to other words as well.

The state bar refers to me as Respondent.

To the police, I am Suspect.

If indicted, I will be Defendant.

I am accused of convicting a man through fraudulent evidence and am under investigation for murder. If the prosecution is successful, I will be disbarred and could become a long-term resident of the Virginia state penal system.

My lawyer.

I have a lawyer.

He is good. One of the best. He has been my colleague and friend for a dozen years. A former prosecutor, his skill in the courtroom and dedication to preparation are unmatched.

He has been patient with me, but I have strained the bonds of our friendship. I've behaved like a typical criminal client, calling repeatedly, venting about my unfair predicament, seeking any reason I can find to give me hope. Worse, I have not been fully truthful with my lawyer. Despite that, I seek the comfort of his counsel, telling me everything will go away and that one day I will have my life back.

He and I both know he cannot provide this relief.

My predicament is of my own making. Like Icarus, flying too near the sun, I have offended the gods of ambition. Some might say it was flavored with a too-strong dose of arrogance. Combined with a modicum of success, it created a lethal elixir that now threatens to poison my career and even deprive me of the liberty I have taken for granted.

Throughout my career of more than a decade, I have protected the community I call home. As a prosecutor, my purpose has been to discern the blameless from the culpable, separate the malignant from the benign, to speak for victims and pursue punishment of the guilty.

My lawyer has instructed me to write down what happened rather than merely telling him at our first meeting. He has found this method more likely to produce a clear rendition of the facts, as I see them, for him to best understand the case before he interrogates me and begins pretrial preparation.

This report will form the foundation of what he analyzes when we have our first serious attorney-client conference. It will also force me to confront the repercussions of my actions.

I will soon learn whom I can trust.

***

Memorandum

To: Eugene L. Cresswell, Attorney

From: William R. Duncan, Client

Re: Pending Charges; Attorney-Client Privileged Communication

Part I

Enclosed and following is the memo you requested. It has been more challenging than I'd expected and will take several installments. Thank goodness for the attorney-client privilege.

Restitution

If this correspondence ever sees the light of day, a good number of people will be out of luck (and probably out of work, if not forced to leave the jurisdiction).

I will try to cover all the bases. You may see something in my words that I have missed. Perhaps you can tell me where my instincts let me down, what details I've overlooked and how by trying to get a miserable miscreant off the streets I became a defendant myself.

You have been my good friend for many years. I will try not to abuse that, but when I do, please have patience and just remember that I am depending on you to save my ass.

Chapter Two

Hand Off

Few places on earth reek of tension more than the lobby of a courthouse in the hour before trials begin. The air is thick, humid and full of the steady hum and rattle of people in various stages of peril. They wander from bulletin boards to the information desk, seeking the location of their tribunal. They are here for cases ranging from traffic infractions to murder, corporate disputes to divorce. For all these individuals, today's date has been circled on their calendars for months, their lives held in place until the issues involved have been decided. Lawyers pull clattering carts, loaded with boxes of binders representing years of work and trial preparation, all done under the abiding pressure and fear of losing. While others have ground through their daily lives, groping with personal challenges, these lawyers have spent countless days and nights immersed in the evidence that form cases, which will forever impact their clients' lives.

My office is on the second floor. I look down from the atrium outside it onto the teeming excitement of another day's dramas, tragedies, and occasional comedies. The police stand at the windows that line the front of the building, sipping coffee as they watch pretty girls silhouetted by the morning sun, shining across the courtyard and through their summer dresses. Detectives shepherd their witnesses; bailiffs herd potential jurors, and bail bondsmen seek out their own clients, ensuring that they have returned as promised. People in suits, who understand the importance of showing the court its due respect, mingle with those who dress as if their next appointment is on a construction site.

I leap into this boiling pot of human energy every day. I look forward to it each morning and miss it when I'm away. I am the Deputy Commonwealth's Attorney, a prosecutor for Jefferson County, second in command of the office and doing the job for which I'd trained and hoped for years to secure. On good days, I swear I could do it forever.

It's not just what I do. It's who I am.

I never planned on being a career prosecutor. Doing it for a few years, getting plenty of trial experience and then moving on to private practice always seemed like the direction I'd follow. Countless other Assistant Commonwealth's Attorneys – ACAs – including my own lawyer, have followed that path successfully. But the cases kept coming, the months stretched into years, and after a decade I was still having way too much fun.

Gene Cresswell, of all people, appreciates that.

The standard refrain we always heard from former prosecutors who entered private practice is "you won't make any money at it, but you'll never have more fun practicing law." The compensation, if one can call it that, lies in the rush of trying and winning cases. A crime is committed, a bad guy is charged, the case is built and prepared, twelve people from the community that was victimized by his actions are summoned to sit in judgment and, if we do our job properly, they're convinced of his guilt beyond a reasonable doubt. Through my efforts he will be dispatched to the penitentiary, exiting through the side door of the courtroom in the hands of bailiffs, my name and face among his last memories of freedom.

I send no invoices and bill no hours. A good job has been done and I conclude the day drinking with my fellow prosecutors, laughing about the things ostensibly normal people do and say in courtrooms, celebrating that we are the finest trial lawyers in all the land and will do this forever, even though we know that several of us will depart each year for less frantic and more highly paid endeavors.

We resemble a ragtag athletic team more than a law firm, and our boss, Mason "Mac" McGuire, revels in that, too. Reconvening in the back of the office after hours, in that so-called library where we gather, putting our feet up on the table and recounting the things we've seen and occasionally done in court that day, can't be described to or understood by outsiders. We regale each other with what defendants and witnesses say, tricks that defense lawyers think will work, rulings that judges make and oddball questions that cops ask us. Where else can someone go home at night, sides aching from laughing so hard at what passes for work?

***

It was no great surprise one day when Casey Butler caught me in the hallway outside our offices and reminded me of a pending trial. He often found a way to get out of a case that he'd brought upstairs, based on the slender hope that the defendant would plead guilty. He'd covered a preliminary hearing for me a couple of months earlier and lost track of it. I'd forgotten about it as well, and the office docket indicated it was scheduled for a guilty plea. It turned out to be set for a three-day jury trial, beginning in two days.

It was my case at its inception, and as it was logged on our calendar as a guilty plea, I was still assigned to it. The general rule in the office is that if it goes to trial, the prosecutor that put on the preliminary hearing tries the case upstairs. You touch it, you keep it. But Casey turned out to have a scheduling conflict, which led him to me, so I agreed to take back the case.

I asked about the charges. I know what any normal person, let alone a lawyer, would be thinking: why take it before I knew anything about it? But that's how this goes. One of us was going to get stuck with it, probably me, and besides, I'll try just about anything. Half the fun of this job is slapping it together at the last minute and on the fly, preparing as quickly as possible.

The charges were attempted rape and malicious wounding. Casey's other trial was a check-kiting scheme. He loves that stuff. He reminded me about this case as he gave it back. A young girl got picked up by a guy named Hausner at the Noncommissioned Officer's Club over at the local army base, who then beat the daylights out of her when she declined his romantic overtures. She ID'd him in a line-up and her co-pilot for the evening did, too. It looked winnable.

I pulled the file. That should have been the second time I got suspicious. I had no idea what was up, but it was clear that something wasn't right. I remembered asking Casey to cover the preliminary hearing because I had been in the middle of another trial. As with most sex crimes, all he had to do was put on the victim, have her summarize the event and point out the culprit in court. But it had to be one of the more serious cases Casey had ever handled, even at that stage. Despite that, the file was thin, containing only the blue sheet that the office administrator gives us when felonies are assigned, and a copy of the indictment. I found the names of the defendant and his lawyer, the charges, and that's about it. Casey had written a few notes from the prelim on the blue sheet, like the names of the victim and the corroborating witness, but little else.

What was also missing was a pre-trial discovery motion and order. That meant the defendant didn't make a formal request to get access to the evidence. If he had, Rule 3A:11 entitles us to know if he was going to present an alibi along with a summary of what it was. That would

7

give us an opportunity to investigate, corroborate or disprove it. Not seeking discovery to hide an alibi was a risky tactic but one occasionally used by sharp defense attorneys. The file made the case looked like a guilty plea, but nothing in the file confirmed it.

Then I saw the name of the defense attorney. Tommy Shea, "Tommy the Titmouse," as he was known, an ornery little Irish pit bull. I winced when I thought about having to put up with his ingratiating brogue for three days, the trial's time estimate. The more confident he gets, the thicker it comes out of his weaselly little mouth. There was no doubt in my mind that he had an alibi up his sleeve. No way he'd settle for just challenging the victim's identification of the defendant. As obnoxious as he can be, Shea wouldn't have forgotten to seek discovery or rely on our generosity with evidence. If he was taking this to trial, he had a plan and didn't think he needed any discovery from us because his plan included a well-constructed alibi. That's the only thing that made any sense.

Shea can't be underestimated. He's been in this business for a long time. Probably more than twenty years. President of the state criminal bar a couple of times and, if we're to believe his boasting, he has the ear of the governor when it comes to appointing judges. When it comes to close cases, that rumor alone gives him a few points with the local bench.

At least the detective's name was in the office file. J.R. Dixon. I'd worked with him in the past and even though I've been underwhelmed by his work ethic and attention to detail, he didn't like to be embarrassed so he usually brought a tight case.

I called Police HQ, Criminal Investigations Bureau, to track down Dixon and his file, because I sure wasn't getting anything out of Casey's. It was well after five by then, and there was no way Dixon would ever be working late. But the shift supervisor pulled the detective's file for me and left it at the duty sergeant's desk. I headed right over.

I had plans to see Charlotte that evening, but when I tried to beg off, she insisted on coming over and helping me prepare the case. She worked in a big law firm doing corporate contracts, real estate development documents, and other high-brow transactions all day.

"The chance to dig my hands into some real cops-and-robbers stuff is more than I can pass up," she said.

Sometimes I think what she really enjoys in our relationship is hearing about the crazy things people do, the trials, the lawyers, and most of all, the judges. She had been a judicial law clerk, right out of law school, so she was familiar with the Jefferson courthouse and its motley inhabitants. She volunteered to pick up dinner and meet at my place to help me prepare this mess for trial.

She arrived at my home with enough Chinese food to feed a family and scampered upstairs, eager to begin. As good a lawyer as she has proven to be, she is an even better girlfriend. Instead of being affronted by my unexpected need to work through a date, she leaped to help prepare the Hausner case.

Dixon's file was a lot thicker than the minimal one Casey had left me. There were over a hundred photographs, plus pages and pages of notes, some handwritten and some typed.

"Holy cats!" Charlotte said. "Look at these pictures!"

Many were of the crime scene, but she held the ones showing the victim's injuries. The young woman had been cleaned up at the hospital, but the lead officer had been sharp enough to take some shots before she was wrapped in bandages and plaster. There were tire tracks on her left arm and leg.

"Who's the current heavyweight champion?" Charlotte said.

"That's a pretty odd question," I said. "Why?"

"Because it looks like this girl went a few rounds with him," she said, "and he must have been really angry."

Chapter Three

The Case

I live in the perfect place for a young, single, underpaid lawyer. The Sandersons, old family friends, have an estate of nearly twenty acres, mostly wooded with perhaps a quarter of the land cleared. The main house sits on its highest point. Behind it lies what they call their carriage house, formerly a barn to shelter maintenance equipment, which now serves as my home. The Sandersons travel most of the year, so I have the run of a tennis court, a pool, an outdoor kitchen and grill behind the main house, and the pond. My rent, such as it is, consists of looking after the property and providing evidence of regular activity.

The carriage house is bigger than the home where my parents raised my three brothers and me. It has two stories. The equipment and tools have been removed from the ground floor and it has been refurbished into sitting rooms and a library. I live on the upper floor, where French doors fill most of the walls, all opening to balconies on the front and back. The kitchen, dining room and the only bedroom are also on this level.

Charlotte and I spread out Dixon's file in the dining room and worked through the witness notes. She is a smart lawyer, good at figuring out important details and getting to the meat of a case.

"I need you to help me establish the facts and which witnesses are the best ones to get them into evidence," I said.

She'd spent two years as a law clerk, watching trials, huddling with judges in chambers and listening to them bore in on salient facts, relevant nuances that confirmed or demolished credibility, and determined the success or failures of lawyers like me.

"The elements of the crimes are simple enough and the victim should be able to testify to almost all of them," I said. "But the jury needs to see more. The investigation, motive, opportunity. All that stuff they've come to expect in a serious case."

"My God, Bill," she said, still staring at the pictures. "What kind of animal is he?"

There was a hospital report consisting of the usual abbreviations and sterile review of the victim's condition.

"Broken facial bones, along with her right arm and femur, and lacerations on her body consistent with tire tracks," I read. "The report also indicates she had a blood alcohol content of .26 when they got her to the Emergency Room."

Charlotte looked up at me with raised eyebrows.

".26?"

"Yeah."

I sat back in my chair.

"Once Shea finds out, he'll hammer her. He'll argue that there's no way they can believe her memory, let alone identify her assailant. He'll be aiming the jury toward reasonable doubt from the beginning of this trial to its godforsaken end."

I put the report on the table.

"You can't hide it," Charlotte said. "There's no question it'll come out eventually."

"I know. I'll have to get it out there on my own, and I'll show that Hausner is the one that fed enough drinks to her over the course of the evening to register such an absurdly high BAC. If I let Shea bring out her blood level on cross-examination, the jury will think I was trying to hide it from them."

Charlotte turned pages in the file.

"Amanda Fontaine, aged twenty."

She looked up at me.

"Underage civilian. How did she get on the base and into that bar?"

"Keep reading," I said.

After a moment she nodded.

"Daughter of a retired general. Went there with a friend, also a military daughter. Amanda's father was stationed at the Pentagon for his last assignment and now runs some sort of a defense consulting firm."

"I read the notes about the incident date," I said. "Check those and tell me what you think."

She tapped a pencil against her forehead.

"She danced with several soldiers until one particular guy noticed her. He bought her all those drinks and hung with her the rest of the night."

"Not exactly original or creative, but a tried-and-true strategy," I said.

"Does it work for you?" she said. "Never mind. Her statement indicates that they left together some time after midnight. She thought they were going to his place. Instead, he drove her to a nearby park, and by then it was raining. He turned aggressive, got brutal, and somehow, she escaped from his car. Then he ran her over with it."

"There's a time lag between the offense and arrest," I said. "How did he get ID'd?"

"It looks like he got scared off by some kids who'd been out driving around and went to the same park. Probably had in mind a little of what Hausner was planning but with more cooperation. Anyway, they saw the girl get hit and the car drive off. One of them said it was a light-colored Bonneville. They wrapped her in a blanket and took her to County ER."

"Good thing they came along," I said. "That girl would have died out there and we'd have had no witnesses to any of it."

Charlotte held her head.

Dixon's file showed that the police arrived at the scene soon after and the rain had stopped by dawn. The photographs they took indicated where Hausner's car had been parked and the path he'd followed, chasing Amanda, and fleeing out the gate. By linking up the pictures, we could see each of the curbs he'd hurdled and scraped, leaving debris in his wake as he ran down that poor girl. Rust and dirt from the bottom of the car and some mulch and grass from the medians stretched across the parking lot. The final picture showed a soaked blouse, mashed into the asphalt, tire treads still embedded in it.

"How did they find Hausner?" Charlotte said. "It had to be a cold trail after that night."

I read deeper into the investigation notes.

"It took the police a while to figure out it was Hausner. He owns a Ford Explorer, but his wife drives a silver Bonneville," I said. "So, they didn't even identify the correct vehicle for quite a while. That's why there are no prints, blood, or DNA evidence. Here are some photos."

I handed them to Charlotte.

"They show the bottom, all scratched, and look—the inside of one of the front wheel wells is damaged."

I pointed to one photo in particular.

"It's partially disconnected and missing a fastener, or a bolt of some kind."

"Here's something else," Charlotte said. "One last piece of evidence. The night shift clerk at a 7-Eleven, which is not far from the crime scene, found some of the girl's clothing and her purse in the store's dumpster the next morning. He put the time they'd been dumped at somewhere between midnight and six a.m., because that's when he'd put trash in there himself. He found Amanda's things on top of the first load when he went to leave the second."

I sat up.

"Where's that 7-Eleven?"

"Get this. Just a mile from the park, and on the corner of the main road and Brinkman Court, which is a dead end. Hausner lives in an apartment on Brinkman not more than a hundred yards from the dumpster."

She flipped through the file.

"Here's the map. Coming from Riverside Park, he'd have to make a left turn into Brinkman and there's the 7-Eleven. The dumpster is on the edge of the parking lot. Quite a coincidence that her stuff got tossed there, just down the street from the suspect's home and within a few hours of the offense."

"Charlotte, if this lawyer thing doesn't work out for you," I said, "try being a cop. You love this stuff."

Chapter Four

Victim

Amanda's home number was in the file, so I called. A man answered.

"Hello, this is Bill Duncan of the Jefferson County Commonwealth's Attorney's office. May I speak with Amanda?"

As a rule, this conversation should have happened long before and in person, but thanks to Casey Butler's inattention, I had no alternative but to do it on the eve of trial, by telephone. I held the phone so Charlotte could hear Amanda.

"One moment," the man said, and I listened as he put down the telephone. "It's a prosecutor, honey. Do you want to talk to him?"

I heard voices deeper in the room, and what sounded like weeping. Then she picked up.

"This is Amanda."

I gave her a moment to collect herself and explained that the prosecutor she'd met at the preliminary hearing had another trial that was running over, so I was stepping in for him. I assured her that I was Casey's senior and that she was in good, experienced hands.

It's a conversation I dislike but have had more times than I can count. No victim wants to think that her case has been handed off to another lawyer at the last minute. They're left feeling that this event, the most significant of their recent lives, isn't important enough to merit our complete attention. Their testimony often suffers accordingly.

"Let me move to a different room," she said.

"Sure."

Describing a sex crime is never easy for a victim under any circumstances, let alone within earshot of a parent. When I asked, she admitted she was drunk when she left the NCO club, which was consistent with her BAC a couple of hours later.

"He gave me a few drinks, fancy ones with little umbrellas. Tequila Sunrises, I think. And we danced. He was a really good dancer."

"Where did he say he was taking you?"

"He asked if I wanted to listen to music and if I'd like to go to his house."

"Why did you leave with him?"

I had to ask her that and the silence gave away her answer.

What she hoped or expected to happen there was irrelevant for our case, so I left it at that. Without any doubt, reasonable or otherwise, she didn't leave the NCO club with the intention of being raped and beaten nearly to death.

"Did you know where he took you? Did you recognize it?"

"No. I don't really remember much of that. I was really wasted."

"Tell me what happened there. I know it's hard, but we need to be clear enough for the jury to understand. Can you do that, Amanda?"

I used her first name in the hope that she'd feel comfortable and trust me.

"Oh, okay. I'll try."

I could barely hear speaking above a whisper.

"I thought we were going to his house. Suddenly the car stopped, and he turned off the engine. We kissed a little. A lot, I guess. He started to grab me, like really really hard. Then he said, uh, he said . . . he wanted me to do stuff."

Amanda began to cry, her voice creeping up higher and higher until it was nearly inaudible. It was a tough conversation, but I had to make her tell me. She would be saying these same things in an open court-room two days hence to total strangers.

17

Charlotte wrote furiously, taking down what the girl said, noting her own questions.

"When you said 'no,' Amanda, tell me what he did next. You know that I have read the file and understand. But I have to hear it from you. There is no reason to be ashamed and if we're going to make sure he gets what he deserves, you need to be able to say it and be clear."

She whimpered, blew her nose, and began again, speaking in halting, measured words, trying not to cry.

"He called me a stupid bitch. Then he grabbed my hair and pushed my face against the dashboard. I tried to get my hands up to protect myself but somehow, I couldn't. He was doing it so fast I couldn't reach out. All I could see was red, and I hurt, and I could hear my head banging against the dashboard."

Her voice broke again, and she went silent for a moment. Charlotte was agitated, got up and walked around the room, gripping her head in her hands.

"I really thought I was going to die in that car," Amanda said. "I couldn't see anything, and blood was in my mouth so I could hardly breathe."

She sobbed. I gave her a moment to breathe.

"How did you get out of his car?"

"I'm not really sure," she said. "I thought he was tying me up or something. You know, I was so drunk and hurting. But then I realized he was ripping off my clothes. Then, he just kicked open the door and shoved me out. I was cold, it was raining, and the pavement hurt. I thought he was going to grab me again, but he didn't get out of the car, so I got up and tried to run away."

"Did he say anything else to you at that point?"

"I don't know. If he did, I couldn't hear it. But, like, you know, I thought he was going to kill me in that car so I got away as fast as I could. I saw the lights of another car and tried to run to it."

I looked at Charlotte who appeared shocked.

"Do you know how it is in nightmares, when you try to run or scream and can't do either one?" Amanda said. "That's what it was, like I could barely move my feet. I couldn't scream. I just tried to keep moving. Then his car hit me."

She stopped talking and began crying again.

"That's all I remember before all the lights and doctors at the hospital. I still don't know how I got there. I don't remember."

I gave her another moment before asking my last question.

"Amanda, the file says that when you got to the hospital you told them you'd been raped. Do you remember that?"

"Not really, but later the next day a detective asked me about it. He told me I'd been screaming that," she said. "But look, I was drunk out of my mind, he'd beaten me bad and, you know, I just didn't know what all had happened. But, I mean, that guy took off my clothes and was, you know, touching me and . . ."

"And you figured that meant rape, is that it?"

"Yeah. But, you know, that didn't happen. He sure tried, though."

Piecing this together, it seemed like Hausner had every intention of raping Amanda in the front seat of that car, and just when he had gotten her clothes off the other vehicle showed up in the park, headlights right on him. Hausner panicked and kicked Amanda out. He must have realized the danger he was in and tried to kill her before she could say what had happened. Maybe he'd planned on killing her anyway. But once those kids showed up, he couldn't risk staying at the park long enough to be identified.

My mind was racing with the details, so I slowed down to go over courtroom procedures, like jury selection, with Amanda for a few minutes. We agreed to meet at nine a.m. in my office two days later, on the morning of the trial.

When I hung up, Charlotte spoke right away.

"What do you think of Amanda?"

I thought for a moment.

"Probably a normal girl. She got careless, did exactly what every parent says not to do, and the worst thing *almost* happened."

Charlotte took a breath.

"I'll guarantee you; she won't leave a bar with a stranger again," I said. "Ever."

"I don't know how you do this stuff, Bill. I couldn't handle it. It's one thing to read about it or watch the trials. But this, the right-in-there, up-close-and-personal stuff, with victims ... I nodded and kind of shrugged.

"Anyway," she said. "That was hard."

"I guess. But it has to be done before every trial. Girls like that, the last thing she ever expected that night when she was getting ready to go out, putting on make-up and wondering who she'd meet, was that she'd wind up in the middle of a serious felony trial, telling strangers about practically being raped and killed."

Charlotte tapped her pencil on the table.

"How did they find Hausner, anyway?"

I raised an eyebrow.

"That is where this case gets interesting. Good police work. Amanda didn't know his name but she and her friend, Laura, came up with a decent description. The problem was that no one like that was stationed at the base. After a while, they figured him to be a guest, but since nobody the police questioned offered up a name it seemed that the trail had gone cold. That's when Dixon got a bright idea. He assigned April Winston to troll for the guy."

April was one of the first policewomen to make it past issuing parking tickets for Jefferson County. She is above average in height but slightly built. This belies a hidden quality. She is fearless.

"Sort of a stake-out. Detective Winston kept company with Laura at the NCO club every weekend for about a month, hoping to see the guy again. No luck. They called it off, thinking that he might have been an out-of-towner that wouldn't return. It made sense, to figure a guy like that would never come back to the scene."

I read her notes.

"One Saturday night, a couple months later and after April had quit coming to the club, Hausner showed up. Laura was there and saw him. She called April, who got there within an hour and quickly sidled up to him at the bar. He bought her a drink and danced with her a little."

I laughed. "Didn't try to take her home. I can't wait to needle her about that. But she got a good look at his face and then his license plate when he left. That gave her the chance to pull his DMV photo, put it in a line-up and show it to Amanda."

Charlotte nodded.

"Bingo," I said.

I put down the file. I always like working with April. Thorough, relentless, and smart.

"It didn't take April long to get the information she needed on the guy. Jason Hausner, former Army infantryman, employed and living nearby. When she connected his address to the 7-Eleven on the corner, she knew she had her man. The police picked him up. He denied everything and hired the Titmouse."

Solid police work.

"April dug further, and after interviewing the kids from the park who saw the incident, she checked more DMV records. That's how she learned that Hausner's wife owned a car, the same model the kids saw that night. She waited until it was parked outside Hausner's apartment building and did her own exterior search. She photographed the underside and all four of the wheel wells."

It was her pictures of the Pontiac I found in Dixon's file. I shook my head.

"What?" Charlotte said.

"Well, as some supervisors will do, April got bumped. Not completely off the case, just subordinated to a senior detective. Absurd. She'd been the one to close it, not Dixon. But he took it back."

"What was so important about this case that it called for a new detective in charge?" said Charlotte. "Isn't that unusual?"

"Go back to what you read earlier, and it might become clear. What did you say Amanda's father did?"

Turning to the section of the file containing the telephone notes, I related the information on Amanda's family. Her father wasn't just a consultant; he was the CEO of Global Solutions International, a major defense contractor headquartered near the Pentagon. Nothing was betrayed in the notes, of course, but after working with cops for ten years I knew something was up, and it wasn't dissatisfaction with April Winston's investigation.

"Charlotte, a case like this only comes along every so often. Most cops work their twenty years then spend the next twenty supplementing their retirement with assorted jobs. Police work someplace else, high school coaching, or maybe even courthouse security. You know, as bailiffs. The detective who brings to justice the man who damn near killed a general's daughter might just have an opportunity awaiting him."

"What do you know about this general?" Charlotte said.

"Not a thing. But defense is big business around here, and it's in the nature of those companies to have security divisions within them. One of the first lessons I learned when I started out working on criminal investigations was that there are no coincidences."

I pulled a page from the file.

"Here. The telephone log shows an inordinate number of calls to General Fontaine, keeping him apprised of the investigation. As a rule, cops think that victims and their families get in the way of police work, often to the point of sheer rudeness. To call this girl's father three to four times a week was either extremely polite or heinously pandering."

I knew Dixon. He didn't even have the manners of a footstool. He'd found a nest already feathered for him. He pulled rank and reassigned the case to himself, overseeing April, of course, and all he had to do was coordinate bringing the witnesses and evidence to trial. All the heavy lifting had been done.

At around midnight I closed the file. Charlotte and I cleaned up and put away the dishes.

"One last question, counselor," she said. "What if you lose?"

A simple question, but one that every trial lawyer avoids asking.

"It's like what the mothers of Spartan warriors told their sons as they went off to battle," I said. " 'Come back with your shield, or on it.' I can't think about losing. Between now and when that jury gets the case in a few days, the fight is on. Every ounce of my focus has to be on winning this thing."

I closed a cabinet door and turned to Charlotte.

"I don't have time to think about losing."

Before leaving the kitchen, she handed me a fortune cookie.

"Tell me what it says."

She smiled. I read the slip of paper.

"Life holds many mysteries."
Indeed, it does. And then some.

Chapter Five

Evidence

I met April Winston a few years ago. A serial rapist had been haunting the Rulonne area of the County for two years and when all the police dragnets and profiles failed, the department sent April out to walk the bike trails and parks at night, armed with a radio transmitter and a pistol. This was an act of desperation, not confidence. After the "Rulonne Rapist," as the papers named him, struck for the tenth time, defying any hope of capture, traditional procedure was cast aside.

She volunteered, of course, still trying to be one of the guys and hoping to prove she wasn't afraid of anything. The department had employed female officers for several years, but April was the first to be elevated to detective and she wanted to dispel any suspicions that she just filled a quota. No one called her "the quota babe" after she brought home the Rulonne Rapist, however, although they did come up with a few more nicknames.

After a week of acting as bait for the culprit, she'd finally established a pattern and a familiar path. She figured that the guy was not acting at random, hence his ability to avoid capture for so long. She started walking in the same area at the same times. The night he finally slipped out from behind a tree was the last time anyone took April for granted.

He grabbed her by the forearm, quickly twisting it behind her as his other arm went around her neck. He pulled her among the trees that lined the adjacent municipal golf course, away from any lights, and ordered her to keep quiet or he'd kill her. She waited for the right moment, when he pushed her to the ground. That's when she put the Glock barrel in his face and grabbed a fistful of his hair with her other hand. Using that moment of surprise, she pulled him over so that she straddled him, keeping the gun in place. No one knows what she said to him, but when he tried to escape, she beat him half to death with that pistol.

The surveillance crew was stationed at a distance, of course, and heard nothing from her on the radio. They were alerted by the man's wails of pain. Running as fast as they could, they arrived to find April standing over him, reciting the Miranda warning. Her left arm hung limp at her side, elbow dislocated. He lay on the grass, unconscious, still un-cuffed and soaked in his own blood.

"I think he'll come peacefully now," was all she said.

When I met with April to prepare for the preliminary hearing, she told me she'd never taken off her pistol's safety.

"Might have shot myself," she said. "Besides, he never knew."

I liked her a lot after that. When I saw that April had been on the Hausner case I figured it was a good investigation. They set her up with a base ID and she started hanging around the NCO club with Laura, Amanda's friend, looking for a guy about 6'1", 180 pounds, white and sporting a couple tattoos. That narrowed it down to just about 80 percent of the guys on base.

But just like in Rulonne, April found her man.

As I write these notes to Gene, I am seeing events in a different light than when I was living through them. I hope he can make heads or tails out of it because it has me perplexed.

***

Every case has problems that arise at the last minute, and in this one, the first issue was that 7-Eleven clerk.

The day before trial I'd put in a call to Dixon and left a message to confirm that the guy was coming. That night, I called the number in Dixon's file over and over. No answer. Not even a recording. A subpoena had been issued for him, but it was posted on his apartment door and not served in person. That was valid service for court purposes, but it was possible he didn't know about it. A decent detective keeps tabs on his witnesses. Dixon never called me back. The location of Amanda's purse and other belongings in the dumpster, right there within sight of Hausner's apartment, was looking pretty critical. Without the clerk, I probably couldn't get those things admitted into evidence, and without them the relevance of proximity to Hausner's home disappeared, too. Again, I was pretty sure the Titmouse didn't know we had it since it looked like the 7-Eleven guy didn't testify at the prelim.

I tried to figure a way to get those things admitted into evidence without the clerk, and even had Charlotte do some research for me on that. No luck. I couldn't prove the chain of custody of the evidence without the clerk because he'd taken it out of the dumpster before the police arrived. He thought he was doing them a favor by bringing it inside since it was raining. Instead, he just made himself indispensable. Charlotte suggested I consider requesting a postponement.

"I don't like the idea of showing any weakness to Shea," I said.

"You don't want to risk losing this case because of a missing witness, do you?"

She could be annoying that way.

The last thing I did that night was take a long, hard look at all those photos. Charlotte wanted to pick out the good ones, but I was going to be the one standing in front of that jury, trying to beat Tommy Shea, and overcome the mountain of reasonable doubt he would construct. I had to be the one to pick out the photos to use as evidence.

The victim shots were easy. The jury would see her in person, seemingly recovered, so the pictures had to demonstrate the destruction Hausner had wreaked on her face and body. The parking lot was a little tougher because the crime scene officer had taken so many. I settled on a few that, when strung together, revealed the path Hausner's car had taken, jumping the median curbs and running down Amanda on his way out. The trail of scrapings and crushed clothing would show just how hard he tried to kill her.

I took a final run through the pictures, looking for something I could link to the Bonneville's damaged wheel well. Then it happened—one of those moments every trial lawyer hopes to experience from time to time, like a gambler drawing to an inside straight.

There it was, lying in the midst of scattered rust scrapings, mulch, and dirt—a single, solitary, all by its lonesome greasy bolt. There was only one photo of it. The rest of the parking lot was pristine, since it had been paved and striped only a few days before the incident.

This was it. Between the damaged undercarriage of the Bonneville and the scrapes over the cement medians, the bolt couldn't have come from anything but the car belonging to the unlucky Mrs. Hausner. Since Shea hadn't asked for any discovery, I figured he knew nothing about it. There was no mention about it in the file, either. Not a single word.

Dixon, in his typical fashion, had probably just taken the photos he'd gotten from the crime scene guys and April and stuffed them into a folder, never looking at them closely. No one on the scene would have known the significance of that single small bolt since Hausner wasn't ID'd and his car wasn't checked out for several more weeks, revealing that it was damaged and missing a fastener. April might have noticed it eventually, if only she'd been left on the case. Casey Butler sure hadn't.

In that moment, I realized I was the only person who knew about this thing. I buried the picture in the string of photos that would bring to life the story I would tell the jury in the morning. This is the place where Jason Hausner attempted to rape and kill Amanda Fontaine. Here is where she thought she would die. Here is how she looked when he failed to take her life.

Things were shaping up.

My guess was that the Titmouse wouldn't look closely at the pictures when I asked the crime scene officer to identify and show them to the jury. Shea would try to stake out the high ground with his usual routine.

"It's a shame what happened to this young lady," he'd say, "out and about picking up stray soldiers, but it wasn't Mr. Hausner who did this to her."

That would probably be his line of defense, endearingly delivered in that damned brogue of his. Closely reviewing or objecting to pictures of the crime scene would be inconsistent with that approach and would imply that he had something to hide.

As I finished drafting my witness questions, I had everything lined up except that 7-Eleven clerk. How tough could that be? All I needed was a few minutes with him. I'd tell him he'd need to identify the stuff he'd pulled from the dumpster. We'd show a map of the crime scene, the location of the 7-Eleven, and where Hausner lived just down the street.

All neat and tidy. What could go wrong?

Chapter Six

Witness

The night before a trial I find it nearly impossible to sleep. Preparing up to the last-minute leaves my mind racing, combing through the facts and legal hurdles long after I have put aside the books, files, photographs and cases to seek a few hours of rest. It is not uncommon for me to turn on the light, get up and return to the kitchen table to re-read a case or jot down notes. This happens several times in what little remains of the night.

When I do finally sleep, it's not for long, because once I wake up I immediately calculate how many hours remain until the trial begins. It's never enough, so I give up and get dressed and head to the courthouse.

On the day of the Hausner trial, I still had some unresolved matters to address before entering the courtroom for what promised to be a battle. The trial would undoubtedly go for at least two days, possibly three, and I needed to assemble jury instructions. These are the statements of law that the judge will read to the jury just before the two lawyers make their closing arguments, after which the jury will be taken away to deliberate. They are comprised of standardized recitations, setting out the so-called "elements of the crime," the things the jury must find that the defendant did in order to convict him of the offenses he is accused of having committed. They also contain certain directions and explanations, such as what jurors should consider and ignore, like the opinions of their friends and family members.

But chief among the things I needed to do was find Ronald Whitacre, the 7-Eleven clerk, and determine how to get Amanda's possessions, the ones he found in the dumpster, presented in court and put before the jury. Once I did that, I would show him the evidence, refresh his memory, coax his recollection of how and when he discovered them, and then quickly go over the questions I intended to ask him on the witness stand.

After depositing the files and my notes in my office, I made a beeline to the Police Liaison desk, where officers and detectives who will be in court that day must report and sign in. I checked the morning's docket, too, hoping to find which judge had been assigned to the case, but it wasn't posted yet.

Dixon had already arrived and was at a far table nursing a cup of coffee. Spread out before him were the contents of a box, with each item in a zip-lock bag and labelled. These were Amanda's purse and the clothing, found in the 7-Eleven dumpster.

"Have you found him? The clerk, what's his name?" I asked Dixon without pausing for any morning salutations.

"I called his number until nearly midnight."

Dixon looked up slowly with undisguised and weary impatience. Many of the career cops care little for the prosecutors, whom they view as opportunists using law enforcement as a stepping-stone to higher career aspirations. In fact, some of my colleagues are rude and dismissive of the police, whom they see as their inferiors, generating a sometimes impenetrable tension between members of what should be a unified team. Developing the respect and trust of the police, which is far more difficult but important, takes not only years but concentrated effort. I learned that long ago through the advice of my elder Assistant Commonwealth's Attorneys and began riding with officers at night, seeking their insight into the criminal world, buying them breakfast at all-night diners and taking their calls at home, no matter the day or the hour.

"He ain't here," Dixon finally said. "He ain't gonna be here."

"What the hell happened? He's under subpoena."

I spun through what now had to be revised before the trial began. The opening statement: could I mention the purse at all? Amanda: could I show the items to her so that she could identify them if the clerk was not there to say he'd pulled them from the trash only hours after she was stripped of them and run down?

"He's Air Force. Got transferred. Someplace in Georgia. He was probably gone before the subpoena was put on his door."

"Dammit! This screws up everything."

I looked around the room without speaking. This was my case now. Not Dixon's. Not Butler's. I began to regroup.

"Is there any way we can get that stuff into evidence without him? What's his name?"

"Ronald Whitacre," Dixon said. "Why don't you just ask Shea to stipulate to it? Save time for everyone, no need to call the clerk. You can spin him a little."

It was an idea. Hallway discussions of how to handle evidence, even among opponents, was not unusual. Neither side would yield an inch and would do no favors. But if a subtle advantage could be gained by conceding something that was likely to happen anyway, a smart tactician would often take advantage of it. Not objecting to evidence might convey to the jury that one has nothing to hide and no fear of the truth. Still, I couldn't see Shea going for it.

"Why would Shea do anything to help us? How does agreeing to the admission of our evidence help him in the least?"

Dixon shrugged.

"I don't know. You're the lawyer."

So far, Dixon had lived down to my expectations. His case, his witness, but my problem. Perhaps another angle was in order.

"Is there any way that we can get Amanda's things in through another witness?"

As little as I liked the notion, Dixon was the only person at that moment who might have an idea of how to connect the loose ends of this critical evidence and the defendant.

"Maybe I could make it. I was the one that got the call from dispatch, and I went to the 7-Eleven and met Whitacre," he said.

This was quite an admission for Dixon.

"Damned early on that Sunday morning, too."

I pondered this for a moment.

"But to provide evidence that Amanda's personals were found in the dumpster, we need a witness to say he saw them there. Whitacre's the only person able to do that."

Dixon wasn't persuaded.

"If you asked the question the right way, I could say I took possession of them at the 7-Eleven, where they'd been found in the dumpster down the street from Hausner's apartment. Kind of infer it looks like I was the one took 'em out of the dumpster myself."

That might work, unless Shea cross-examined Dixon in any detail. Even a cursory line of questioning would expose the lack of an essential witness, unless Dixon just lied, and then I'd have to pull the plug on it. If we just danced around it carefully and the Titmouse figured it out, he'd flog it over and over, demanding why the person who supposedly found Amanda's things wasn't present in court to own up to it in person.

No explanation of where Whitacre was, sweating his ass off in Georgia, training to become a better cook or some such thing would be admissible because Dixon was relying on hearsay as to his whereabouts. The admission of Amanda's purse would be denied, and not only would we fail to introduce it, we'd appear to have tried to slip improper evidence to the jury.

The Titmouse would remind them of it all day long. Besides, "inferring" something that wasn't true was something expected of defense lawyers, not prosecutors. Once we've lost their confidence, juries punish us.

Another possibility was that I could get Amanda to identify the purse and other items, then put Dixon on the stand after her to testify that he received it at the 7-Eleven from the clerk. We could establish Hausner's address separately, giving the effect of linking up the crime, purse, 7-Eleven and his home.

Perhaps I wouldn't even attempt to introduce her things, leaving the identification of it and Dixon's testimony hanging out there, waiting for Shea to draw more attention to them by objecting. Whether the purse was actually admitted would be irrelevant, once the jury had heard all that testimony.

There was still a risk. As damning as that purse could appear to be against Hausner, Shea would have good reason to scream about our failure to get it properly admitted and accuse the police and prosecution of trying to patch together a weak case in order to convict an innocent man whose only crime was having danced with the daughter of a general, who by her own admission was drunk and carousing with soldiers, even willing to go home with one of them.

I'd seen the Titmouse in action for years. He had no hesitation when it came to accusing us of stacking a case. It would call into question everything else we had.

I decided against it, and after giving it all the consideration I could muster in about thirty seconds, I took the direct route. I tracked down the eminent Thomas Eoghan Shea.

Chapter Seven

Titmouse

Tommy Shea grew up in New York City, the child of first-generation Irish immigrant parents. He rode the subway while attending City College of New York so that he could work in the family tailor shop between classes. When the draft saved him from a life resembling that of his father, he leaped at the opportunity. After serving a tour in Vietnam, he re-enlisted and was sent to Europe, where the chances of a healthy survival were much improved. A scrape or two introduced him to the Army lawyers, Judge Advocates Generals, and his interest was piqued.

Shea's story was well-known and he told it often. He decided that his fortunes lay not with the military but in the law. The former had simply too many rules and people telling him what to do. The latter had a structure that permitted his rambunctious character the flexibility to calculate, to improvise and most important, to perform.

He parlayed his GI benefits into finishing college and then a law degree in Virginia, where began his career in the Justice Department as a federal prosecutor. There, he honed his courtroom skills and when the first good offer came his way, he bolted for the other side to do criminal defense. At first, he took everything: drunk driving, shoplifting, bar fights—anything for a fee and experience. But before long, he focused on serious felonies: murder, theft, embezzlement, bribery, and even espionage cases came his way as his reputation grew. The general rule was that if someone was truly guilty and in need of a top lawyer, he went to Tommy Shea. If there was a chance of acquittal, Shea would find it.

He dressed impeccably, always wearing a suit, even to traffic court. French cuffs, gold tie clasp, silver hair perfectly cut and combed. He had put his family's humble immigrant past behind, now effecting the more respectable "lace curtain" Irish.

He got the nickname "Titmouse" from one of my colleagues, Kenton Raker. In the midst of a heated argument outside a courtroom but in full hearing of several onlookers, including members of the local bar always eager to disseminate courthouse gossip and slander, Shea was doing his routine. Arms waving, voice rising in pitch as well as volume, he denigrated Kent's case and a particular witness. His gambit was to intimidate the prosecutor into a plea deal without incarceration. But as stubborn as Shea was by nature, he'd met his match. When Shea took to pointing his finger into the chest of the much taller man, it was all Kent could stand.

Grabbing Shea by the wrist, Kent uttered the words we'd recount and repeat over drinks for years to come.

"Try it or plead it, you little titmouse," he said. "I'm done with your shanty Irish crap."

Shanty Irish, everything Shea had tried to escape for years. Kent later said that he figured Shea was never going to try that case, as hard as he was working for probation, so there was little to lose and perhaps something to gain by inciting him to lose his temper. But Shea never forgot the humiliation and every contact with him by any of us in the office resurrected his antagonism. No opportunity to embarrass us, any of us, would be missed.

It was with this in mind that I sought out the Titmouse forty-five minutes before trial. He was in the courthouse cafeteria, awaiting his client. I was relieved to see that Hausner hadn't arrived. I didn't want to talk to Shea in front of him or await the conclusion of their last-minute pretrial conversation. At least one thing was going right this morning.

"The honorable Mr. Shea. Good morning."

I held out my hand, and he took it.

"Why, Mr. Duncan, how are you this fine day? My favorite Scotsman. Or is it Englishman? I can never remember."

That was his way of staking out the high ground. He was 5'5" at best, in shoes, and it seemed to bother him, especially when he confronted others, like Kent or me, who were taller than six feet.

"Now, Mr. Shea, there's no need to be insulting at such an early hour. You'll certainly remember, I told you that 'Duncan' was originally D-U-N-Q-U-I-N, from the small town in County Kerry by that name."

I forced a smile, which was not exactly returned.

"I'm sure we've had this conversation before. That part of the Emerald Isle closest to America. Where the old kings of Ireland were, and all that."

"Oh yes, yes. I forgot. Age will do that to you," he said. "What do you have on for today? I've got a little tilt with your friend Butler this morning."

I took the seat across from him.

"That's why I tracked you down. Casey is wrapped up in a case of vastly more importance than this one and I've inherited the Hausner trial. It seems that you and I are together this morning."

Shea never let his eyes break from mine, but plainly considered the change this might impose on his strategy. He slowly turned his cup in circles before he spoke again.

"I scared him off, did I?"

He chuckled, his famous brogue starting to come out.

"But it appears that now I'm up against the first string. Is there anything we can do here, Billy, any way to resolve this unfortunate matter?"

"Well, Mr. Shea, what lies between a conviction for trying to rape and kill a girl on the one hand and walking out the back door of the courtroom? There's not much common ground as I see it."

"Yes, yes, I see your position. And, of course, I have no authority to speak for my client in this way. But I think he would heed my advice if you and I could reach an agreement."

He paused, eyes on me the entire time.

"I was thinking of a misdemeanor. Assault and Battery, twelve months with eleven suspended."

I would starve if I sought to make a living playing poker. I couldn't tell if he was serious. Had I missed something so grievous that I should consider watering down a case of two serious felonies to a single misdemeanor and thirty days in jail, something akin to what a repeat shoplifter might receive? I responded by smiling and saying nothing.

"Here's the way I see it, Billy," Shea finally said, breaking the silence. "The kids these days, they're all out there sleeping around, doing God-knows-what with total strangers. This girl got herself in a predicament with someone she didn't know, and mind you, I'm not saying it's Mr. Hausner, and she got herself hurt. Drunk, going home with strange men. What did she think was going to happen, a poetry reading? My goodness."

One lesson I learned early and the hard way was not to say too much at moments like this. But I couldn't let Shea's minimalization of the case stand.

"Breaking a dozen bones and running over Amanda with a car is a little more than a misunderstanding about who's in the mood for love, Mr. Shea."

The Titmouse feigned discomfort. His brow furrowed and his lips tightened in a grimace.

"How about this?" he said. "Amend the Malicious Wounding to A&B, thirty days to serve, *nolle pros* the other, and my client will make a civil admission on that business with the car. He has a $300,000 auto insurance policy and his statement would give her a direct claim against it."

This presented a turn of events I hadn't expected. Still, it showed that Shea was wary of the risk of conviction. I considered a moment before speaking.

"With the testimony of the witnesses we have, she has a shot at a civil claim anyway, with or without his admission of liability. I don't know much about this civil stuff, Mr. Shea, but I suspect that neither of us can bind his insurance company. She'll still have to wrestle with Robbins & Scanlan or one of those other defense firms. Heck, some of those guys are nearly as tough as you."

He chuckled at my subtle refusal of his offer while seeming to compliment him. Pissing on his leg, we prosecutors call it.

"Well, have it your way. The offer stands until we get to the courtroom. You know we've drawn Judge Fairchild."

Walter O. Fairchild. "Wally" for short and derisively so, as he was known to hate that nickname. He was the chief judge of the circuit and seemingly more concerned with clearing a docket than doling out any semblance of justice. I was surprised because the trial was scheduled for three days, and it was well-known that to avoid having him sit on a case one needed only to ask for more than a single day when it was set. I wondered how Shea knew who had the case, since the docket hadn't been posted yet.

"And good for both of us," I said. "He'll have the case to the jury by lunchtime today."

I tried to hide my disappointment.

"Perhaps, but if we're done that soon it's more likely he's pitched your case in the can. But what was it you came to see me about? You said you'd been looking for me. What can I do for you, Billy?"

"A simple stipulation, Mr. Shea. I have the witnesses lined up and ready to go. All but one. He may still appear, as he's been subpoenaed, but I've not put my hands on him yet."

Shea sat back and smiled. He knew he'd been handed a present, the value of which was undetermined but clearly important enough to lead me to him, hat in hand.

"What might this witness supply to the Commonwealth that my stipulation will assist?"

"He's just one link in a chain of custody matter. The girl's purse. It was found about a mile from the park and the man who picked it up gave it to the police. Since your client denies having anything to do with this unfortunate event, what difference will it make to him?"

"And if we decline to assist the Commonwealth," Shea said. "What happens?"

"The witness is under subpoena. By statute, I'm entitled to a continuance. And the next time around, when he shows, the exact same line-up will testify about that purse. Nothing different. But if Wally refuses my motion, and I have to *nolle pros* the case, you know it will come back at the next grand jury and Hausner will be re-indicted. He'll have to post bond all over again, and from what I saw in the file it will cost him about $25,000—again."

A cash bond of $250,000 would have to be posted, or ten percent of it gets paid to a bonding agency as its fee for risking the balance on behalf of a defendant. Those without enough cash on hand keep the bondsmen in business.

"He won't get personal recognizance on two felonies, even in circumstances like this," I said. "Nobody does."

Shea pondered this turn of events, once again slowly turning his cup in circles.

"Do you know that aside from 'Not Guilty,' the words *'nolle pros'* are the most beautiful syllables a defense lawyer can imagine? It means another day of freedom, possibly followed by another retainer fee. That pleasant and temporary dismissal, even though without prejudice to be relitigated, offers a brief respite and hope for us all."

He sat smiling at me, but I didn't respond.

"And what kind of courthouse is it where a man can't even have a morning cigarette? Billy, I've heard that the judges still smoke back in chambers."

The parrying was over. Shea was inclined to turn me down but wanted to buy time to consider whether it was better to try the case against me today or possibly against Casey Butler in a few months. If he had any idea of the lack of interest Casey had in this case, it would be worth $25,000 to Hausner, or whoever had paid the bond for him, to go through the process all over again. I didn't tell him I was keeping this case, no matter when it was tried.

"I need to meet witnesses upstairs, Mr. Shea. We're ready to go. Just let me know your position on the stipulation when we get up to the courtroom."

"And you talk to that girl about making a personal injury claim, and how a plea to A&B helps her get $300,000."

You little weasel. Trying to put me in a position of advising a witness in a criminal case as if she were my client in a civil one.

"She's not my client, Mr. Shea. The Commonwealth of Virginia is who I represent. And the Commonwealth gets quite jealous if I express my affections elsewhere."

I stood and tried to leave with a smile on my face, but with a sense of finality and firmness.

"And you know how stubborn Kerrymen are."

Chapter Eight

First Punch

There is only one way to succeed in this trial business. Prepare. Prepare. Prepare. And then prepare some more. If I've earned credibility with the judges in this county, it's because I've built a reputation for being ready when it's trial time. If nothing else, I learned that from Gene Cresswell, way back when.

It takes at least five hours of preparation to be ready for every single hour of cross-examination. Know the facts, know the law, and never be surprised, or if and when it does happen, never show it. The close calls go your way when the judges think you're right, and they'll only believe you're right if you're ready. The confidence that goes along with that comes across in the courtroom.

But this time that confidence put my ass in a sling.

***

When we got up to Wally's courtroom, Shea acted like we'd never spoken. I slid over to his side of the room and asked about his position on the stipulation, and the Titmouse, standing next to his client, scoffed at the notion that he'd ever agree to such a thing. He didn't even revive the subject of a plea agreement, so confident that the case would not go forward.

He played it well, I must say.

Wally came into the courtroom at precisely ten o' clock and asked whether there were any preliminary matters. I stood up and made my motion for a continuance, even though I was somewhat reluctant. By then I really wanted a piece of the Titmouse.

"Yes, your Honor. The Commonwealth moves to continue the trial of this matter. I realize the Court has a general policy of not postponing trials but in this case a witness under subpoena has failed to appear. We do not know why and efforts to reach him have proved fruitless. The statute provides that the Commonwealth is entitled to a continuance under these circumstances."

Wally didn't even ask Shea to respond as he growled into the microphone.

"I don't know how the Commonwealth can bring serious charges like this and not be prepared for trial, Mr. Duncan. I have to deny your motion."

I continued to argue.

"Your Honor, the Commonwealth is prepared to go forward and try this case. All required actions have been taken and procedures met. The witness is under court order to appear and his absence is not the fault of the Commonwealth. With all due respect, a review of the statute will confirm our entitlement to . . ."

"Mr. Duncan, I have made my ruling. Do you have any other motions?"

Any other judge would have granted it without a second thought. Wally just shook his head and invited me to *nolle pros* the case, turning him loose for the rest of the day, and Hausner for who knows how long he'd stay free. Wally knew the prosecution had no right of appeal and he used that fact like a club.

I sat. Shea was still standing, briefcase in hand, ready to head for the door. Once the jury was called, it would be too late to change my mind. The Double Jeopardy Rule would come into play and I'd be in this trial until the end, win or lose.

I started to look over the list of prospective jurors left on my table by the bailiff, trying to appear as if I were still ready to try the case and didn't care that Wally had surgically excised a critical part of it. It was plain that he expected I'd make a motion to *nolle pros* the case, not knowing or caring whether we re-indicted Hausner. Either way, he figured this three-day jury trial was done and he would be free to head to his country club by eleven that morning. Weekday golf was not uncommon in his schedule. Nor was disappearing with Nancy, his young clerk.

"Mr. Duncan?"

"No, sir. No other motions."

***

Looking back, if I'd just *nolle prossed* that damned case none of this would have happened. Hausner might never have been re-indicted, Amanda might never see her assailant go to trial, Wally would have dumped on us once more, Casey Butler would have skated on a hard case and I might never whip the Titmouse again. Who knows? But one thing is for sure: I'd have never gotten flogged just for winning this damned thing.

Chapter Nine

Jury

Wally was stumped. We were still on. He waited a moment, seeming not to understand what just happened. I was aware that I'd be fighting with less than our full armament, but between Amanda's testimony, the kids in the park, the photos of the injuries and the picture of that single bolt, I figured I had a good shot.

"Mr. Bailiff, bring in the panel of prospective jurors," he said.

Voir dire is that part of the trial when the jury is selected. It means, literally, "to speak the truth." Questions are asked of the panel of jurors, and they are required to answer in order that any perceived slants, attitudes, biases, experiences, or prejudices may be unearthed and used by the lawyers to disqualify or "strike" those whom we do not want to serve on the jury.

We begin with twenty potential jurors and each side is entitled to four strikes. No reason need be given. If a potential juror indicates a specific reason why he cannot serve, the judge may remove him and call another. *Voir dire* is the only time in the course of a trial when the lawyers may converse directly with the jurors and them with us. A savvy lawyer will use this opportunity to establish a connection, a rapport, with these individuals. Depending upon the judge's patience it can sometimes go on for hours. Wally was not patient, so I tailored my questions to be succinct and targeted.

It is easy to consider the panel as a singular group, but in fact it is rare that any of the jurors have ever met one another before this day. They will bond quickly, however, and as people tend to do they will pick friends and enemies just as fast. They will view the judge as their ally and protector. The lawyers are a different story. The jurors know that both sides will exhort them to find in their favor. Simple human nature will lead them to conclude that only one side is telling the truth. The early stages of a trial give the lawyers a chance to convince the jury of their own trustworthiness.

Wally gave the jurors the preliminary instructions. They were to answer all questions posed by the lawyers truthfully. There were no wrong answers. His words seemed to calm the candidates, judging from the nervous smiles and nods he elicited. Some, on the other hand, seemed not to have heard anything and were annoyed at being inconvenienced.

The prosecution always goes first. My practice is to use *voir dire* as an additional opening statement, at least as best as I can within the bounds of the rules and the leeway granted by the judge. Sheltering my rendition of the case within my questions, I intended to tell them about our case and attempt to guide them before Shea ever spoke. I would reveal the nature of the case and plant the seeds for the result I hoped to reap by the end of the trial.

"Ladies and gentlemen, good morning. I am William Duncan, representing the Commonwealth of Virginia and Jefferson County. Your community. We are here today because the Commonwealth has charged this man, Jason Hausner . . ."

I paused, turned slowly, and pointed to him, seated next to his lawyer. If I wanted the jurors to believe he committed the acts of which he was accused and send him to prison, I had to make them look at him, recognizing that he is a person and not just a term, in this case, the "defendant," and accept that he did do what Amanda Fontaine was about to describe. I would repeat his name several times, and rarely refer to him any other way.

". . . with the crimes of Attempted Rape and Malicious Wounding. These crimes carry maximum sentences of ten and twenty years in prison, respectively."

I looked briefly at every one of them. This was the first they'd heard of the charges or their severity. They glanced at Hausner, and I knew each of them was wondering if that neatly-dressed, well-groomed young man was capable of such things.

"Is there anyone here who would be unable to sit in judgment of such a case?"

No one, of course, raised his or her hand.

"Is there anyone who will be unable to convict Jason Hausner of these crimes if the Commonwealth proves that he has committed them?"

Again, no hands were raised. It was a simple question and one virtually impossible to answer in the negative. But at the conclusion of this trial, in my closing argument, I would remind them of this pledge as I recounted each gruesome element of the offenses. Even if they were hesitant to convict Hausner, I would insist that they promised to do so, once the evidence supporting it was on the table.

"Is there anyone who would be unable to impose the maximum sentences if you are convinced of Jason Hausner's guilt?"

Again, no hands. They knew virtually nothing about the case, but they understood that crimes have ranges of penalties. At this point, they had no reason to think that this case wouldn't warrant a lengthy sentence. And again, I would remind them of their answer in my closing.

Hoping to deflate some of what I knew Shea was sure to describe, I delved into the potential weakness in our case. Better they hear it from me than the Titmouse.

"The evidence will show that Jason Hausner attempted to rape Amanda Fisher. When he was unsuccessful, he beat her and then drove his car over her."

I let that sink in.

"They met earlier that evening at the Noncommissioned Officers' Club at the Army base. Does the fact that these two people, adults, met in a bar and had several drinks cause any of you to be unable to render a verdict in this case?"

Knowing that Shea would try to make Amanda out to be a tramp that got what she deserved, I tried to get the jurors to compartmentalize any judgment or disapproval they might have of her social choices and focus on the brutality of the crime. Once again, no hands.

"The panel is satisfactory to the Commonwealth, your Honor."

I directed my response to Judge Fairchild as I said that and then turned my attention back to the jurors.

"Thank you for your candor, ladies and gentlemen."

I would demand compliance with their answers later, but at that moment I needed to show them respect and my agreeable nature.

Shea's turn. Thanks to television and movies, people expect defense attorneys to be flamboyant characters. Knowing there was still a long way to go, however, Shea took an understated tone. Because he couldn't deny the offense occurred, his case would rest upon making the jury believe that Amanda identified the wrong man.

"Ladies and gentlemen of the jury, my name is Thomas Shea, and it is my honor to be here today with Mr. Hausner. He is a former member of our nation's armed forces, honorably discharged. He stands accused of terrible deeds. Terrible."

He frowned and shook his head in seeming distress. Then, the theatrics began.

"We will make no argument about what the Commonwealth says happened to this poor girl."

Shea paused, allowing that to wash over the twenty attentive people in the jury box. He paced along the railing that divided them from the open court.

"But we vehemently deny that it was Mr. Hausner who did it."

I stood to object, if for no other reason than to interrupt Shea's rhythm and imply to the jurors that he was already breaking the rules. Sure, it was almost exactly what I had done, but he was more blatant.

"Your Honor, I apologize for interrupting, but is there a question within Mr. Shea's *voir dire* or have we progressed to opening statements?"

Judge Fairchild was not pleased by my objection but had to address the matter since it had been raised.

"Mr. Shea, you'll get an opportunity to make an opening statement. Please inquire of the panel whatever you need in order that we may conclude *voir dire*."

He then turned back to me.

"Mr. Duncan, I'll take it from here."

The judge made sure to show the jury that he had chosen no favorites and that perhaps I was out of bounds as well. Shea restarted in earnest, initiating what would be his three-day assault on Amanda's credibility.

"As you have heard, Miss Fontaine was at the NCO club. If the evidence demonstrates that she had been drinking, is there anyone who will be unable to consider whether her recollection of the events of that evening was, perhaps, clouded?"

Put so mildly, no one raised a hand. The first brick in his foundation had been laid.

"If the evidence demonstrates that in fact Miss Fontaine was inebriated, is there anyone among you that will be unable to question her recollection of the events of that evening?"

No hands.

"If the evidence demonstrates that at first she claimed that she had been raped but later acknowledged that she had not, is there anyone among you that is unable to consider discounting her testimony altogether?"

Some of the faces frowned, eyes darting between Shea, the judge and the gallery, perhaps searching for who they thought might be Amanda. No hands.

"The panel is thoroughly satisfactory to Mr. Hausner, your Honor."

Shea made his pronouncement, turning to the jury and bowed. Then, for the first time that day, he gave a hint of his beloved brogue.

"And thank you, ladies and gentlemen, for your patience and honesty. You appear to be a collection of this community's finest citizens. A fair trial cannot be had without honest people such as yourselves."

I cringed, having to weather this obvious pandering. This kind of speech to the jury at this point was completely improper and far worse than mine. But I refrained from objecting. To what end? It's already out, and no amount of arguing by me can take it away. And what would my objection be?

He's complimenting the jury already, Judge! Make him stop!

In the part of the voir dire process when strikes are made, the prosecution again goes first. Tucker, Wally's bailiff, handed me a copy of the list I already had, and I marked my first strike. He took it over to Shea, who then noted his.

The clerk's office provides us little information on these people. We are given names, ages, addresses and employment. Since the people are taken from the rolls of registered voters, we know that none of them are felons, but without asking questions that may embarrass them or encourage them to lie through silence we do not know if they or their family and friends have ever been on the wrong side of the law.

In the right circumstance, the prosecutor and defense attorney will penetrate that subject. The Hausner case, however, hinged on one simple question—not whether a crime occurred, but whether Jason Hausner was the one who did it. If Amanda presented herself as a believable witness, and if I could tie the Hausner Bonneville to the asphalt parking lot at Riverside Park, none of those unasked questions would matter.

I struck two women over fifty. I had no idea what or how they think, but experience told me that women of my mother's generation take a dim view of young girls going to bars and are even less enthusiastic about their going home with men they barely know. In a close call I feared that they would fall for Shea's oblique theme and conclude that Amanda had it coming.

My other two strikes were of a twenty-five-year-old fellow who was still in college, and a female social worker. Playing the odds, I suspected that the boy had seen his share of single girls he met in bars and could imagine being the recipient of a false accusation arising from a drunken grope. I tossed the social worker because long ago my boss said never to trust them: they think they know better than the rest of us and won't follow the law. For all I knew, this one could have been a real law-and-order enforcer, but if I lost this case or she caused a hung jury I'd never find the words to explain to Mac why I left her on the panel.

Shea played a similar game. He struck young women who could possibly identify with Amanda, and men with military service. At first blush, one would think that Hausner's past enlistment would mean he wanted servicemen on the jury. But Shea served as well, and he knows that soldiers see reprehensible behavior in the ranks on occasion and would have no trouble believing that Hausner, a man they did not know, could be capable of this atrocity. Besides, the absence of men with military experience would enable Shea to argue things that former soldiers would never believe.

Once we'd picked the twelve jurors they were sworn to their task—to faithfully try the case of Jason Hausner, hear the evidence and follow the court's instruction on the law.

The fight was on.

Chapter Ten

Opening Statements

"Does the Commonwealth have an opening statement?"

I stood, thanked Judge Fairchild, and walked to the center of the courtroom where I faced the jury box and began my effort to bring Jason Hausner to justice. My objective was to convince the jurors as quickly as possible of his guilt so that Shea would be fighting uphill for the remainder of the trial. The jury had already been told not to discuss the case, even with each other, until the conclusion of all the evidence. They were instructed not to form any opinions until, at the end, they retreated to the jury deliberation room together. Shea and I knew full well that each one of them would make up his or her mind within the next few moments. They might change their opinions later, but only if overwhelmed. As always, I used no notes and spoke directly to the jurors as if we knew one another.

"Members of the jury, this is my opportunity to tell you what the Commonwealth will prove."

I avoided using terms like "beyond a reasonable doubt," "victim," "defendant" and "alleged." I wrestled to make the words as direct, believable, and convincing as possible. My task was to tell them that Jason Hausner was guilty. Later, in closing, I would be more detailed and forceful as I recounted the testimony they would have heard and the evidence they'd have seen.

"On the night of May 15, Jason Hausner took Amanda Fontaine to Riverside Park. There, he demanded that she engage in sexual relations with him. When she refused, he brutally beat her, pushed her out of his car and ran her over."

I stopped for a moment, letting those words resonate.

"Ran her over," I said again.

The momentary silence coupled with my stare at them made the jury focus on that horrific scene.

"Amanda suffered multiple broken bones, the loss of several teeth, and her vision in one eye remains diminished to this day."

I paused again and looked at each of them, expressionless. I wanted them to look at me as I described the events of that night, to imagine the peril that this young woman endured. I was all business, with no sign of collegiality or pleasantry.

"Amanda will tell you how she suffered. She will tell you she believed she was going to die. She will tell you that this is the man."

I pointed deliberately at Hausner again.

"This is the man who did this to her."

I let that sink in and walked the length of the railing between us.

"Amanda will admit to you that she was drinking that night. Drinks, she will tell you, that Jason Hausner gave her. Strong, powerful drinks, not beer or wine. At least five, too. The fact that she was under the influence of alcohol, her judgment diminished and physically weakened, was no accident or coincidence. Jason Hausner, as the evidence will show, knew perfectly well what he was doing."

I stopped at the center of the jury box and looked at every one of them.

"She will tell you that she will never—never—forget the face of the man who did this to her. She will never forget Jason Hausner."

I returned to my seat at the prosecution table, purposely having declined to describe all the evidence and testimony we would soon introduce, preferring to keep the jury interested by the suspense and thereby paying attention to details about which they had not yet been told. But more than that, I didn't want Shea thinking too much about the photographs.

The judge nodded at Shea.

"Mr. Shea. Opening statement?"

"Your Honor, may it please the court, we do. Thank you."

He stood up, all five-and-a-half feet of him, and slowly walked to the same spot where I had just concluded my opening statement.

"Ladies and gentlemen, I know that you will pay close attention to the evidence, so I need not speak to that. I know you will follow the court's directions, so I need not speak to that, either."

At this point, Shea clasped his hands behind his back, looked downward and assumed a look of distress. Pacing slowly along the jury box railing, he effected a visage of grave concern.

"What I do need to address, however, is the serious matter at the heart of this case. We make no argument nor dispute that Miss Fontaine was the victim of a terrible, terrible deed. An attack. The details of it remain somewhat murky but be of no doubt that she was seriously injured."

His voice became quiet and measured.

"The critical question is whether we can believe that she has identified the proper man. You will learn that she did not know the name of her assailant, a man with whom she voluntarily left the NCO club, intending, we understand, to go to his home. She could not describe the make, model or even the color of the car in which she rode to the park, was attacked, and which eventually ran over her."

He stopped pacing, turned to the jury, and pointed his finger in a general direction over their heads. Then, he turned the volume up a notch.

"She told the police and the hospital personnel that she'd been raped, but they will tell you that she was not violated. Beaten severely, yes, but not raped. The records will show that she was intoxicated, her blood alcohol at .26, more than three times that of the legal driving limit."

How did he know that number already?

More pacing. Shea stared down the jurors, one by one, pointing at each of them and punctuating every one of his words.

"Mr. Hausner was not arrested until nearly three months had passed following May Fifteenth, the night of this incident. At that time, after being handed the photographs of several men in their late twenties, all with short haircuts, none of them with distinguishing facial characteristics, she picked out one and said, 'That's him.'"

He stared at the jury with a look of disbelief.

"There will be no evidence that she and Mr. Hausner ever met before May Fifteenth or saw each other again after that night. She cannot identify anything else, but we are to believe, months later, that she is certain that she has picked the right man, one of many she saw that night, a night on which she was severely intoxicated."

The Titmouse had the jury in his grip, but there was nothing I could do or say since I'd already had my turn. Shea then turned toward me. Once again, I was looking down and writing, appearing to be focused on my notes, trying to convey to the jury that nothing he said was a surprise and nothing had diminished my resolve.

"The Commonwealth has brought charges that, if they result in a conviction, could imprison Mr. Hausner, a war veteran, for up to thirty years."

He'd taken our case head on by describing the enormous risk and penalties faced by Hausner. In doing so, he had dared the jury to believe a drunken trollop. Still looking at me, he held out his arms, hands open with an expression of dismay. Refraining from speaking to me directly, which even Fairchild would not tolerate, he gave the jury a moment to absorb this salvo. Turning back to face them, he assumed a soft, almost hushed voice as he finished.

"When this matter comes to a close, members of the jury, we will ask you how in the world can you believe that poor, beaten, intoxicated and confused girl beyond a reasonable doubt when she blames this man, a veteran, a man that served his nation honorably, a man with no previous criminal record, of these terrible deeds?"

His gaze fixed on the jury, Shea walked backward to the defense table. Just before taking his seat, he practically whispered his closing pitch.

"Beyond any reasonable doubt."

The judge broke the silence in the courtroom.

"Mr. Duncan, call your first witness."

Chapter Eleven

Amanda

Shea's strategy weighed heavily on the identification issue. But by not contesting the crime he gave me an opening. I pushed some evidence through, making it seem like it wasn't too significant since we were only there to decide if Amanda had pegged the right guy, not whether a crime occurred or where it happened.

Trying to build the substance and framework of our case early, I called Ted Bowen, the crime scene officer, as our first witness. He had taken the photos of the parking lot I'd assembled the previous night, showing the location of the car when Amanda was beaten and the path it followed as it hurdled the curbing, ran over the discarded clothing, and eventually her. Inserted in that string of pictures as Exhibit Number Seventeen was the photograph containing the bolt.

I presented about twenty-five pictures to Bowen as a set. He testified that he'd taken all of them in the early morning hours of May 16th and that they accurately portrayed the parking lot and the debris. He knew nothing of the actual crime, had not interviewed the victim or had anything to do with tracking down the perpetrator. It gave Shea the opportunity to appear magnanimous. He barely glanced at the photographs of the parking lot.

"No objection, your Honor," he said. "I'm certain Officer Bowen did his usual thorough and meticulous job."

He was performing up to my expectations, and I hoped to use those words against him at the end of the trial. Judge Fairchild admitted all twenty-five of them into evidence. I made no sign to indicate our case was nearly home free, but inside I could hardly contain my delight. The bolt—the link between the crime scene and the car belonging to Hausner's wife—was buried in the evidence like a ticking time bomb, set to explode during closing arguments. Shea probably wouldn't look at Number Seventeen again until I put a spotlight on it at the end of the trial.

When I showed Bowen the pictures of Amanda, her shattered face, broken limbs, and the tread marks across her flesh, Shea threw me a curve.

"Objection, your Honor. I must protest. These photographs are highly inflammatory. Indeed, their probative value, if any, is overwhelmed by the prejudice they present to the Defendant. I say, 'if any,' of course because we have stipulated that Miss Fontaine was indeed assaulted."

To my utter amazement, Judge Fairchild sustained the objection before I could respond. I persisted.

"Your Honor, with all due respect, the Supreme Court has ruled that the 'handiwork of the criminal' cannot be the basis of an objection merely because it is horrific. In *Commonwealth v. Heydenreich*, just a few years ago ..."

But, as he had done with my motion for a continuance, he just shook his head.

"I have to agree with Mr. Shea. These pictures are inflammatory and will not be admitted. That is my ruling, Mr. Duncan."

That was classic Wally, always concerned about a risk of reversal on appeal. I never knew what irritated him more: the embarrassment of getting reversed or having to take the time to handle a case twice.

I was angered, in a way, but also pleased by the ruling. Angered because the pictures showed a broken young girl that I was certain was unlike anything the jurors had ever seen but pleased inside because

Shea was so worried about the pictures of Amanda's injuries, and focused on them and not the crime scene.

I had purposely put up a fuss, knowing I had no chance of getting Wally to change his mind. The struggle to get them admitted, however, told the jury that Amanda's condition had to be grotesque. I counted on their imagination being more colorful than the actual photos or testimony.

We worked our way through Amanda's friend, Laura who testified that Hausner spent most of the evening with his victim.

"Do you see the man that bought Amanda those drinks?" I said.

"Yes," she said, pointing at Hausner. "That's him right there. He must'a gotten her five or six of 'em."

Shea shook her a little on cross-examination since she'd been dancing with other guys and had let Amanda out of her sight some of the time.

"But that's the guy she left with. I got no doubt about that, Mr. Shea," she said. "He put his arm around her and took her right out the door. I went home alone, after that."

April Winston took the stand and was right on target. She described getting the call weeks later and going to the NCO club to get a look at Hausner. She tracked him down through the car she saw him drive away that night, his Ford Explorer, and then discovered the other one, the silver Bonneville, through DMV records. That's when she knew she had her man.

"And did you do an inspection of the other car, the Bonneville, Investigator Winston?" I said.

"Yes. It was parked on the public street. I confirmed it was the same one that DMV records showed belonged to Mr. Hausner's wife, Delores. I took photographs."

She identified the pictures she'd taken, including the ones of the sagging wheel well. When I moved them into evidence, Shea objected.

"Your Honor, there is no foundation. No search warrant was issued. These photographs were improperly taken. The police have violated Mr. Hausner's constitutional right to be free of unreasonable searches."

The judge turned to me.

"Mr. Duncan?"

"Your Honor, the testimony was clear: this car was parked on a public street when Detective Winston inspected it. Everything she photographed was in plain view. She never sought to enter the car, which might have required a warrant, but that is not at issue today."

"Objection overruled," he said. "Proceed."

Shea had to know that his objection would fail, but he had tried to insinuate that the police had been surreptitious, sneaking pictures of Hausner's car without his knowledge. He must have been puzzled as to why we cared about the wife's car, but alibi or not, he was going to challenge the integrity of the investigation at some point.

I finally called Amanda Fontaine to the stand.

Some prosecutors prefer to get the victim up early in the trial, maybe even first, leading with the most powerful testimony, then backing her up with the rest of the case. Not me. If she's a good witness, I like to make the jurors wait a little while and build anticipation. By the time Amanda walked in to testify, they'd heard all about where this thing had happened, how we'd tracked down the culprit, and seen many pictures of where it had occurred. But they'd yet to hear from the one person at the center of this tragedy or what took place that night between the two of them. They would hang on every word she spoke.

Still, I had concerns. Amanda had been camped outside the courtroom in a witness room with April, unable to hear what was being said by the lawyers and the other witnesses, and I knew she was getting more and more nervous. She was shaking as she took the witness stand and, even as she clasped her hands, she couldn't hold them still. All I really needed from her was what happened and who did it, by then, so I asked her to identify Hausner immediately, getting that out of the way.

"Do you see in court today the man that took you to Riverside Park?"

She was hesitant to look at him initially, but then found her nerve.

"That's him," she said, looking and pointing at Hausner, her voice breaking slightly. "Right there. That's him."

"Tell us how you met Jason Hausner, Amanda."

I kept my voice firm and direct. She gathered herself, bowed her head for a moment, then looked at me.

"I was there with my friend, Laura. We talked to some of the soldiers, then he—him . . ." She pointed at Hausner again.

"He offered to buy me a drink. And then we danced. I'd never had much hard liquor before that night. Tequila Sunrises. He said I'd like them, and I did."

A few chuckles could be heard in the courtroom.

"How many drinks did he buy for you, Amanda?"

"As fast as I was drinking them, he was buying the next round."

More muffled laughter.

"After the dancing and drinking, what did you do next?"

"At around midnight, because they were closing up, he said we could go to his place." She paused.

"To listen to music."

I didn't buy that one the first time I heard it and didn't think anyone in the courtroom did, either. But everyone could believe that's what he'd said. They found their way to his car. She didn't remember walking to it, what it looked like or how she got into it and drove off the base.

"Do you remember arriving at Riverside Park?"

"No. I mean, I remember the car stopping and him parking. I was sort of out of it by then. I wasn't paying much attention to where we'd been going, and I was hazy after all those drinks."

I lowered my voice and softly asked her the next question.

"And then, Amanda?"

I did this for two reasons. First, to gently keep her focused, understanding that I was her guardian for the moment. But also, to inform the jury that the next words would be significant.

"He started unbuttoning my blouse and pulling up my skirt. Then, he said what he wanted me to do."

Her voice began to break again, ratcheting up into a sorrowful cry. Even in her drunken stupor, she'd known she was in the wrong place. Hausner liked it a little weird and even a .26 BAC wasn't enough to get Amanda interested.

"I just wouldn't do it, what he wanted," she said, sniffling. "Then he got really angry."

"What did he say he wanted you to do, Amanda?"

I pressed her gently.

"He said . . . he . . . he . . . do I have to say it?"

She was slipping away, and with Shea waiting for a shot at her I decided not to pursue Hausner's perverse intentions. Let the jury speculate. Once again, I trusted their imaginations to be vivid.

"I'm sorry, Amanda, but you have to say it."

She bowed her head and paused.

"Amanda?"

"He wanted to have sex, right there, but in a nasty, ugly way. Do I have to say any more?"

"No, Amanda. What happened next?"

"He slapped me, then grabbed my hair and slammed my face against the dashboard, hard. I don't know how many times he did it. I couldn't see, and I thought he wasn't going to stop until I was dead."

She looked down, starting to cry.

"Take a moment, Amanda."

She needed to collect herself and finish, but I also wanted to show the jury that we were going through it all because the case required it. After a moment, I asked again.

"And then what did he do?"

"He called me a stupid bitch and ripped open my blouse. He tore it off me. Then he yanked my skirt off, over my head. I couldn't really see, and I was coughing up blood. He pulled off my under . . . you know, things. He was screaming at me, saying he was, you know, going to do it to me whether I liked or not. Then he stopped and said, 'Oh, shit!' "

She glanced at the jury.

"I'm sorry, but that's what he said, and then he pushed me out the door. Right onto the pavement."

"Do you know why he shoved you out of his car?"

"I didn't then, but I do now."

"What happened to make him stop?"

"Some people drove into the park, and they must have seen us."

"Once you were out of Mr. Hausner's car, what did you do?"

"I didn't know what he was doing, but I just tried to get away. It was raining, and I could see the other car's headlights, so I tried to run to them."

"Did you get to the other car?"

She shook her head.

"I kept stumbling and falling, and then I blacked out. All I remember next was being in the hospital, with bright lights and lots of people holding onto me."

"Amanda, what injuries did you suffer that night?"

"Broken nose, broken cheekbone. I lost two teeth. My right arm and leg were broken when the car ran me over and I can't see very well out of my right eye even now."

The jury wouldn't need to see the excluded photographs to have an idea of how she must have looked that night in the hospital.

I stayed at the podium for a moment, delaying Shea's cross-examination briefly to give Amanda a chance to take a breath before he pounced on her. I slowly gathered my notes and witness file, buying an extra minute or two.

"Thank you, Amanda. Please answer Mr. Shea's questions."

Shea had plenty to work with when it came to gaps in Amanda's memory, and he used every ounce of it.

"Miss Fontaine, I am Thomas Shea, and I am here to represent Jason Hausner. I have to ask you some questions so that we may get to the truth today."

He was a pro and knew that Amanda had the jury's sympathy, and he set up his cross-examination so that the jury understood his role. He had to get them to question her ability to identify her assailant without crossing a delicate line, and without minimizing her injuries. That would risk alienating the jury.

"Jason Hausner. You say you met him for the first time that night?"

"Yes."

"That was the only time you saw him at the NCO club?"

"Yes."

"You think you danced with him?"

"Lots of times."

"How many?"

"I . . . I . . ."

"Could it have been two times?"

"More than that."

"Three?"

"More than that."

"How many more?"

"I don't know."

"So, maybe three, four?"

"I guess. I don't remember."

"And this man that you accompanied when you left the club, Miss Fontaine, you did not know his name?"

"I don't remember."

"Miss Fontaine, you admit you were intoxicated. You admit that you did not know the name of the man with whom you danced several times and later left the club. How many drinks did you have that evening?"

"Uh, I think five," Amanda said.

"Is that what you were told, or do you remember?"

"It ... I ... I think it was five. I don't remember for sure."

"And the automobile. You got into an automobile driven by this man. Didn't you tell the police you thought his car was a truck, or a jeep?"

"Like I said before, I don't remember."

Shea paused, looking at the floor.

"Miss Fontaine, at the hospital you told the medical professionals that you had been raped, did you not?"

She looked to me for help, but I couldn't offer any. Any nod or signal from me would be seen by the jury and I couldn't risk them thinking that Amanda's testimony was in any way orchestrated. She had to get through this on her own.

"Miss Fontaine?"

"Yes. But I'd been beaten, stripped naked and run over by that man, that man right there," she said, pointing at Hausner again. "I . . . I thought . . ."

She put her face in her hands and wept.

"But you had not been raped, had you?"

She sobbed.

"No."

"No more questions, your Honor."

Shea had made his points.

"Thank you, Miss Fontaine. I am very sorry for what you endured."

He returned to his chair, but before sitting he added one more note.

"Whoever it was that did it."

Shea was good. No denying that. I stood for a brief re-direct.

"Amanda, before this horrific experience, did you know the legal definition of 'rape'?"

She blew her nose.

"No, of course not."

"No more questions, your Honor."

It was the best we could do at that point, and I wanted Amanda off the witness stand while the jury could still feel sympathy for her.

Shea's gambit was still in play. He'd been tough but honest. The questions were the right ones to ask. If the jurors didn't want to believe her, they had a reason. Amanda left the courtroom. As I watched her depart, a man who had been seated in the back row got up, put his arm around her and took her through the door. I had seen him earlier but mistook him for a potential juror. He was tall, wide in the shoulders and had white hair, cut very short. General Fontaine, I figured.

Our best witness was Boyd Wetherholt, the young driver who had scared off Hausner. He was about Amanda's age, and sported what we used to call a skateboarder's haircut. It was faddish, almost immediately out of date. But he had an athlete's build, was slender, tanned, with strong looking hands and an easy bounce in his stride.

"Mr. Wetherholt, please tell the jury how you came to be in the Riverside Park at about midnight on May Fifteenth," I said.

"Well, me and my buddy, Bryan, we'd been to the movies with our girlfriends. We just pulled in there, you know, just for a minute. On the way home, you know."

"Please tell us what you saw."

"The place looked empty, at first. Then I seen a car, over at the other side of the parking lot from where we were. I turned so's my lights were on it, and then all hell . . . I mean, we saw it happen."

"What happened, Mr. Wetherholt?"

Sometimes, witnesses need the facts pried out of them.

"The passenger door opened up and a naked girl fell out. Right on the asphalt. Like she'd been shoved out. She crawled for a ways, then tried to get up and run. She kept falling down."

"What did you do while this was happening?"

"Nothin'. We were, like, in shock. We just stared. We didn't know what was goin' on."

"What happened to the girl next?"

"Wow. It was like, incredible. She was sort of coming our way, stumbling-like, and suddenly, the other car's headlights came on and he started, like, going at her."

"How far were you from the other car at that time?"

"Maybe twenty-five, thirty yards."

"And then?"

"He drove over some of the curbs in the parking lot. I could tell because the lights kept going up and down and there were sparks flying from under the car. Then he hit her! I was like, no way! But she flipped up onto the hood. He backed up in a hurry, and she fell off. Then he ran over her. We were all, like, screaming and stuff, because we thought he'd killed her, but he only got her arm and leg. Then he drove out of there. Real fast."

"How close were you to that car as it left the park?"

"Right next to me. We were still in the driveway coming in. He had to pass right by me."

"Did you get a good look at it?"

"Oh, yeah."

"Could you tell the make and model?"

"For sure."

"What was it?"

Shea saw it coming and had one last chance to stop me from tying Hausner's car to the crime.

"Objection, your Honor. The prosecution has laid no foundation for this witness's expertise as to automobile identification. I object to his testifying as to the make and model of the vehicle."

Judge Fairchild turned to me.

"Mr. Duncan?"

"Your Honor, not only is expert testimony not required here; it is not even permitted. The Virginia rule is that expert testimony is allowed only when the subject matter is beyond the scope of common experience. Thanks to incessant advertising and countless commercials, the make and model of virtually every automobile is within the common experience of everyone in this room."

A few chuckles rippled through the jury box.

The judge looked at me and sighed.

"Objection overruled."

Shea's point had been made, despite the failure of his objection. He'd raised the issue with the jury.

Can you believe this young man when he testifies that he can identify a speeding car, at night, in the rain?

"What were the make and model?"

"Pontiac Bonneville, maybe two years old."

"And the color?"

"Either white or silver. I couldn't tell 'cause it was, like, nighttime and rainin'."

"No more questions."

Shea scurried to the podium.

"Mr. Wetherholt, that parking lot was not lit, was it?"

"Uh, no. I don't think there's any lights there."

"And it was raining, was it not? Heavily, in fact?"

"Yes."

"And you could not see the driver, could you?"

He shook his head.

"No."

"But you are certain of the color?"

"Yep."

"It could not have been gray?"

"Nope."

"It could not have been, perhaps, light tan?"

"Nope."

"And why not?"

"Because Pontiac didn't make 'em in those colors that year."

Shea could take no more. Foiled in his earlier objection, he refused to let the youngster upstage him.

"And how do you know this, sir?"

Wetherholt finally relaxed. He leaned back, smiled, and answered Shea's challenge.

"I work in an autobody shop. I seen 'em all."

I had gambled and not asked him about his work experience with cars, hoping that Shea would be lured into asking one too many questions. By my count he'd asked two.

After Boyd Wetherholt stepped down, I called the DMV witness to certify the documents showing that a silver Bonneville with the same license number April Winston had photographed was registered to Hausner's wife, who lived at the same address on Buckman Court.

I still did not know what Shea's defense would be, since he hadn't hinted at it during the opening statement, other than to attack Amanda's ability to identify Hausner. I thought it possible that he might just rest his case, not put on any testimony, and rely on the holes he'd poked in Amanda's recollection. Boyd Wetherholt's testimony did enough damage that he had to do something, however. We reached the end of the day and the judge sent us home.

A woman had been sitting right behind the defense throughout the trial, in the first row. She and Hausner had spoken briefly during a recess but there wasn't enough interplay between them for me to determine if that was his wife. There were also three soldiers in uniform waiting outside in the hall. It looked like Shea had an alibi lined up, and of course I didn't know what it was because Shea hadn't sought any pretrial discovery that would entitle me to get it. Since the woman had been in the courtroom all day, she was barred from testifying.

I asked April to get me the DMV photograph of Mrs. Hausner and find out what she could about her by the next morning.

Charlotte called me at home, asking about the trial and offering to come over and help me get ready for the second day. I declined, even though I'd have welcomed her company, especially after a day in the ring with Wally and the Titmouse. But I had to stay focused and prepare for whatever was coming. She pleaded that she could fix me dinner, help with the case, and then stay over to fix me a decent breakfast in the morning. Weighing the risk of getting ambushed by Shea against the pleasant distraction of Charlotte for a few hours, I reluctantly chose to spend the night alone.

Expecting an alibi of sorts, I sketched out several lines of attack against his witnesses. But much of this I couldn't articulate. I had to guess and hope to probe their stories when I cross-examined each of Hausner's witnesses on the fly.

Part of my task was to show the jury that nothing they said came as a surprise to me. I needed to demonstrate that any tales purporting to put Hausner elsewhere were far-fetched and irredeemably false. I spent the next few hours thinking of what I would want witnesses to say if I were Tommy Shea.

But what was he going to do about that Bonneville?

Chapter Twelve

Alibi

I slept little.

On the morning of the second day of trial I arrived at the courthouse early, hours before the case would reconvene. I had spent the previous night trying to anticipate the alibi Hausner's witnesses would spin for him, the good character by which he was assuredly known, and who knows what else.

I'd worn a dark blue suit on the first day, trying to appear formal and official, the essence of "in charge." This day, when Shea took center stage, I sought to be in contrast with him. Eschewing another dark suit, I wore a light gray one, with a white shirt and blue tie, but no jewelry, such as cufflinks or a tie clasp. I don't know how much attention jurors pay to these things, but I believe they expect lawyers to dress properly. Still, I wanted to look like someone with whom they would be comfortable as I challenged the alibi witnesses. Shea, of course, would be wearing all his accoutrements: gold cufflinks, matching necktie bar, and Rolex watch.

Shortly after 7:00 a.m., Judge Fairchild's bailiff appeared in the doorway of my office. Tucker—I never knew his first name; everyone called him "Tuck"—was like many in the courthouse security division: a retired police officer working toward a second pension. He had spent most of his first career as a homicide detective. An old-style cop, he was short on words and broad of frame, with hands resembling catcher's mitts. He betrayed a minor limp, the result of more tussles with recalcitrant suspects than he could remember.

"You had the old man going yesterday," he said.

I liked Tuck. He understood what the police and prosecutors confronted each day, and his two decades on the force seemed to put us both on the same side. It was not unusual for him to whisper to me during a trial, offering a seasoned insight as to how it was playing out to the jury or judge.

"Tuck, I'm stunned. I thought I had him eating out of my hand."

He laughed, a muffled snort that came with his smoker's wheeze.

"Just don't let him eat that hand right off your arm. He ain't happy, settin' there all day watchin' you and the Titmouse wrassle."

He slowly shook his head.

"You figure to get it to the jury today?"

"It's not up to me, Tuck. I'm done, but Shea has a bunch of soldiers lined up and I can't say how long he'll take."

Tuck's face descended into affected grief.

"You know he's gonna blame you if this carries over a third day."

He shook his head mournfully.

"My God, I may have to call in sick if that happens."

I could see how it would go. If I took too long cross-examining the defense witnesses, the judge would interrupt, trying to hurry me along. It could look to the jury as if I were wasting their time, floundering, grasping for weaknesses in their stories. I needed to be concise and make my points quickly before Fairchild undermined me again.

"Thanks, Tuck. How about I just let Wally ask the questions? That ought to get us out of there by lunch."

His wrinkled face twisted into a smile.

"Ooh, don't be callin' him that. You know he hates that name."

He waved at me as if swatting flies and left.

***

The trial resumed with Shea calling the soldiers. One by one, they testified that they'd known Hausner for about a year. He was a civilian but had previously served in uniform and his present job put him in contact with some of the Noncoms. They treated him as one of their own, and he enjoyed their affinity because of his service in Iraq.

They frequently invited him to the NCO club. He told them, they said, about his adventures in the desert. Shea was clever, bringing out Hausner's military service through the soldiers rather than the defendant, allowing him to bask in humility while the witnesses portrayed him as an unparalleled war hero.

They were all there on the Fifteenth of May, they said, and after carousing with the available women for a couple of hours, they'd left together for an all-night greasy spoon.

"Oh, yeah," the first one recalled. "We all went to a local diner after the NCO club closed. Jason was there, for sure."

"And there is no doubt in your mind he was there?" Shea said.

"No doubt, no Sir."

They all followed suit, and not surprisingly each of them could recite what they ordered, exactly what time they arrived and departed, and every one of them recalled seeing Amanda left back at the base. She showed up drunk, they said, and made a play for every guy in the NCO club. Hausner had been polite and danced with her a couple of times, but no more. He might have bought her one drink, but he certainly did not leave with her, they said. Of the dozens of guys at the club that night, almost all of them were white, and most fit the same general description as Hausner. Surely, they insinuated, she mistook someone else for him.

Cross-examination of witnesses such as these must be done carefully. The questions asked should be those for which there is no good answer. The objective is not so much to learn any untold truths or incite a breakdown and confession, like on television. Rather, it is calculated to make the jurors question the veracity of the witnesses and draw their own conclusions as to the truth. Those are conclusions that I planned on helping them make.

The cross of each witness was similar, as was their direct testimony.

When did you first learn that Hausner was arrested?

Around late August.

And the first time you were asked about your recollection of the night of May 15th was about that same time?

Yes.

And you're certain that you left the NCO club at midnight?

Yes.

But you had no cause to discuss that time or even that date until three months afterward?

Right.

What happened on the night of May 8th?

Pardon me?

The night of May 8th, one week earlier.

I'm not sure.

Did you go to the NCO club?

Umm . . .

Was Jason Hausner with you that night?

May 8th?

Right.

Uh, not sure.

How about May 22nd?

When?

May 22nd, one week later.

Not sure.

No more questions, your Honor.

There were a few additional questions I wanted to ask but I refrained because I knew Wally would run out of patience.

Who paid the check?

Was there a receipt?

Who was the waitress?

And where was Hausner's wife all this time?

Despite the rule on witnesses, forbidding them to discuss their testimonies with each other or Hausner, I had no doubt they would cover every question with each other in detail, out in the hallway, when given the chance.

But I withheld some questions in anticipation of Hausner taking the stand, so that he would have no warning or chance to calculate those answers, which conveniently explained away the implications I hoped to convey to the jury.

When Shea said he was calling Hausner as his final witness, the judge took the afternoon recess. It is standard practice to break approximately every ninety minutes. It gives the jurors and the judge an opportunity to visit the restroom and walk about for a moment. The last thing any trial needs is those people distracted by physical distress or drowsiness when witnesses are testifying. It also gives lawyers a chance to prepare their witnesses for what lies ahead. Shea and Hausner huddled in the hallway, with the diminutive lawyer driving home his final instructions, jabbing his finger into his client's chest.

Even though juries are instructed that each defendant has the constitutional right not to testify, there is something just plain unacceptable to people about someone who wants them to believe he was somewhere else during the commission of the crime but won't take the stand to tell them himself. It was a standard belief in our office that an alibi could never be successful unless the defendant was willing to tell the jury to their faces exactly where he was when the crime was committed.

And so, Jason Hausner, having heard his drinking pals lie for him, took the opportunity to tell the jury a tale that was consistent with what the soldiers had said. Shea lathered him up, first asking about his prior military service, lack of criminal record, and then finally about the evening of May 15th.

"I met Miss Fontaine," he testified. "But I didn't know her name or spend much time with her. She'd been drinking already, before she got there, I'm pretty sure."

"And did you seek her out, Mr. Hausner?" said Shea.

"No, she came on to me," Hausner said. "I did dance with her once, but that was it. She tried to get me to hang with her, but I wasn't interested. I mean, I'm a married guy. One dance, maybe. But nothing more. I was just having a nice time with my friends, like they said."

"Did you drive an automobile to the base that evening, Mr. Hausner?"

"Yeah. My Ford Explorer."

"What color is it?"

"Black."

Shea shifted behind the podium.

"You heard Detective Winston testify about your wife's car, did you not?"

"Yeah. She has a Bonneville."

"What color?"

"Silver."

"But you were driving your car that night, correct?"

"Right. The black Ford Explorer."

"Did you take Amanda Fontaine to Riverside Park and do the things she described to the jury yesterday?"

"No, of course not."

Shea bowed slightly.

"No more questions."

It has been well-documented that the most anticipated moments in a trial are when the opposing lawyer rises to cross-examine a witness. If there was ever to be such a time in this case, this was it.

During the afternoon recess, April had handed me a manila envelope containing the picture of Hausner's wife. Despite the DMV's best attempts to ensure no license photograph ever resembles its owner, it was clear that the woman seated in the first row behind the defense table was Dolores Tiffany Hausner. She couldn't testify, having been in the courtroom for the entire trial, so I knew she wouldn't be part of any alibi. I could only guess as to why, at this point, and it would be dangerous to gamble. Jurors expect mothers and wives to protect their criminal sons and husbands, and instinct told me to steer clear of attacking her directly. Indirectly, however, was fair game.

Hausner had been cool and comfortable answering Shea's questions, of course. I was certain they'd rehearsed them repeatedly. He had shown no fear or nervousness, despite facing charges that could send him to prison for three decades. It seemed unlikely that he would make any serious mistakes, so my task was to make his comfort look undeniably calculated, practiced, and deceitful.

"Mr. Hausner, have you ever been mistaken for another man on the base?"

After a pause, during which Hausner looked over at Shea and then back at me, he responded.

"No, not that I know of."

"Then we can also conclude that you were not mistaken for anyone else at the NCO club on the night of May 15th."

He shifted slightly in his chair and smirked back at me.

"That's correct, Mr. Duncan."

"Then it is also safe to say that you are the only one that looks like you—who was at the NCO club on the 15th of May?"

This question was purposely convoluted, and I anticipated that he would ask me to repeat it. That gave me a chance to drill it into the minds of the jurors a second time.

"I'm sorry, I don't understand. Could you repeat the question?"

Every lawyer advises his clients to take this escape route if they are ever unsure of a question and its possible answer. Rather than make a mistake, and even to buy a little time, one can delay committing to a position for a few moments by seeking clarification. But it works both ways.

"Let me try it a different way, Mr. Hausner. We've established that you have not been confused with anyone else on the base, have we not?"

"Yes."

"And we've established that there was no one at the club that night for whom you were mistaken."

"Yes."

"And so, isn't it true that we've therefore established that there was no one who looked like you in the NCO club on May 15th?"

Shea saw where I was heading and tried to derail my line of questions.

"Asked and answered, your Honor. I object. This is bordering on argument with the witness."

Judge Fairchild turned to me.

"Haven't we heard this before, Mr. Duncan?"

There he was again, getting in the way of my trying this case. Tucker was right. Wally was still angry at me because I'd kept him in court a second day. Possibly at Shea, too, but any retribution toward the defense could create an appealable error so I would be the sole beneficiary of his wrath. But even though I could see he was going to let Hausner off without answering the question directly, my response could do almost as well as his.

"Your Honor, as a matter of fact we haven't. If you will recall, I posed this question in a different fashion and Mr. Hausner was unable to answer. I've merely asked him if we can agree that there was no one who looked like him in the club that night."

"I think we can move on from here," he ruled. "Ask your next question."

At moments like that, I am tempted to glance at the jury, shrug my shoulders, roll my eyes, and practically say to them, *What else can I do?* But any hint of improper communication from me to the jury would be met with instant retaliation by the judge and possibly a mistrial.

I picked up some of the photographs from my table and laid them on the podium in front of me. Hausner couldn't see what I had, but I figured he'd presume it was evidence already admitted.

"Your testimony was that you were driving your Explorer, not your wife's Bonneville?"

"Correct."

"Where was the Bonneville that night, Mr. Hausner?"

"In North Carolina. My wife was visiting family and drove it down there."

"Do you know of any other silver Bonnevilles on the base?"

He rolled his eyes.

"No."

"Then I presume you have no explanation as to how a silver Bonneville could have been the car that drove Amanda Fontaine off the base that night."

He looked to Shea, hoping for an objection, but none was forthcoming.

"No."

Holding the photos in my hand, I pretended to be examining them closely.

"Can you tell us how the scrapes on the underside of your wife's Bonneville came to be there?"

He paused, searching for an answer that would foreclose further questions about the car.

"Speed bumps. There are speed bumps at the apartment where we live."

"I see. And did the speed bumps cause the damage to the front right wheel well?"

Again, he stalled.

"Must have. You'd have to ask her."

"Who?"

"My wife."

He'd presented me with a gift. In his meticulous attempt to navigate the minefield of cross-examination, he had committed a grievous error. I had other questions but thought better of them. I had to play this card deftly and quickly before Shea realized what Hausner had done.

Picking up my notes and the photographs, I turned back toward my table and slowly moved behind it. But before I sat down, I stopped, turned, and looked at him without speaking. I shifted on my feet, dropped the notes on the table and put my right hand on my hip. I wanted the jury to think I'd just thought of something significant. I asked one last question.

"That's a good point, Mr. Hausner. Why have we not heard from Mrs. Hausner about her use of that car on May 15th?"

He froze. He knew she couldn't testify since she'd been in the courtroom throughout the trial. He'd created a trap for himself and then walked into it. Shea leaped from his chair.

"Objection, your Honor. Mr. Duncan knows better than that. I am the lawyer here, not Mr. Hausner. I make those decisions, and I alone."

Turning to me in manufactured rage, he continued.

"He has no right to ask such questions and he knows it."

He shook his fist in the air.

"This is an outrage, your Honor."

The judge was perplexed. I could tell he wanted to back up the Titmouse, but my question was proper, and I had every right to ask it. The defense put forth the alibi and I was entitled to explore it. A defendant is protected by the Constitutional right not to testify, but not his wife. The message to the jury, I hoped, was clear: she would not, or could not, corroborate his alibi.

This time, the judge didn't give me a chance to respond, perhaps fearing that my retort would do even more damage to Hausner's defense. Ever mindful of risking appealable error, he turned to me.

"Mr. Duncan, is your cross-examination concluded?"

It was not, of course. I wanted the answer to my final question. But the furor that it had caused was far more valuable than Hausner's denial.

"Yes, your Honor. Thank you," I replied, with a slight smile. "I believe we have every answer we need."

I glanced toward the jury.

"Every single one."

Still seething, Shea attempted to repair the damage on re-direct.

"Mr. Hausner, do you love your wife?"

"Oh, yes, Mr. Shea. She's everything to me."

"And are you a faithful husband?"

"Yes, of course."

"Is that her, seated loyally behind you throughout this trial, this terrible experience?"

Hausner nodded toward his wife.

"Yes, sir. That's her."

"And have you ever, during your entire marriage, given her any reason to suspect you of infidelity?"

Again, Shea was sharp. Since the wife couldn't testify, I'd never cross-examine her to find out.

"Absolutely not, Mr. Shea. Not ever. Not at all."

He carefully avoided the points I'd made, seemingly hopeful that he could bury them beneath this heap of marital froth.

When Shea rested, the judge asked if I anticipated any rebuttal evidence. For once, I did not. I was still sitting on Exhibit Number Seventeen, the picture of the missing bolt. It had been admitted into evidence earlier on the first day, of course, and it had remained quietly at rest among the other crime scene photographs. I was waiting until closing argument to bring it to the jury's attention and hammer it home. We recessed until the third day.

Chapter Thirteen

Closing Arguments

The next morning April Winston was waiting for me at the courtroom door.

"I found something."

We slipped into a witness waiting room.

"We do closing arguments in about two minutes. What do you have, April?"

"This," she said, handing me a manila envelope. "Hausner's wife was in North Carolina the night of the crime, just like he said."

I put down my files and opened the envelope.

"Okay. So?"

"She got a ticket for an illegal turn in Raleigh that night. But check out the car she was driving."

I had seen hundreds of traffic citations and knew where to look. Three quarters down the page was the automobile description: Ford Explorer.

"DMV records confirm that the Hausners have only two cars. He was driving the Bonneville that weekend for sure."

This was all I'd need to eliminate all doubt, reasonable or otherwise. It would place his car over two hundred miles away, put Hausner and Amanda in the Bonneville and, most of all, prove him to be a liar.

Except that it was too late.

"April, we rested yesterday. You've seen what Wally did to me already. Denied the continuance, kept out the photos of Amanda's injuries, halted my cross-examination of Hausner. There's no way he'll let me reopen the case now."

"Can't you try? C'mon, Bill. You can't fold now."

This ticket could eviscerate Shea's defense and send Hausner to the penitentiary.

"Do we have anyone from Raleigh? The issuing officer? Anyone from DMV?" I asked.

She sat, sighed, and cursed silently.

"No, of course not. I just found this late last night. I got to thinking about why his wife wouldn't testify and took a flyer. I found the charge in the Raleigh traffic court records and this morning had a clerk fax me a copy. I only received it a few minutes ago."

I sat down next to her.

"You're a fine cop, April. But you see where I'm going, right?"

"Yeah. Hearsay. An out-of-court statement, no opportunity to cross-examine the source, therefore unreliable. I know the drill. Even if Wally lets you reopen, Shea will object and that gives the judge a way to screw us again."

"If I could find an exception to the rule and get this copy qualified as a court-record, I still need someone from the Raleigh clerk's office, or better yet the officer that wrote it up, to authenticate it. If I can't do it, that's just one more opportunity I'll be giving Shea to claim we're trying to stack the deck."

She bowed her head.

"And I suppose asking for a one-day continuance is out of the question."

I looked at her. She raised a hand.

"Never mind. Even I can answer that one."

"It's good work, April. Hold on to that. If this jury hangs, we'll have this in our back pocket and bring the officer up the next time."

I put my hand on her arm. She was a pro. Some cops figured their jobs were done when the arrest was made. The good ones know it's not over until the verdict is read.

"Let's go inside. I can't keep the jury waiting or Wally will send Tuck out to arrest me."

Shea and Hausner were at their table when I got to mine. Tuck was standing by the door to the judges' chambers behind the bench, waiting for me.

"All ready to go, Mr. Duncan?"

I nodded.

When Judge Fairchild entered, he scowled in my direction, enough to let me know he was aware that I'd caused a slight delay.

"Any preliminary matters, Counsel?"

"No, your Honor," Shea said, standing. "The defense is ready for closing summations."

"Bring in the jury, Mr. Tucker," the judge said, not waiting for me to respond. If I needed an affirmation that my instincts were right about how he'd react to a request to reopen the testimony, I'd gotten it.

***

Closing arguments can be overrated. Nothing new in the way of evidence comes out, and the judge always tells the jury that the lawyers aren't witnesses. All we're doing is telling the jurors what we think the testimony they already heard really means.

But those people in the box expect a performance, too. They've probably made up their minds already, even though they've been admonished not to do so, but in a close case the lawyers can make the difference between guilt and exoneration. Even then, the defense attorney only needs to instill doubt in their minds, not convince them of the defendant's innocence.

My task was to give them the confidence they needed to send a man to prison, perhaps for decades. They are normal people with normal lives, most of them reluctant to speak to a neighbor about an annoying dog. And yet, I was about to demand that they decide how a man would spend most of the rest of his life.

Because the prosecution has the burden of proof, we get the last word. I would speak first, make my summation, and then Shea would get his turn with the jury. That was his only chance to tear into our case and create enough questions in their minds to make them comfortable with releasing Jason Hausner back into the community.

When he was finished, I would have one final opportunity to reach back to that rainy night in May, when one human being savagely brutalized another in a deserted parking lot, leaving her for dead, and somehow balance what we call the scales of justice. Shea's reputation for pyrotechnics in closing arguments was well deserved. There was little point in attempting to out-perform him early. My second shot, during rebuttal, would be the right time.

The judge read the instructions to the jury. These set out what they can and cannot consider in reaching a verdict and what they must determine has been proven. Most important, the instructions identified each element of the crimes for which Hausner stood accused.

In my closing I held them up and ticked off the evidence that supported each. There was no reasonable doubt, I told them, as to any of the components of the offenses. The only real question was whether Jason Hausner was the perpetrator, as there had been no contest as to the occurrence of the crimes themselves.

I challenged the alibi, noting that the witnesses told identical stories but could not recall a single moment of the previous or following weekends.

I kept my words and pace even keeled, reminding them of every one of the promises they'd made at the beginning of the trial during jury selection. I made sure, however, that they knew I'd get one more chance speak to them after Shea was done.

"Members of the jury, we have reviewed the evidence you heard over the past two days. Amanda Fontaine was taken to Riverside Park and nearly killed. No one disputes this. She has identified the perpetrator as Jason Hausner. She has no doubt. Her friend, Laura, also identified him and corroborates the fact that Amanda and the Defendant left the base together. Mr. Hausner himself acknowledged that there was no one at the NCO club that looked like him, and he knows of no other silver Bonnevilles on the base. He does, of course, deny that he was in his wife's car that night, but Boyd Wetherholt told you that it was a car identical to the one owned by Dolores Hausner that he saw run down Amanda Fontaine."

I took a final moment to pause and let that sink in, and then I did something I reserved for special cases.

"Mr. Shea will speak to you in a moment, and I challenge him to convince you that all of those facts, somehow, are wrong. Because if he cannot dismantle every single one of them, there is only one verdict to return. I will have a last opportunity to speak to you when he has concluded, and I will ask you whether he's done it."

My closing had been understated and controlled, but by throwing down that gauntlet at the last moment, Shea had no chance to prepare. I hoped to disrupt his delivery.

He was true to form, starting hot and then really lighting up. He chastened the police for the photographic line up he claimed was designed to aim Amanda's identification toward Hausner. He ridiculed April for sneaking around taking pictures underneath the Bonneville. He reserved his greatest scorn for Amanda Fontaine, the brazen little tramp that showed up at the NCO Club, already drunk, and who at the end of the evening left with someone she didn't even know. It was a terrible shame, he agreed, but what did she expect? Carefully walking a fine line between blaming the victim for a criminal's act and questioning her credibility, he shook his finger in my direction and insisted that her injuries did not entitle her to convict the wrong man.

He then berated me for not respecting the stature of a former soldier, who had served in combat and was now reduced to defending himself against the baseless claims of that girl. And not only did we rely on the word of an admittedly confused victim, but with all this time to develop the case we had never found blood, fingerprints, or DNA to properly tie the Hausner Bonneville to the events at Riverside Park. He was far too thorough to let those pass.

Boyd Wetherholt, the auto body mechanic, had seen a silver or white Bonneville, Shea noted, but had not been able to read the license plate or even determine its identifying state. He and his passengers had not seen the driver. The fact that the vehicle was similar was not enough to overcome the reasonable doubt so plainly apparent, he concluded. His face red, hands shaking in outrage, Shea practically ordered the jury to return a verdict of not guilty.

"You cannot, ladies and gentlemen, absolutely cannot wipe away reasonable doubt on the say-so of a girl that was admittedly so drunk that she didn't even know the name of the man with whom she left the NCO club, the kind of car in which she rode, and somehow suffered such traumatic injuries."

The Titmouse took a moment to breathe, staring at them one by one.

"You cannot sentence this honorable soldier, who defended this country, you and your families, on such flimsy testimony."

I waited for Shea to sit and took another few seconds before standing, allowing, I hoped, for the temperature to cool. As I began my rebuttal, I slowly picked up the dozen photographs I'd selected the previous night. Culled from all the pictures introduced early on the first day of trial, they showed the parking lot, the trail of destruction left by the Bonneville, the underside of Dolores Hausner's car, the loosened wheel well, and of course, Exhibit Number Seventeen, the one revealing the bolt.

I walked to the railing at the front of the jury box and placed the pictures along it as if I were dealing cards. The jurors peered over each other to look at them. I took a step back and paused, letting the fury of Tommy Shea's outrage subside.

I looked slowly at each juror and then began.

"Jason Hausner testified. He sat right there," I said, pointing to the witness stand. "He sat there and told you he didn't take Amanda from the NCO Club, and he didn't try to kill her. He didn't have to testify, but he did."

I walked beside the railing, beginning with facts no one disputed. This would narrow the scope of what the jurors had to determine was truth or false.

"Both he and Mr. Shea identified Mrs. Hausner. She sat right behind her husband throughout this trial. But you will recall that she didn't sit over there."

I pointed back to the witness stand again.

"Was there nothing she could say to corroborate her husband's alibi? She was in North Carolina, he said, with her Bonneville. But you must ask yourselves, why didn't she tell you that herself?"

I knew that I'd gone about as far as I could on the subject of Delores Hausner's failure to testify and didn't want to risk Wally's wrath in front of the jury—again. This was my final chance to convince them I was trustworthy. If the judge censured me at this point, I knew I could lose them for good.

"Simple. That car was here, in Riverside Park, running down Amanda Fontaine. How do we know that? Boyd Wetherholt saw it. Could it have been another silver Bonneville? No. Jason Hausner himself sat there," and again I pointed to the witness chair, "and told you that there are no others like it on the base."

I looked at each of them again, lowering my voice.

"And there's one more reason. The Hausner Bonneville left a calling card back at the park."

I stared back and let that sink in. Every juror was watching me. I walked a few steps along the railing, eye to eye with them.

"Members of the jury, Mr. Shea has tried to give you a simple task. Decide whether you believe that Amanda Fontaine could identify who it was that took her from the NCO Club and tried to rape and kill her. He says, if you do not accept that she was capable, then you must acquit Jason Hausner."

I raised my voice.

"It's all about Amanda Fontaine, he says, how drunk she was that night and how unreliable she is today."

Amanda was seated in the first row, behind my table, right where I wanted her. The jury had to look at her, too, when deciding who to believe.

"But there's more to it, ladies and gentlemen. A lot more. Jason Hausner told us he was driving a Ford Explorer that night. But someone was driving a silver Bonneville. Someone drove a silver Bonneville into that park at midnight, with Amanda Fontaine in it, and whoever that driver was, tried to rape and then kill her."

I'd created an expectation and held their attention, keeping them in suspense. Once again, I walked along the railing next to the photographs. The jurors were following me closely, but began glancing at the photographs, looking from them to me and back again, waiting for me to tie it all together. They had waited long enough.

"When you go back into the deliberation room, ladies and gentlemen, take a look at Exhibit Thirty-two."

I picked up the picture of the damaged underside of the Bonneville.

"Look closely at this picture and see not only the scrapes but the damaged wheel well. It even hangs low due to a missing bolt."

I held up the picture and pointed to the empty hole.

"And when you look at the other pictures, the ones that Officer Bowen brought us two days ago, the ones that trace the path of mayhem that the silver Bonneville left across the parking lot that night, bouncing over the curbs, crushing Amanda Fontaine, leaving tracks across her clothing . . . when you look at them, pay close attention to Number Seventeen."

I picked it up. In my peripheral vision, I watched as Shea and Hausner looked at each other and shifted in their seats. I paused for a moment, holding up the picture as I walked, meeting every juror's eyes again.

"Look at this one, Exhibit Seventeen, and see what lies in the debris left behind by that silver Bonneville. The missing bolt, the one that previously held the wheel well in place, is lying right *here*."

I halted, pointing to the bolt in the picture, as several of the jurors leaned over each other to see it. I gently laid it back on the railing.

That move unsettled everyone. The jurors peered at the photo, trying to see the bolt. The audience gasped. I stayed focused on the jury but could feel Shea stirring. I knew that I had only a moment before he tried to break my grip on them, so I took aim at the heart of the case.

"Jason Hausner used his wife's car to abduct a young girl and meant to rape and kill her. That car wasn't in North Carolina. It was right here, in Jefferson County, in that parking lot. He used his wife's Bonneville to commit these crimes but left a piece of it behind. That's why his wife didn't testify yesterday. That's why she sat silent for three days. But the Bonneville, here in Jefferson County, not in North Carolina, has spoken to you through Exhibit Seventeen."

Shea finally erupted.

"Your Honor, I object! This is highly improper. We were told nothing of this so-called missing bolt. This is a fraud on the court. This is an outrage. This is . . ."

"Mr. Shea," Judge Fairchild interrupted.

Then he turned to me.

"Mr. Duncan, may I see that exhibit, Commonwealth's Number Seventeen?"

"Of course, your Honor."

I handed it to Tuck, who walked it to the judge. He glanced at the picture and turned it over, reading the notes on the back.

"Mr. Shea, that exhibit was entered into evidence two days ago without objection."

He knew that Shea had gambled in his strategy, but it seemed as if he had drastically miscalculated. Like everyone else associated with this case, except me, he had missed the bolt in that picture.

"Objection overruled. Mr. Duncan, you may proceed."

Shea's oversight was his own problem, the judge seemed to be saying. I could not have written a script for this performance any better than what had just transpired.

I turned back to the jury a final time.

"There is no doubt, reasonable or otherwise, about who took Amanda Fontaine to Riverside Park. This case, at long last, is in your hands. The Commonwealth, your community, now relies upon you to do the right thing."

***

The word came from Tucker.

Nearly four hours had passed since Judge Fairchild sent the jurors and the case into the deliberation room. As a rule, I stay away from the courtroom after that door closes. Each minute seems like an hour, and everyone in the vicinity is on edge. The lawyers ponder every question they asked, the answers they got in return, the arguments they made or, just as often, wished they'd made. They try to calculate the why and how the jurors will ignore the contrary factors and still find in their favor. But none of this anxiety makes any difference. None at all.

And so, I stayed away. I retreated to my office, where I busied myself with anything at hand. The other assistants stayed away, as we all did when one of us had a jury out. It was bad luck, we believed, to talk about a case while it was being deliberated. After a while, Tuck leaned his head in my door.

"They're back. Best come upstairs now, my friend."

It has always seemed to me that the longest of times is what passes between the delivery of the news that a jury has reached its verdict and the moment when it is announced. The lawyers, parties to the case, and the judge must be located and brought back to the courtroom. The jurors gather up their jackets and purses and file into the box. The formalities follow.

When everyone had taken their seats, Judge Fairchild spoke.

"Mr. Foreman, has the jury reached a verdict?"

"We have, your Honor," the man said.

He handed the form to Tuck, who glanced at it and passed it to the judge. Fairchild read it to determine whether the jury had followed his instructions, then gave it to his clerk. I had an inkling as to the result when I saw Tuck whisper to another deputy, who then surreptitiously moved behind Shea and Hausner and pulled out his handcuffs. Beneath the table I made a fist, congratulating myself.

"Please stand, Mr. Hausner," said the judge.

His clerk began.

"In the matter of the *Commonwealth of Virginia v. Jason Hausner*, we, the jury find the Defendant guilty of Attempted Rape, and fix his penalty at ten years in the penitentiary."

His wife wailed, and Hausner, ever the gentleman, turned to her and barked.

"Shut up, you idiot."

"My car, my car . . ."

She was moaning, seemingly oblivious to the verdict.

"You did it in my car!"

The clerk continued.

"In the matter of the *Commonwealth of Virginia v. Jason Hausner*, we, the jury, find the Defendant guilty of Malicious Wounding and fix his penalty at fifteen years in the penitentiary."

Hausner continued to curse, and his wife collapsed in tears as the bailiff secured the handcuffs on her husband. Another deputy opened the side door of the courtroom and Hausner was led out, to be taken to the jail below the courthouse.

I looked for Shea, as win or lose it is a matter of professional courtesy to acknowledge the efforts of one's opponent after a trial. He was attempting to console the despondent wife, surrounded by some of the witnesses, so I gathered what was left of my files and headed back downstairs without speaking to him. I intended to call him later.

Maximum sentence on Count One, and just shy of it on Count Two. Even without seeing how Amanda looked in the hospital, they nearly maxed him out. Twenty-five big ones. Not a bad day at the office.

Amanda hugged me, her tears soaking into my jacket. April shook my hand. Dixon nodded, didn't say anything, and left.

The first person I saw downstairs was Casey Butler. His jury was still out in that check kiting case, but he looked genuinely relieved that Hausner had been convicted. If we'd have lost, I would have excoriated him for the poor way he'd handled the preliminary hearing and follow-up. As it was, I was flush with victory.

The Greatest Trial Lawyer in all the Land, as we called ourselves in the aftermath of a hard-fought victory.

A few of the other ACAs and I headed over to the Holiday Inn for the evening happy hour and, as is the custom, I didn't pay for a single drink.

***

I tried to reach Charlotte to tell her the news, but the call went straight to voice mail. At about nine o'clock, I left the bar and headed home.

Any concerns I might have had for her whereabouts disappeared when I arrived. Her BMW was parked in the drive. The house was dimly lit inside and when I opened the front door, I saw why.

A series of small candles zig-zagged up the stairs to the living area, and, strewn nearby, I saw various items of hers. A blouse, skirt, and assorted lacy things. As I closed the front door, her voice cascaded down to me.

"If that's the Greatest Trial Lawyer in all the Land, it's about damned time."

I reached the top of the stairs and found a few more candles set around the room, and an ice bucket with a bottle of champagne.

"Come here, big boy. It's time to celebrate."

She rose from a chair, wearing high heels, and eased herself out of my robe.

Chapter Fourteen

Charlotte

Charlotte was slender and lithe, with runway model looks and shoulder length auburn hair. To me, she was the sort of woman who seems to exist at an unreachable distance.

She'd been selected for a clerkship at the Jefferson County Circuit Court after graduation from a west coast law school. Those are coveted positions, as law clerks work directly with judges on pending cases. They spend countless hours helping them wade through the factual and legal mazes constructed by trial lawyers, where the competing interests can be measured in civil millions and criminal years. These young clerks, who spend a year earning their judges' trust, become prized recruits for the top firms and are rewarded with commensurate salaries and perks. Their employers get associates with credibility already achieved, along with friendly relations with the bench.

We'd met at a Jefferson County Bar Association event shortly after the Hausner indictment. I had seen her on occasion during her clerkship, in the courthouse cafeteria, but she'd always taken her lunch in the judges' dining room.

This time, it was an evening seminar, and I had been on a panel addressing the rules and subtleties of drunk driving prosecution and defense. She was getting some of her required continuing education credits and approached me afterward.

"Mr. Duncan, could you spare a moment for a couple of questions about the whole breathalyzer certification routine?"

"Bill, please," I said. "And you are . . ."

"Charlotte Spencer."

She smiled and extended her hand.

"I'm an associate at Winchester & Ford."

"Nice to meet you. I'm not sure I've ever seen anyone from that firm down in traffic court."

She laughed. It was pleasant, almost musical, and came from deep inside. It sounded like she enjoyed laughing.

"We have a few big shot clients that get themselves in trouble on occasion. We refer them to the usual lawyers. In fact, a couple of them were on the panel with you tonight. But I'd like to make myself, let's say, more important to the firm. You know, do what I can to keep the business in-house."

"And get closer to those big shots, too, I would imagine. I'm guessing an associate has limited contact with the firm's high rollers."

"Mere rumors," she said, smiling slyly. "I'm sure they know me quite well from my initials on the monthly billing statements, even if we've never met."

"Well put. What can I tell you about the breath machines?"

She smiled again.

"Care to talk about it over a drink?"

I smiled back.

"Oh, the irony."

"I said *a* drink, not enough to get us doing field sobriety tests in front of a cruiser on the side of the road. But just in case, can I get a note from a prosecutor?"

"Sure."

"Will that work?"

"No, but it will make for a great story tomorrow morning during arraignments."

We took our conversation across the street, where we talked about a variety of things over vodka and tonics, none of which involved Alco-

Sensors, breathalyzers, or sentencing guidelines. I told her stories of courthouse antics and she laughed long and happily, pleading for more. I coaxed her to reveal the judges' secrets, but she demurred. Someday, she said, I'd hear things that would astonish me. It was a subtle way to ask me to see her again, I hoped. But that night she held firm and protected her former employers.

I also learned that Charlotte enjoyed the piano, spending late evenings playing after long days grinding away in her office. It was a reach back to her pre-lawyer past, enjoying the comfort of classical music and a healthy separation from work. Each morning, she rose early and ran, biked, or visited a gym. She'd been on her college tennis team, and while she still played occasionally, she confessed to being so competitive that it was difficult to enjoy a friendly match. Nor did she have the time to keep her skills as sharp as she liked. I took it to mean she lost too frequently for her taste.

She had revealed little of herself, but enough to entice me to suggest we reconvene on a weekend. Her response came quickly enough that when I later considered it, I realized she'd already decided to accept my invitation before I'd asked.

One Saturday morning, when our schedules finally permitted, I took her to the reservoir where I'd arranged for a pair of kayaks. She had insisted on packing our lunch, no doubt allowing her to demonstrate her culinary skills. I came to learn that while she enjoyed and appreciated fine restaurants on significant occasions, she preferred planning and preparing a meal at home, accompanied by music and a glass of wine. Or two.

I took note.

The day on the water was idyllic. No cell phones, no office chatter, and the farther we floated the less we heard but for the sound of our paddles slicing through the water. She wore the top half of a swimsuit, running shorts and sandals. As she aimed her kayak ahead of me, I watched the muscles and sinews in her arms and back flex methodically. She was smooth and feminine, but well-toned, with an athlete's graceful ease.

We stopped at a small island where we ate the lunch she'd prepared. Sitting on a blanket, we talked and laughed between bites of fruit and quiche and sips of beer.

This is the way one spends a perfect day.

By the time we returned the boats it was near dusk. We had talked of families, schools, sports, and music, but never the law. Still, I felt that there was so much more to learn about her. I was entranced but leery. How could a prize like her still be available? Was she? There had been no mention of other men. Smart, pretty, successful and cultured, she presented a rare but exceedingly attractive combination. It was the sort of question I knew needed asking eventually, but I declined for the moment. The answer would be informative, but perhaps awkward, so I left it alone. The day had gone so well I just didn't want to risk unsettling it.

There are few transferrable skills that a trial lawyer can bring to a social setting but knowing when *not* to ask a question is one of them.

Over the ensuing weeks, we met for drinks after work, occasional courthouse cafeteria lunches, and spoke by telephone almost nightly. I finally summoned the nerve to invite her to my home, the carriage house, for dinner.

On the appointed day, I looked after the grounds early, seeing that the lawn was mowed and trimmed. The view from the second story back deck, where I keep a grill, includes a descending stretch of grass leading to what the Sandersons call their lake. It is just a large pond, bordered on three sides by forest. In the center is a floating wooden platform put there years ago so their children could swim to it and dive from its perch. After an occasional long day of outdoor work, I sometimes swam out to it and relaxed in the solitude it offers.

Charlotte appeared, radiant in a light blue dress. It was simple but refined, made by some famous designer of a satin-like material, and it probably cost more than a closet full of my best suits. She brought a salad and an exotic dessert from her favorite French bakery. I grilled salmon flanks, vegetables, baked a couple of potatoes and poured wine, all within the narrow constraints of my cooking talents.

"So, did the Sandersons adopt you, or are there incriminating photographs someplace?"

"Nice hovel, huh? No, Prescott and Betty are just old family friends. When he retired, they wanted someone they knew to keep an eye on the place. They travel, and so I do a walk-around each day, check on the main house and keep the grounds in good order. I'll turn on a few lights, drive their cars now and then, just to keep the place looking lived in."

"Where do you find time to do all the landscaping?"

"I don't. There's a groundskeeper for that. But I like to get outdoors when I can and sitting on a John Deere for a couple of hours is a good way to clear away the fog of a week in the courthouse."

"A true Renaissance Man."

"You got it. Brains and brawn, that's me."

I smiled.

"And I cook, too. And read books. And listen to music."

Knowing her affection for piano, I played a collection of Mozart solos. I broke my own house rule, that when permitted good music one should listen and not talk through it. But a pleasant meal is enhanced by sounds of romance, not those of chewing or just silence. I compromised and kept it low. She appreciated the selection and, perhaps incorrectly, credited me with a modicum of refinement.

After dinner, we sat on the deck and talked, watching the sun set behind the trees surrounding the lake, until she finally posed the question I guessed had been on her mind since that day at the reservoir.

"So, why are you still single?"

I had expected the question to arise at some point. Still, it caught me by surprise since thus far, we had avoided probing each other's romantic histories.

"Love gone wrong."

She raised an eyebrow and looked at me.

"Did someone write a country music song to commemorate it?"

That cajoled a smile out of me, remarkable in that the story had been the source of such heartache years earlier.

"It would take an entire opera to do it justice."

"Oh, now you have to tell me."

"The short version: boy meets girl, boy loses girl, boy decides not to jump off a cliff and instead becomes a famous county prosecutor."

She poured us both another glass of wine and settled into her chair, pulling her feet up beneath her.

"And now, the long version. The director's cut. All the scenes."

She leaned in and flashed a sly grin.

"You are a sadist."

"I'll be gentle."

I thought for a few moments and wondered if I could speak of Marshall at length without boring Charlotte or, worse, coming unraveled.

"I'm sure it was like so many other relationships that simply don't work after a while. It just took me a long time to accept that when it ended, it was really and truly over and lost."

"As in, you were the loser?"

I winced.

"That's your idea of gentle?"

I told her anyway. Marshall—she went by her middle name, a family tradition—and I had been together for several years, laboring through professional schools at the same time. She was in a postgraduate program up in Baltimore and I studied law in Virginia. I told Charlotte about how we had become close friends, then lovers, and how before then I'd never thought it was possible to be so happy.

"I felt like I had completely surrendered to her. I allowed myself to yield and give her the power to lift me up or crush me, and it was wonderful. It was like falling off a cliff into an abyss and landing on a soft bed of feathers."

"That's not very romantic," Charlotte said, wrinkling her brow.

"Oh, but it was. That's why they call it 'falling in love.' I just fell in, eyes wide open, voluntarily, and gave up my heart."

The things we say after a couple of drinks.

"How did she respond?"

I will always love you, I'd said. *No one will ever love you more than I do.*

I remembered only that Marshall smiled and embraced me that night.

"Come on, Bill. Don't hold back on me. What happened?"

My chest tightened.

"Everything was fine. At least I thought so at the time. Things were so fine that I anticipated that we'd be married after we were done with school and had our degrees, so I pillaged my finances to buy a house. We both grew up nearby and I wanted to come back. I took out the maximum student loans possible and after getting hired by Mac McGuire, the Commonwealth's Attorney, I made the down payment. But instead of getting married and sharing the cost, well, we didn't. She never came home to Jefferson."

It turns out that forever just isn't that long after all, I'd thought at the time.

Charlotte silently considered my answer, and I recalled times and emotions I hadn't felt for quite a while. Feelings I thought had been buried years earlier turned out to be lurking just beneath the surface, waiting for the opportunity to rise up and haunt me all over again.

"I had to get out of that house since I couldn't begin to afford it alone, but I took a bath on the deal, selling it so soon. The Sandersons were long-time friends of my family and when they found out about my predicament, they offered the use of this place until I got back on my financial feet. It's worked out pretty well, so I'm still here."

"Free rent?"

"As an old coach of mine was fond of preaching, 'free is better than cheap.'"

Charlotte was quiet.

"No warning?"

I looked at my glass.

We'd have been perfect for each other, Marshall had written. *If only we'd been different.*

"Not that I saw at the time, but you know what they say about love."

She looked away and nodded.

"Blind. Right."

"Looking back, I guess there were cracks in the foundation. But let's not dwell on that. Not tonight."

It was time for me to be silent. Truth may bring us comfort or pain. We can't control it, but we do control whether we recognize and accept the truth at all, something I had failed to achieve for so long after Marshall left.

"And you've been flying solo ever since."

I lifted my glass.

"Well, I never said I joined a monastery."

"If only these walls could talk, right?"

She playfully waved her hand at the room.

"They'd spin quite a tale."

She laughed.

"An old one, but I walked into it. So, tell me. How did it all end with Marshall?"

Hearing Charlotte say her name echoed like a note off-key, something unusual, as if it somehow introduced the two women to each other with me present in the room. It made for an uneasy feeling, and I looked away from Charlotte and out toward the lake, where the stars were shimmering in reflection.

So much time, so many nights alone, so many times I'd stood here on the deck and relived that final moment, that loss of hope.

"Just a letter. We spoke one last time and I used all my mighty talents as an advocate to make a case for us. I don't think she could handle another conversation, so she just wrote it."

I looked at my empty glass instead of Charlotte.

"I came to understand that some people are just right for us at one stage in our lives, but not the next one. I haven't seen her since."

"Like Humphrey Bogart in *Casablanca*, standing in the train station."

Charlotte got up to bring the wine from the kitchen and offered to pour me another.

"I never liked that movie, after . . ."

I put a hand over my glass.

"And why am I telling you all of this? I'm being cross-examined, and you haven't told me anything about your own past. I'm sure there's a battlefield out there, littered with broken hearts and failed attempts to win your affection."

She sat and edged forward in her chair.

"We're built on our failures and losses, not just our triumphs. The good times make for nice memories but it's the cuts and bruises that make us what we are. Those are the things in life that mold us. I want to really know you, Bill. I want to know what hurt you, and what made you strong."

She pried into me, not with a crowbar or even a knife, but with an easy view into my soul. It was like she'd listened to my thoughts even before we'd met.

"Fair enough. When is it going to be my turn?"

She smiled.

"How is it you're still single?"

Leaning back, she looked away.

"Maybe next time. I know a little about heartache, too."

As she turned to me, her eyes narrowed.

"But there's only so much room for that in one evening. Now, enough of that lovey-dovey stuff. I need to know about one more thing."

She looked over her glass at me.

"How was she, you know, in the boudoir?"

I sputtered.

"There are some things . . . my God, Charlotte."

"Nonsense."

She insisted, laughing at my embarrassment.

"Tell me."

Another frontier to be crossed.

There had been winter nights when we huddled in the darkness beneath layers of blankets, holding each other close as if the world were empty, except for us. I thought of quiet summer afternoons, a warm breeze gently billowing the sheer curtains in her bedroom as it cooled the sweat on our skin.

But no.

Charlotte accepted my non-answer.

"Even if she broke your wallet right after she broke your heart, I suppose some things ought to be left alone. I'm just . . ."

She drifted, waving her hand back and forth.

"Curious? Scouting the competition? I set the bar pretty high, I warn you."

I smirked.

She laughed again, that deep musical laughter I came to cherish, and went to the kitchen to gather her things.

"I should be going."

I shrugged, not knowing how else to respond.

"It's late, and it's been wonderful, Bill. Thank you for going to all this . . ."

"Trouble? None. I do this every night."

"My luck to be on the guest list, I suppose."

I walked her to the car. Charlotte carried her purse and the empty salad bowl, clutched in her arms and against her chest. She leaned forward and kissed me, a brief brush against my cheek, and slid into the front seat before I could reach to embrace her.

"Let's talk tomorrow. I'll be at the office early."

She started her car.

"It's Sunday, for goodness sake. Don't you people ever take a day off?"

"Captains of industry, pal. No rest for the weary."

And she was off.

I finished cleaning the kitchen and turned on music again before I returned to the deck to savor the evening. For a moment, I considered a collection of Puccini arias.

Not yet. The man that composed La Boheme *and* Madame Butterfly *knew heartache better than anyone. Not just yet.*

I put on Mozart and poured a small glass of the Sandersons' best bourbon.

What am I doing? She's a country club girl in a white shoe law firm, making twice what I do. We make each other laugh, but she left with little more than a handshake. Could she possibly know the way she makes me feel? What is she thinking? What the hell am I thinking?

This gradual slide into vulnerability, this descent into exposure. I knew the more I opened myself to her the more it would hurt if once again I was wrong.

I savored the bourbon as the moon rose and stars sparkled down on the lake, a mirror of flickering, rippling lights. Fireflies darted over the freshly mowed lawn.

Don't do it again. Don't let her in. Don't do it.

***

Later that night, just after two o'clock a.m., the bedside telephone woke me.

"Hello?" I mumbled, fumbling in the darkness and expecting a police officer's voice. It was not unusual to field calls from them during the heat of a case investigation, even in the middle of the night.

"Are you in a coma? I've been knocking on your door for ten minutes."

"Charlotte?"

"Who were you expecting?"

"Here?"

"This is Bill Duncan's house, right?"

I stumbled down the stairs and opened the door. There she stood, wearing the same light blue dress as she had earlier that evening, but barefoot.

"Nice pajamas," she said, noting my gym shorts. "Let's go."

She took me by the hand.

"Uh, go?"

"Come on, idiot. This is too perfect a night to waste sleeping. Look at that moon."

It was high in the cloudless sky. She pulled me around to the back of the house and jogged across the lawn, down toward the lake. I followed her, still shaking myself out of the depths of sleep. She let go of my hand and dashed to the water.

Turning to face me, she ran backward for a moment and laughed at my clumsy staggering. Spinning back around, she crossed her arms, grabbed her dress at the waist, pulled it over her head and tossed it aside, all the while still running and laughing, revealing a white bikini. She ran on and on, down and across the pier and dove into the lake. As I reached the edge, I watched as she swam easily but quickly to the floating platform.

I followed.

When I reached Charlotte she was in the center of the platform and resting on her elbows, hair pulled back and face tilted upward. I held onto the edge, still in the water.

The moonlight gave her wet skin a silver sheen, with beads of water reflecting like tiny stars. The bikini, I realized, was nothing more than tan lines. All she wore was a smile and dripping water.

"I can't believe you don't swim out here every night."

"I probably would, if I could count on beautiful naked women being out here."

She smiled, her teeth shining in the moonlight.

"Give it time."

I crawled onto the platform as she lay back, and sidled against her, leaning on one elbow. Her demeanor had changed from when we were on the deck just a short time ago. Calm, quiet, she lay next to me without a word. I touched her face, drawing a line with my fingertip on her eyebrows, draining away the droplets of water. Stroking her silky hair, I looked at her closed eyes and delicate face, watching her breathe. The sounds of the outdoors in the middle of the night rolled over the lake from the woods. Frogs croaked, cicadas chirped, the breeze rustled leaves in the surrounding forest and water lapped against the side of our wooden island.

I had to wonder why I wasn't out here every night.

She opened her eyes and turned to me.

"Are you over her, yet?"

Ever confident, she demanded center stage.

"Over who?"

"Good answer. You can kiss me now."

I leaned down, and my lips met hers as she reached an arm around my shoulders, pulling me close.

"Now get out of those silly shorts."

I never showed good judgment at times like that.

***

Afterward, we swam back to the shore. I saw that she'd spread a blanket on the grass before knocking on the front door. In my sleepy haze I had missed it earlier, trudging right past it. Two folded towels lay on it. We wrapped ourselves in them and collapsed.

She put her arms around me. I lay on my back, her head nestled against my chest, her wet hair across my shoulder. The moon had sunk behind the trees, but the stars still glittered between passing clouds.

My thoughts drifted until I wondered once more if I could give away my heart again. But I paid no attention to those doubts and fears and sank into the quicksand of a welcome blindness as surely as I did Charlotte's embrace.

I peered over the edge of the abyss and joyfully hurled myself into it.

Chapter Fifteen

Post-Trial

I awoke before dawn the morning after the Hausner verdict as Charlotte was getting dressed. She was heading off in her gym clothes to spin, lift weights, do yoga or whatever she else did with such unimaginable effort.

"Oh, come on," I whispered hoarsely. "Keep a poor trial lawyer company for just a moment longer."

Even in the dark I could see her smiling at me.

"Nope. You slack government types can lounge around all day but those of us who work for a living need to pay some bills."

She leaned over and kissed me, then headed for the door, carrying a garment bag in one hand and her high heels in the other.

"This was big. You'll get some press for this one. We need to talk about getting you into the big game."

She meant well, chiding me to go into private practice, and perhaps I will at some point. But not today.

Not being assigned a courtroom docket, I slept until eight o'clock. I fixed a pot of coffee, picked up my robe from the living room floor, showered and drifted into the courthouse around ten. I hadn't been near my office for several days and hoped to catch up before the weekend.

I'd barely entered the lobby when Dolly, one of the receptionists who doubled as my secretary, looked at me and froze.

"You need to see Patty. She's had us calling you. Did you lose your phone?"

The thought of my cell phone hadn't crossed my mind. I'd left it in the car when we went to the Holiday Inn the previous evening and never took it into the house when I arrived home, perhaps distracted by the sight of Charlotte's BMW. The battery was certainly dead. Besides, I hated that thing.

"Where is she?"

"Back in her office, I think."

Down the hall I headed, wondering what travesty had erupted while I was tied up with Shea. Patty was the office manager and probably knew more about prosecuting than most of us, even though she'd never practiced law a day in her life. She'd been with Mac since the beginning, more than twenty years.

I knocked on her door, already open, and went in.

"You lookin' for me?" I mumbled, an old joke between us.

"Oh, man, where the hell have you been? Shacked up with that honey of yours? Oh, man. There is some shit goin' on today. You have really fucked up this time. Oh, man."

Patty and I were friends, but she was never one to restrain herself when upset.

"Patty, what are you talking about?"

"That Hausner case. Wally is rantin' and ravin' about some stunt you pulled, and Tommy Titmouse has already got Hausner sprung. He's back out on bond."

There are moments of unexpected terror in everyone's life. This was one. My back suddenly ran cold with sweat, rivulets running down to my belt.

"Patty, I don't know what . . ."

"Prosecutorial misconduct," said a voice behind me. "Failure to produce *Brady material*."

Mac McGuire had walked into the office.

"Shea says that you put on bad evidence, sandbagged him and Wally, and this morning he filed a motion to set aside the jury verdict and dismiss the case."

I just stared at him.

"Wally is taking it under advisement. He let Hausner back out on bond, pending a hearing. Didn't even give us notice."

He clenched his teeth.

"Anything you care to tell me?"

I drifted to the old, well-worn wooden chair in the corner of Patty's office and sank into it. Countless prosecutors had sat in this spot over the years, sometimes laughing with Patty, sometimes being scolded. Careers had been launched and derailed in this place.

"Yeah. Something here isn't right."

I looked at Patty and Mac.

"This stinks on ice, Boss."

***

Shea was smart, I had to give him that. Overnight, he had figured a way to get another shot at acquitting Hausner. Despite his waiver of pre-trial discovery and the chance to examine the prosecution's evidence, he was relying on the case of *Brady v. Maryland.*

I was certain there was nothing wrong with our evidence or the way I'd presented it to the jury. I was under no obligation to produce it to him prior to the trial. But Shea wasn't whipped until every last ounce of fight had been drained out of him.

Brady, as it is known, created a precedent in 1963 when the United States Supreme Court ruled that prosecutors have an affirmative duty to reveal to defendants any evidence that tends to prove their innocence or even casts doubt on their guilt.

Robert Malvais Brady had confessed to his involvement in a murder but denied that he was the actual killer. Unknown to him, his partner in the crime admitted to the slaying. The police and prosecutors made sure that this detail remained concealed from Brady, and he was convicted of first-degree murder. When the previously withheld confession came to the attention of Brady's lawyers, they appealed but the Maryland Court of Appeals affirmed the conviction. The Supremes took a different view.

To hear the defense bar tell it, prosecutors are obligated to help defendants get acquitted. *Brady* didn't go quite that far, but it does require us to produce anything that is inconsistent with our theory of the case, especially if it could instill reasonable doubt in the minds of jurors. In my view, of course, the bolt was a clear link between Hausner and the crime scene.

I read Shea's brief. He argued to Judge Fairchild that I must have known there was at least a possibility that the bolt portrayed in Exhibit Seventeen was inconsistent with the ones used in Bonnevilles. But by springing it on the defense at the last minute, during my rebuttal, I left no chance that he could disprove our theory, or even put a question about it before the jury.

Now, he claimed, he had an expert witness ready to testify that the bolt came from a different make of automobile altogether. Shea demanded the case be dismissed, as not only had *Brady* been violated but a fraud had been perpetrated on the court. A hearing on this new view of the evidence, however, must be held. His expert, as yet unnamed, would supposedly testify and prove that the bolt came from a car other than a Bonneville.

Our office was in a scramble. I was anxious to have the police department forensic staff blow up the picture and show that the bolt matched what Pontiac put in its cars. I was certain it came from Dolores Hausner's car, but the stars were lining against me.

Mac told me not to handle the evidence or speak to witnesses. I steamed, but it was the right call. I was likely to be a witness in the hearing, and therefore couldn't be the presenting lawyer, too. Most of all, there couldn't be even a whiff of deceit. We couldn't give Shea the opportunity to accuse me of falsifying any photographs or strong-arming our expert witnesses. Since he had handled the case at the outset, Mac called on Casey Butler to resume control. Worse, Detective Dixon was put in charge of marshalling the evidence and coordinating with Forensics. I pointed out to Mac that April Winston was the detective who had made Hausner's conviction possible and that she was the only one who should be trusted now.

My entreaties fell on deaf ears. Everything—Hausner's conviction and the allegations against me depended upon two people performing their jobs as well as possible, and they were the same two people who had shown themselves to be poorly equipped or inclined to do so in the first place.

As the cacophony of the morning eased into a late Friday afternoon murmur, the euphoria of the previous evening became a distant, faded recollection. For the first time in memory, no one went to the Holiday Inn. Or at least no one invited me to go. We worked, fought, and played as a team, but that night there was no laughter, no joking insults, and no toasts.

I couldn't call Charlotte on my way home since my phone was dead, but found the one bright spot in an otherwise dismal day when I pulled into the drive. Once again, her BMW greeted me. My delight was dampened only slightly when I opened the door and found no candles or articles of clothing on the steps. Music was playing on the second floor and the aroma of simmering tomato sauce drifted down the staircase.

"That had better be one hungry lawyer," Charlotte shouted from the kitchen. "And I'm going to pour out this wine if he doesn't drink it soon."

I bounded up the steps and into the kitchen. A glass of pinot noir awaited me as she prepared an Italian feast. Salads were on the table, and I could smell bread warming in the oven.

"I guess you've heard," I said. "Shea has sprung Hausner and . . ."

"Yeah, I know. And you rigged the jury, or ate Shea's homework, or some such bother."

I was assured by her faithful ridicule of today's calamity. I couldn't tell if she was truly uninformed of the seriousness of the situation, yet, or was just trying to lighten the mood.

"You're right. It's probably nothing. The worst that can happen is I could get disbarred and not work anymore. I could use the time off."

"Fiddlesticks. You'll fix it. You always do."

Charlotte stayed focused on the bubbling vats of pasta and sauce.

"Who's your forensic expert?"

"Whoever he or she is, it won't be mine. When the hearing comes up, I'll be sitting in the hall with the other witnesses outside the court-room, while Casey Butler is in there, presumably fighting the good fight."

She stiffened and turned slowly from the stove.

"Butler?"

She pointed a wooden spoon at me and splashed tomato sauce.

"Butler? You've got to get Mac or Kent to take this case. You need to tell them Butler can't handle it."

I took my eyes off her for a moment, ostensibly to pick up my glass, but really just to break away from the glare she was boring into me.

"This is your career, William Duncan, and you've only got one of those. You've built a reputation for being a damn fine trial lawyer. People trust you. Judges believe you. If that simpering idiot blows it, Hausner goes free and you're out on the street. You have to get a grip on this thing."

She was shaking. The spoon dripped sauce on the floor, but she continued pointing it at me and growled.

"Don't let them do this to you, damn it. Be smart for once."

Words are my tools, the scraps of imagery and persuasion I use to make a living. There are times, however, when even I know there are none that will perform the necessary task at hand. I set down my glass, took the spoon from her hand and tried to wrap my arms around her. She pushed me away.

"No, none of this honey-dearie stuff. Now's not the time."

She turned away from me, hands on her hips.

I looked at my shoes, shaking my head. She was right.

"I know, sweetheart. I know. I . . ."

Before I could finish, she tore off the apron, threw it into the sink and stormed down the stairs and out the door. I heard the BMW's tires squealing for a good quarter mile.

Chapter Sixteen

Teammates

If Friday had been a bad day, Monday was one for the record books. I arrived at my office in the courthouse early that morning before everyone else. With no trials scheduled for the coming week, I expected to take my turn in the rotation, covering traffic and misdemeanor dockets.

A knock on the door came as a surprise, and looking up from the mass of files, telephone messages and reports, I saw a welcome and friendly face.

"Hey, Bill. I seen you come in. I brung you coffee."

It was Reuben Lewis, a mentally handicapped man who worked in the courthouse cafeteria. He cleared tables and tended to the endless dishwashing in the kitchen.

"I done it just the way you like it. Honey, no sugar. One cream."

He smiled.

"I seen you make it that way buncha times."

Reuben was a gentle man of unknown age. I knew he was older than he seemed, but his view of the world was seen through the eyes of a child. As a frequent target of ridicule, he gravitated to those of us who offered him a modicum of friendship. He liked old comedies, musicals, and comic books, I learned. After I gave him a collection of Laurel and Hardy DVDs for Christmas one year, he became my devoted admirer. A day in the courthouse rarely passed when I didn't see him and receive a report on the latest offerings at the nearby entertainment shop.

"I gotta get back t' work. I'll see ya lunchtime."

"Hope so, Reuben. Thanks for the coffee."

A copy of Shea's Motion for Reconsideration and Dismissal of Hausner's conviction lay on my desk. I forced myself to read it again, suffering through its exaggerated rendition of what occurred during last week's trial.

Long on accusation and short on facts, the request to vacate the jury's verdict and dismiss the charges rested on the bare assertion that it was at least possible that the bolt hadn't come from the Hausner Bonneville, but the way I presented it to the court led the jury to conclude that it must have.

Well, of course. That's exactly the way I'd planned it. But that bolt sure as hell came from Hausner's car.

Because it wasn't a Bonneville bolt, according to Shea's as-yet-unnamed expert, by not telling the defense that another car might have left it at the scene I had supposedly violated the *Brady* mandate. Intentional, fraudulent prosecutorial misconduct could only be rectified, Shea concluded, by vacating the jury's verdict and dismissing all charges. The reasoning was somewhat circular, but if his expert could back it up and ours couldn't, he likely had a winner.

As I was finishing a second read of the papers, another face appeared at my door. Casey Butler, from whom I had heard nothing since last Thursday evening, had a copy of the brief in hand and looked fretful.

"So, what do you think of Tommy's motion?" he said.

I tossed it onto the desk.

"Hard to say what's more preposterous—that he has somehow lined up an expert witness who's reached such a definitive opinion practically overnight and who the Titmouse is unwilling or unable to identify, or that Wally would actually take this crap seriously."

Butler looked at me without a clue.

"Well, what's your take?" I said.

He stepped back from the doorway, glanced down the hall as if looking at someone else and took a deep breath.

"I don't know, Bill. I think he's got something. I'm worried about this thing. If he can tie that bolt to another car, it could take both of us down, make the office look bad. Shit, the *Post* would have us on the front page every day until Mac ran us off."

I was dumbstruck. He'd spent the weekend worrying about the ramifications of losing and not a moment preparing to win. Pushing back my chair, I got up and walked across the room to him.

"Casey, you've got a tight case."

I pointed a finger at him.

"It wasn't just that bolt. The two girls ID'd that guy. The kids saw a Bonneville. You knew that when you put on the preliminary hearing. And you haven't even talked to the forensic guys. I'm telling you, there's no way that any car but Hausner's left that bolt. You saw the parking lot. Go back and look at all of Bowen's photos. That asphalt was brand spankin' new. It was as clean as your grandmother's living room carpet. There wasn't a damn thing on that parking lot that Hausner didn't leave in his wake. Don't go limp on me now, Casey."

Butler looked at the floor.

"Yeah. Okay. Well, I'll talk to Forensics and see what they can do."

I was done pleading. I watched as he sheepishly walked away.

What was Mac thinking? Giving Butler back this case. What was he thinking?

The morning continued to descend into a cavern of seeming insanity. Just before ten a.m., my desk phone rang. Mac was on the line.

"I take it that you were not invited to the press conference about to take place?"

I slammed down the receiver and ran to his office.

"What press conference?"

He was standing behind his desk, looking out the window to the courtyard below. Standing before a podium with the front of the courthouse as the backdrop stood Jason Hausner. A cluster of reporters were gathered, some holding microphones to record the event. At least one local television station was represented by a fellow with a shoulder-mounted camera.

"I can't hear anything, Mac."

"Me neither, but I don't need to. Here."

He handed me several pages.

Hausner had prepared a press release, no doubt with the able assistance of his lawyer, outlining the evil deeds he accused me of having committed. The language was similar to the motion I'd just read. The font, I noticed, was identical.

"He says they're filing a complaint with the State Bar against you," Mac said. "Depending on what else they find, they might sue us for civil rights violations in federal court."

"Civil rights? Jesus Christ, Boss, where does this lunacy end?"

"It's a bludgeon, Bill. A gambit. Tommy's always been a gambler, like in your case, not taking discovery so he could hide the alibi. But he's also one to prepare impeccably. Maybe he thinks he can force me to cave and drop the case, then finger you if he makes enough noise."

"Blame me for a *Brady* violation then fold on the case? Then you need to have a talk with Butler. He seems to be buying into this stuff."

Mac turned away from the window and sat behind his desk. Perusing photos from another case, he signaled that our conversation was ending.

"Casey's got a chance to show what he's made of," he said. "And I'm watching. By the way, why don't you take a few days off? There's no sense in you even going to traffic court until this blows over."

His tone was clear. There would be no further discussion. But given the choice between working a traffic docket and spending a few early fall days away from the courthouse, there seemed to be little reason to argue.

"Oh, and Rita Mohr of the *Post* has been calling," he said. "Don't talk to her."

On my way down the hall, I passed Kenton Raker's office. He sat with his feet on the desk, telephone at his ear.

"Hold up," he said, beckoning me as I walked by.

He quickly ended his conversation and put down the phone.

"Come in here a minute and close the door."

I hadn't spoken with Kent since Thursday evening at the Holiday Inn, right after the verdict. A recitation of him originally giving Tommy Shea the name "Titmouse" led him to buy several rounds in celebration of the Hausner verdict. A dozen times or more we heard about the finger-pointing escapade and "Shanty Irish" had been roared over and over.

"How's the conquering hero?" he said, chuckling.

"I'm pretty sure they're going to name the courthouse after me. Probably later today," I said. "What's up?"

He put his feet on the floor and slid his chair forward. Leaning toward me, he lowered his voice.

"Keep your eyes on Butler and Dixon."

Kent liked to keep a stack of files in the one other chair in his office. It dissuaded intruders from getting comfortable and overstaying what little time he could afford between trials. I moved it to the floor and sat down.

"Talk to me, Kent."

"Not sure. Butler's been begging for bigger cases for months. He did the Hausner preliminary hearing for you, then dropped the ball. I heard about what was in the file."

He rolled his eyes.

"Nothing. Hadn't given you anything. Then, Friday afternoon, he's back in Mac's office, insisting that he's the guy to bring this thing home. Trying to make up, I guess."

Kent leaned back, resting both hands on the desk.

"Does that make sense to you?"

It was one of those questions that answers itself. But what did it mean? I had done nothing to Butler and while we weren't close friends we'd worked together for several years.

Kent continued.

"Then there's that weasel, Dixon. He's never been reliable, and we both know he cuts corners. Never overly concerned with the truth."

"Why would they try to jam me up?" I said.

"I can't think of why," he said, voice still low. "Maybe it's not all about you."

His crooked smile made me laugh. Still, he made a point.

"There's a bigger picture here, Billy Boy, and we're not seeing it yet."

I pondered this.

Hausner must have powerful friends, and they might be running right over me.

Chapter Seventeen

Marquess of Queensbury

The mail at home brought what I knew was coming. Hausner's complaint, having been vetted by the Virginia Bar Counsel, was officially served on me. Mac got a copy the same day, and he called that afternoon. He gives a lot of orders but not much advice, so when he recommended that I meet with my lawyer as soon as possible, I listened.

Eugene Cresswell has been in private practice for several years. As a prosecutor, he didn't just pass through the office getting some trial experience. He tried every case he could, setting trials with juries when it was easier just to take them to a judge. He took other ACAs' cases when they had schedule conflicts or just plain wanted out of a tough one. In his three years in our office, he tried more juries than most of his stable mates did in twice that time.

It served him well. He had a strong client base and was now known as one of the most formidable criminal defense lawyers in Jefferson. Several corporations kept him on retainer to defend against claims ranging from employment disputes to medical malpractice. Among his steadiest clients was the Commonwealth's Attorney's Association, which paid him to represent its members throughout the state when bar complaints like mine are filed.

I called him.

"Gene, is there anything we can do to counter Hausner's daily speeches? Am I allowed to get ahold of a reporter, maybe Rita Mohr, and give my side of this damned thing?"

"The simple answers," he said, "are no and no. He's not committing a crime by running his mouth, and unless Wally issues a gag order, there's no risk to him. As for you, I'm sorry. The Rules of Professional Conduct prevent you from commenting on a pending bar complaint."

"Thanks for the good news," I said. "Wally won't issue an order like that because there isn't a jury involved any longer. He's the only one who has to make a decision and he'll say he isn't swayed by anything Hausner says. But seriously, I can't defend myself?"

"Only before the panel. Not in public. The people we want to impress are the judges that hear your case. They don't care about press releases, news stories or anything else. They've heard all that stuff before and will decide your case on the evidence alone. It's easy for me to say, but just let it ride. Don't watch the local news."

He let that sink in.

"Have you heard how it's going at the office?"

I was in my living room. Instead of the incessant and usually annoying racket of the CA's office, I was immersed in silence. I seemed out of place, being here at home on a weekday.

"Alright, I guess. As far as the primary case goes, the Hausner post-trial hearing, I'm in the hands of Butler and Dixon for now. Just what I need to rest easy."

"I know. Sorry again. That's not exactly a recipe for confidence. Set up an appointment with my secretary for tomorrow and get in here to talk about this thing."

***

Sitting in Gene's lobby, I found the difference between our offices to be stark. Instead of multiple telephones jangling relentlessly, a quiet tone emanated from a single panel on the receptionist's desk. Leather couches and oriental rugs decorated the room, instead of wooden benches and government-issue brown carpet. Framed artwork covered the paneled walls, as opposed to 8.5" x 11" notices, tacked onto beige and otherwise bare walls.

"Bill."

Gene beckoned from the landing.

"Come on upstairs. Have you been here before?"

"I thought you had a rule against that. Some of your criminal clients might not care to be seen around your former coworkers."

"Those idiots barely recognize me, let alone any of you boneheads. Last week I ran into one of them at the hardware store and he thought I was his old high school principal. Let me show you around."

We reached the top of the stairs where a short hallway led to several offices, a conference room, a kitchen and, finally, to his office. Here the walls were decorated with drawings of him trying well-known cases, the pictures having been shown on television or in newspapers since cameras still were not permitted in Jefferson courtrooms.

"I think Kent Raker has some pictures you might consider putting up here," I said, pointing at some open space.

"Is he still doing that?"

Among Kent's endearing traditions was drawing obscene pictures on the backs of legal pads that he left in the offices of new prosecutors. Mindless of the displays, the neophytes would stand in the hallways outside traffic court, talking with defense attorneys and taking notes without a clue of what was portrayed on the other side or why each lawyer in succession was unable to stop laughing. One assistant completed a felony trial without knowing why the jurors snickered throughout his closing argument, until a bailiff told him later that his notepad provoked questions during deliberations about his personal proclivities.

"Oh yeah he is, and more. Last month, he hid an open can of tuna above a ceiling tile in Pamela's office. After a week or so, it was making her eyes water. I think a county HAZMAT team finally located it."

Gene's suite was large, at least compared to my office. Rather than sit behind his desk he took a chair and invited me to do the same, on opposite sides of a small table. A woman wearing a black dress and white apron brought coffee to us on a silver tray.

"Just like the CA office," I said.

"I wanted you to feel at home."

A copy of my bar complaint lay on the table, marked up and tabbed.

"Well, should I start practicing 'paper or plastic?' or 'you want fries with that?' I mean, do I have a chance at beating this thing?"

The welcoming smile left his face as he picked up the complaint. His tone and demeanor shifted. Jocular friendship was set aside, replaced by serious counsel.

"There are challenges, but this is a fact-driven charge. You and I will talk more later, but the essence of the complaint is that you intentionally withheld *Brady* material from the defense and perpetrated a fraud on the court. This requires them to show two things. First, that you knew or should've known that the evidence, that photo of the bolt . . ."

"Exhibit 17."

"Right, Number 17, didn't really come from Hausner's Bonneville. The forensics guys will likely make or break that one, although if they come back with an inconclusive report, it will be hard for the Bar Counsel to prove you knew more than they do. That would make you careless, perhaps, but not fraudulent. Our position will have to be that the jury could have accepted or rejected the proposition that Hausner left that bolt on the pavement."

I thought back to the night I found that photograph. I'd scoured perhaps a hundred others looking for it because logic dictated that Delores Hausner's Bonneville had banged up its wheel well and shed a bolt. The entire exercise took me about thirty minutes, and when I found it, the last thing I ever considered was that it might have come from another car. How could it? The parking lot surface was immaculate, except for the trail left by the Bonneville.

"The second part of the complaint is that, knowing the bolt was possibly from another vehicle, you surreptitiously introduced it through your first witness, Officer Bowen, then waited two days, springing it on the Court during your rebuttal argument, thereby preventing a full examination of it by Shea and Judge Fairchild. Evidence that might have led to an acquittal, the argument goes, was used instead to ramrod a conviction."

"Oh, come on," I said. "Shea could've looked at it when I introduced it. He was too busy shrugging his shoulders, playing 'who cares?' because his client wasn't there, remember? Plus, he never asked for discovery. That's two shots at that picture that he passed on."

Gene quietly nodded. I realized I was straining his patience. It was time for him to be the lawyer, and for me to be the client.

"I know. I'm just telling you what Hausner has alleged in the Bar Complaint, no doubt ghost-written by Shea himself. Remember, Shea has a problem, too. His strategy backfired. If the Titmouse's client goes down because he overplayed his hand, guess who's looking at a claim of legal malpractice? You can rest assured that Hausner's next ploy will be an appeal based on ineffective assistance of counsel."

"I hadn't thought of that."

"Of course not, because you're focused on the attack against you. This is why you need a lawyer. But back to the complaint. In essence, if you'd treated Exhibit 17 like *Brady* material, which does not require a discovery motion since you're required to turn it over anyway, Shea would have had a chance to get an expert on it prior to trial and sort this out one way or the other. Without a link to the Bonneville, your case would have been weaker. Worse, with any evidence of another car's bolt in the middle of that debris, it would show another man—with a different car—was the perpetrator. Reasonable doubt, followed by acquittal. That's their case."

I had been as certain that the bolt came from the Hausner Bonneville as I was of my own name. I played it perfectly, introducing it along with several other rudimentary scene-of-the-crime pictures that Shea blithely agreed to allow into evidence without objection or even looking at them. Then, I let it sit quietly until the final moment, when he had no chance to challenge it. The craft that Mac, Gene, and I practice and have polished over countless cases had served the Commonwealth just fine that day.

But had it served me? Had I swashbuckled my way into a trap of my own making? Had I been driven by hubris, not guided by honest tactics?

"And if Forensics confirms that it's a Bonneville bolt?"

"You're in the clear. You accurately deduced the bolt to have been broken loose from Hausner's car—identified by your witness, the mechanic—as he scraped over the curbs. The pristine condition of the parking lot supports your conclusion that only one car, the one the witness saw run down Amanda Fontaine, could have left that bolt. You're not obligated to suggest something may be wrong with your evidence and offer a challenge to it. The most the bar counsel could say is that you took a chance, without forensic back-up, but I'll pounce on that. Those guys have never tried a case like this. They've never been in 'the pit,' as Mac calls it, slugging it out with murderers and top lawyers. The judges have seen those battles and they'll be on our side, as long as the CIB Forensics backs you up now."

I just looked at Gene, as it became clear that some guy in a white lab coat down in the basement of the Criminal Investigation Bureau was going to save me or usher me out of the practice of law altogether.

"One more thing," Gene said. "I've heard a rumor that Wally has been talking to the bar investigator."

"My God," I said. "Can this get any worse? I thought judges were prohibited from testifying about anything that happened in a trial where they presided."

"They are. Statute right on point. We can't even make him testify, but you can bet that whatever he says to them will find its way into the disbarment hearing, one way or the other. Other witnesses, whatever. They'll find a way, no doubt, and with Shea's able but anonymous assistance, to be sure."

There was Tucker, the bailiff. Wally would put him up to testifying, and I could only imagine what he'd be told to say. Wally must be afraid that any blowback out of this case will come back on him.

"So, how does this go?" I said. "Closed door, confidential hearing?"

"It could. But my preference is to request a three-judge panel and a public hearing, instead of a closed tribunal. The bar knows I play for keeps. Wally, too. I don't think he'll like the idea of my pushing his buttons in public, even if it is through another witness. He'll know I've figured out what came from him. And don't kid yourself. This will play to a full house."

"Is that good for us?"

"Look at it this way. Hausner is out there braying like a mule almost daily with his press conferences, making you out to be a slime bag lawyer who tried to send an innocent man to prison. He's got the *Post* doing at least one article a week."

I shrugged.

"The Rules of Professional Conduct, on the other hand, forbid you to speak publicly about a pending bar charge. If we beat this thing behind closed doors, what good will that do you? Hausner will just claim that the State Bar covered up for one of the boys. Sure, your license will have been saved, but who will ever trust you again? No, Bill, we need to do this on center stage, shoot down that loudmouth, kick those bar counsels' asses back to Richmond and clear your name."

"And if we lose?"

He shrugged.

"Then it really won't matter, will it?"

We looked at each other as the full impact of his words settled.

"Listen up. I looked at those photos, too. Aside from where Hausner hurdled those curbs and trampled that girl, that asphalt was clean. Like new."

"It *was* new."

"I know. Look, that bolt came from the Bonneville. That was nice trial work and when I'm done with Hausner those three judges are going to want your autograph."

He laughed.

"You haven't soiled my furniture, have you?"

"Not yet, Gene, but it may take me a few minutes to start breathing again."

He smiled.

"Good. It's working. Now, I said I need for you to explain your preparation. What you know, what you did, and why. Not just this photo. The whole trial. Do it in writing. It will make you think about it better than just sitting here, telling me a story. It gives me a chance to analyze it and I'll have better questions for you when we meet the next time."

This was his signal that we were done. Other cases beckoned, and other clients were to be met. But I was motionless in the chair. In this business, we live and survive by facing challenges, showing no surprise and certainly not fear, even when overwhelming evidence is mounted against us. Courtroom gladiators, however, may put their reputations and credibility in jeopardy with every trial, but the battles fought are on behalf of others. It was my hide at stake this time.

Gene was sending me home with an assignment, and now a little hope.

"I'll get to writing," I said.

***

Patty called me at home that afternoon. Mac wanted to talk to me right away, and in person. I went to the courthouse, dreading what was to come during every inch of the drive.

As I walked down the hall, past the small offices of my fellow prosecutors, it was as if I were invisible. No hellos, taunts, or acknowledgement of any kind. I had the feeling that everyone else knew what was coming before I did.

Mac closed his door behind me.

"I have to sit you down, take you out of the lineup," he said.

He looked past the piles on his desk and out the window toward the jail. He hadn't turned toward me, yet.

"You couldn't win a guilty plea."

He was right. I couldn't accept it, of course, but feeling my life collapse around me it seemed that more conversation was warranted, even if it wouldn't take either of us where we wanted to go.

I looked at him for a moment, then turned to gaze out the same window. The sun was setting, leaving the late summer sky a deep red.

Finally, I asked the inevitable.

"Do you think I was wrong? The way I handled that photograph?"

I didn't say it, but it seemed that we were both thinking of the lines that could follow.

You've known me since your first campaign. You stood in my parents' living room when I was fifteen. Now, I've worked for you more than a dozen years.

He spoke slowly and evenly.

"Here in this building, we have a principle of holding people innocent until proven otherwise."

"Boss, we're prosecutors. We decide who's guilty and then set about convincing everybody else."

I walked around his desk, standing in his line of sight, arms folded. He looked up at me, sadness showing in his eyes.

"What do *you* think?" I said.

He rolled his chair back from the desk, stood up and stepped to my side. We stared out that same window together.

"I think . . ."

He paused, not seeming to know where to go with that sentence.

"I think it's a bunch of crap. You were in the pit, and down there we don't play by the Marquess of Queensbury's rules."

He turned to face me before he continued.

"But I haven't seen all the evidence, have I?"

I said nothing. A smile formed on his face.

"Unless, of course, there isn't any."

Chapter Eighteen

Casey Butler

Theodore "Casey" Butler joined the office several years after I did. He came with high marks, having graduated near the top of his law school class, clerked for a federal judge for a year, and spent a couple more doing insurance work defending personal injury car accident cases. When he arrived at our shop he was already an experienced trial lawyer.

He saw himself as a ladies' man back then and still does, one of those fellows that always pauses when he sees a mirror. I noticed on his first day that he combed his hair against his natural part, making something of a flourish, a wave.

Dolly said it best.

"I never trust a guy that spends more time on his hair than I do."

Until the Hausner case, I'd never had a reason to question Butler's trustworthiness. But then again, that may have been because I'd simply never caught him in a lie. His foibles tended toward chasing every available skirt in the county. He had a wife and young child, as well as a seemingly insatiable appetite for women to whom he was not married. This was demonstrated by his endless flirting with the office staff or courthouse clerks, for the most part, and late-night drinks with female lawyers or cops. Sometimes, he dated women he met through cases.

It was one of those that had nearly cost him his job, and his marriage, a few years back. Casey had been working on a drug ring investigation with the undercover narcotics detectives. These were often interesting cases and for prosecutors they presented a welcome change of pace. For one, it got us out of the courthouse for a while. For another, we had a chance to help shape a case and its evidence before the arrests and indictments came down. Once the defense attorneys were involved, our access to the dealers ended. We wrote the search warrants so they could withstand later challenges and ensure that the evidence, developed over months, would one day be put before a jury and not be suppressed by a judge. The drug lawyers always claimed that overly aggressive detectives had violated the Fourth Amendment prohibition against unreasonable searches. Our job was to prevent that from happening.

But most of all, we enjoyed the excitement of the hunt. Trying cases is what we do, but the cops are at ground level, impersonating drug users and dealers, risking exposure and danger every day. The chance to work with them in the formative stages of an investigation was rare, essential, and above all, fun.

Casey liked the thrill, and he knew that when drugs and money were involved there were usually women not far behind.

"I'm toast, Bill," he lamented after his latest escapade had ruined a lengthy investigation. I waited for him to continue.

"Mac will fire me for sure. My wife will leave me. I'll lose everything."

He went on at some length, explaining how his relentless pursuit of "extras," as he called them, had led to a series of ultimatums. This time, he'd become entangled with a confidential informant. She'd used it, however, to thwart the pending bust of her boyfriend, a cocaine dealer.

He cried, he pleaded, and I listened to him for nearly an hour. Despite his travesty, the self-flagellation and despondence he displayed would have brought the coldest heart to sympathy. He blamed no one but himself and professed that he'd never again so much as touch another woman, if only I could see my way to helping him out of this tar pit of legal and domestic disaster.

I'd sent him back to his office with instructions to tell no one until I had thought through it all. On the one hand, his immediate dismissal seemed to be the obvious and necessary decision. On the other, the exposure of his affair with a confidential informant, a C.I., would hurt the credibility of our office, not only with the public but with the police.

I felt sorry for Casey and was angry at him for ruining a months-long investigation, but I was eternally loyal to Mac McGuire. He and I met after hours and came to a decision.

Casey's behavior showed an immense and unjustifiable lack of discretion. He'd been unable to control his passions and he'd exposed our office and several detectives to embarrassment as well as danger. But his error was human, not legal. We'd lost an investigation, but not a trial.

Mac and I decided not to fire Casey. The risk to the office outweighed the damage that would ensue should his misbehavior be made public. We called him to Mac's office the next morning.

"Butler," Mac said, "you have put all of us behind the eight ball."

"Mac, I . . ." Casey stammered.

"Not now," Mac said. "When I want to hear a word out of you, I'll tell you, and I'll also tell you what that word will be. Understood?"

Casey nodded, not even taking the risk of uttering an acknowledgement. Mac's face was red, and veins were bulging from his neck. I had not seen him like this since the last time I'd fouled up a case. I took morbid relief in seeing someone else on the receiving end.

"You blew a good investigation. You put cops in harm's way. You know how those dealers are. With all that money at risk, to say nothing of prison, they might kill someone. You got a detective made. Now he's done with undercover work. Somehow, I need to tell the chief that this guy has to go back to the street in a uniform. His career path has been stymied because you couldn't keep your pants on. What in God's name were you thinking?"

He paused for breath.

"If it were up to me alone your office would already be empty. I can't have a lawyer in this place who thinks more with his pecker than his brain. Think about the cops. Think about your fellow prosecutors. Think about it, Butler. How much dope will be on the street because you were screwing some coke whore?"

Mac was in full closing argument form, towering behind his desk, hands on his hips.

"There are two reasons you're not out on your ass right now," Mac said. "The embarrassment your dismissal would bring to this office, and Duncan has convinced me that you're a good enough lawyer to justify the risk. Personally, I'm not sure. But he hasn't let me down yet."

He glared at me.

"Yet."

He turned to the window behind his desk. I'd seen him do this before when he was winding up the verbal thrashing of an assistant.

"I have a lot of time and training invested in you. I can use a good hand. But for now, it will be Traffic and Misdemeanor Court for a while. I'm also cutting you from an Assistant Three back to a Two. That's about five thousand in salary as I recall."

Turning back to Casey, he concluded.

"You can stay and earn your way back or leave now. It's your choice. Personally, I can live with either one. Duncan says we should keep you, so I'm giving him your felonies."

That was a surprise, but I acted like I expected it. Mac had exacted a price from us both. It was my recommendation, so I got the extra load. Fair enough. He'd owe me.

"Let me know by the end of the day. Either way, get your files to Duncan."

Mac sat down, opened the file on his desk and, without looking up, spoke his final words to Casey.

"You can speak now. And the words I want to hear are, 'thank you, Mr. Duncan.'"

Casey rose meekly and quietly mumbled.

"Thanks, Bill, er, Mr. Duncan."

As he moved for the door, I stopped him. In front of Mac, I shook his hand. He'd taken enough of a beating. If he was going to pull out of this nose-dive, he needed encouragement. I was invested in him, thanks to Mac's terms.

"You can do it, Casey," I said. "Bear down. I know you can do it."

He nodded, bowed his head, and left.

Mac, as was his custom at moments like this, put on his glasses and focused on the documents before him.

"Well, we'll see," he said. "What the hell was he thinking?"

I closed his door on my way out.

What the hell was he thinking?

Chapter Nineteen

Unscheduled Appointment

This is the sort of thing defense lawyers can't stand. If I'd asked Gene for his advice, he'd have said, "Don't do it." In fact, he might have used more forceful and colorful language. I can't justify it now, and just couldn't help myself. When I get to that part of the memo he told me to write, I'll try to make this day sound logical.

The Motion to Dismiss and now Hausner's bar complaint had been eating at me. Shea played hardball, but so did I, and I did it straight up. The claim that I'd sat on *Brady* material and intentionally misled the Court had pushed me past my limit.

I met Charlotte for breakfast, before going down to the valley for a day, and talked to her about it. She convinced me to stand up to Shea and make him talk to me, lawyer to lawyer, man to man, face to face. It seemed out of bounds since the Motion to Dismiss was still pending. But I'd stewed over the incessant press conferences and the allegations in that motion. I went to Shea's office to have it out with him.

I didn't call ahead because I didn't want to give Shea a chance to be out of his office and conveniently avoid me. I figured righteous indignation, surprise, and pride were all on my side and that he'd have to give me a few moments. I had no expectation of talking him into withdrawing the motion but thought I could put him back on his heels and maybe learn something. I might even shame him into second thoughts. Besides, I had become pretty tired of being the last one to know anything about this case.

I'd been to his office once before that day. It's on the top floor of a twelve-story high-rise. I parked in the basement garage, having found the spaces reserved for his staff and clients, and took one. The elevator opened right up into his suite since he had the entire floor and rented offices to other lawyers.

The chairs and couches in the lobby were full. A tall, stout fellow I recognized as a retired cop stood guard. Eckhardt, I thought was his name, and we nodded to each other. We called him Eck. Knowing the sort of clientele Shea had, it struck me that having a guy like that out front was a good idea.

The receptionist glanced at her schedule and asked if I had an appointment.

"Just let Mr. Shea know I'm here. I'll wait."

I made it plain that I wasn't leaving until we spoke.

She buzzed his secretary and in about thirty seconds a little hottie in a tight skirt appeared and led me back to a small conference room down the hall. Showing me to a seat, she offered me coffee, just as sweet as she could be.

Looking back, I guess going there wasn't such a good idea after all.

***

When Shea finally arrived, he greeted me with an outstretched hand. I shook it, and he sat across the table from me.

"This is a bit of a surprise, William," he said.

He'd kept me waiting a good half hour, still showing me who's the boss.

"What can I do for you?"

It didn't seem all that long ago we were sitting like this in the courthouse cafeteria the morning of the trial.

"How long have you known me, Mr. Shea?" I said.

I wasn't there for social pleasantries or the coffee. Just as I had done in the trial, I wanted to establish immediate control of the conversation.

He swiveled his chair sideways and looked out the window.

"When did you start? Didn't we have that one little girl, the one that had the misfortune of accidentally selling contraband to Detective Bashinsky?"

Shea had a good memory. His topless dancer had sold two hundred dollars' worth of PCP to an undercover cop, and they used her to get to a dealer further up the distribution chain. All of that happened twelve years ago.

"In all that time, what have we had, maybe fifteen, twenty cases together?" I said. "Counting DUIs and various misdemeanors, what? Maybe fifty?"

He saw where I was going.

"Now, listen, William, I really should not be talking to you about Mr. Hausner's case . . ."

"Bull. You two are talking to everybody about it."

He leaned back in his chair and turned toward the window. The industrial smoke spiraled silently from a dozen chimneys across town. Beneath them, countless anonymous working stiffs labored. He might defend some of them. I might prosecute them. But now, he couldn't bring himself to look at me.

"William, I know what you want to ask. Have I ever been spun by you? Ever been misled? Sandbagged?"

He lifted both hands, dropped them into his lap, and turned to face me.

"No. You've always been straight with me. That's what makes a case like this so difficult."

"Mr. Shea, this has gone beyond doing your best for that punk, Hausner. Once you've accused me of professional misconduct and started filing bar complaints, it's personal. Tell me. If you've got evidence that shows I broke the rules, let's see it. Whatever you think you've got, I can't go back and change anything. Let's see it."

Having finally made eye contact I held it and leaned forward, staring at him. Tapping my index finger on the table as I spoke, I kept my voice low and put it to him directly.

"You're a pro, Tommy."

I'd never called him by his first name.

"You traded seeing my evidence for not telling me that Hausner and his pals were at the Waffle House. You knew I'd be over there with a subpoena for their receipts, questioning every waitress and busboy in the place. And you knew I'd never find a soul that saw your boys on the fifteenth of May because you and I both know they weren't there."

I paused, still eyeballing him.

"So, you took a chance. A calculated risk. What could go wrong, you thought? Dixon or Butler had told you everything, you thought. You gambled and lost. That's not on me."

He stood, walked around behind his chair, and grabbed it with both hands. Summoning all his acting skills, he pursed his lips, frowned, shook his head and finally spoke.

"William, this is a hard game we play. A man's future, his life, hangs in the balance. We lawyers are charged with playing with all our might until the game is truly over. I wish that I could offer more than my understanding for your position. I like you, William, but I have a duty to my client. Besides," he said, with a slight smile. "You yanked down my pants with that missing bolt trick. Then you tied them in a knot. I'm not letting you get the last word on this one, not without a hell of a fight."

I got up and put my hands in my pockets. There would be no more handshakes that day. He read my signal and began to leave. Standing in the door he turned to me.

"One thing, William," he said. "Did Butler tell you about that bolt?"

I looked back at him, deciding whether to answer his question or just laugh.

"What do you think?"

***

I passed through the crowded lobby a moment later, just as the elevator doors opened. A single passenger stepped out before I could enter.

Jason Hausner looked surprised to see me but put on a smug expression.

"No wonder Shea is in such a hurry to meet," he said. "But shouldn't you be cleaning out your office, Duncan?"

I couldn't tell how many of the people in the lobby recognized us, but I was immediately aware of the silence. All the low murmuring had stopped. Eck stood up. All of this I saw in the periphery because I didn't take my eyes off Hausner for a second.

The telephone was ringing but the receptionist didn't answer it. Every movement we made, every word we spoke, I knew would be remembered and repeated, possibly in a courtroom. Moments like this don't happen often, and never with any warning. Lawyers would hear about it and later claim they were in the room when it happened.

I moved first.

"Don't push your luck, Hausner," I said, putting my finger in the middle of his chest. "I'm not some helpless little girl."

"Fuck you, Duncan."

He pushed away my hand and tried to walk past me, between a Hispanic woman and her sack of baby accoutrements on the floor.

"I'll see your ass in jail and then I'm suing you."

I couldn't stand any more. The guard moved in our direction. I shoved Hausner, and he fell over the baby bag, tumbling to the floor. Eck scurried between us, pushing me away and toward the door.

"Knock it off, boys. Mr. Shea don't like his furniture gettin' busted up."

I shook off Eck's grasp and stood over Hausner, snarling down at him.

"Those guys in the joint are going to love a pretty boy like you."

Chapter Twenty

Old Man and the River

Later that day, after the incident at Shea's office, I took Mac's advice and rather than sit at home, staring at walls and worrying about things I can't control or even understand, I headed out of town and to the countryside.

The early fall is a time I rarely get to enjoy, since its appeal is found outdoors, far from the windowless courtrooms where I spend most of my waking hours. This day was bright and clear. The trees along the two-lane highway had begun to turn yellow and orange, and the temperature was almost summerlike.

Two hours later, I was deep in the Shenandoah Valley. I stopped at a familiar general store as I neared the river. The entrance was through a wooden screen door that was older than I, and the floor creaked and sank beneath each footstep.

Passing the row of old refrigerators lining the back of the store, each labeled with different kinds of live fishing bait, worms and nightcrawlers, I went to the one marked simply "COLD BEER." The six-packs inside were kept at a temperature barely above freezing to accommodate the patrons inclined to drink them on the way home.

"Want you some bait, too?" the proprietor said as I carried my purchase to the front. "Your daddy got some this mornin' and I 'spect he's about fed it all to the fish by now."

"No, but thanks, Claude. I'm just down for a few hours. Didn't even bring my tackle this time."

The older man looked at me. At least I think he did. His eyes didn't aim in the same direction, and I could never remember which was the good one.

"You been in the city way too long," he said, shaking his head. "Come all the way down here on a day like this and ain't even puttin' a line in the water."

"Maybe I'll just sit on the bank and read a book," I said.

I leaned toward him and whispered.

"Poetry."

He laughed.

"Now you messin' with me. G'on down there. He's at the usual place, if I remember what he tol' me this mornin'."

I paid for the beer, bid Claude farewell, and left. The turn off the highway was just down from the store about a mile. Taking the gravel road, I passed a farm, went through a cattle gate, and drove down a narrowing dirt trail to a wide meadow that lay next to the Shenandoah River. A few weeks earlier it had been full of this year's hay. The crop had been cut, baled, and stored in a barn, waiting to be fed to the herd in the coming winter. The field was clear, and across it I spotted a white pick-up truck parked beneath a tree along the bank.

I pulled in next to it, opened the cooler in the back of the truck and put the new six-pack inside right next to a container marked "hellgrammites." Smallmouth bass were said to be helpless to their allure at this time of year.

The river was low, thinly covering rocks that had been laid bare by mountain streams feeding this coursing swath of clear water for thousands of years. In some places, it was no more than knee-deep all the way across to the other side. The high-water levels of spring were long gone. The current was slow, enabling an angler to walk across, wade up or down the river along the bank, and cast his line into every known and familiar spot, seducing the hungry fish with shiny lures or live bait, depending on the word at Claude Shiflett's General Store.

I heard him before I saw his figure. The tell-tale sound of the bale, clicking shut after each cast and just before the line was slowly reeled back. In this quiet of the early evening, no sounds were perceptible other than the gurgling of the river rolling through its stone passageways, and the rod and reel, clicking and spinning, clicking and spinning.

He was on the far side of the river and about a hundred yards downstream. His pattern was to wade down along the other bank in the shallow water, come back across, and work his way up to his starting point. That's where he would deposit any fish he'd caught, restock with bait, and enjoy a beer. Judging by the empty space in the coolers, it looked like the bass were prevailing that day.

I sat on the front bumper of his truck and watched in silence as the water slipped past me.

Away, you rollin' river, I imagined him singing.

"Hey there, young fella."

I heard him holler as he climbed up the bank minutes later, dripping wet in a pair of old shorts and ragged tennis shoes. He ridiculed those who wore hip waders.

"How's the life of a celebrity?"

"I never thought of it that way. I must have tried a few hundred cases in that building but none of them got as much attention as this one."

"Seems like you're in a bit of a fix," he said, leaning his rod against the tailgate. "Is the office backing you up?"

"So far. But I'm on the outside of the case now."

"You're the trial lawyer. I'm just a lowly fisherman," said the re-tired CEO. "But it seems to me that you've got quite a few moving parts you need to get your arms around."

He'd spent a lot of time thinking about my predicament. I wasn't surprised.

"Like?"

"Well, for one, that Shea fellow. I've read about him in the paper and remember that profile a couple of years ago. The thing that stuck with me was a line about his clients. 'They're result-oriented and they pay extremely well for those results.' That's the kind of guy who can't or won't accept a loss."

I nodded.

"Then there's your judge. I've heard you talk about him before. Something of a tyrant, as I recall. For him, being a judge isn't a calling; it's an opportunity. He's got ambitions. A higher court maybe? Raw power? And you have a victim whose father was a general. I've crossed paths with a few of them in my time. Some are fine men. Some are bullies. But none of them accept losing at any level, at any time. That's why they're generals."

He took a pull on a cold beer.

"You lose this case, the guy who damn near killed General Fon-taine's daughter goes free, and all this publicity . . . I don't think there's any place you can hide."

I drained my own can and reached for another.

"You make it sound like I need to enjoy this one because it could be my last."

I popped the tab and waited.

"I've worried about this ever since you called last Friday. Your mother is all worked up. Probably has every little old lady in town pray-ing for you. I know you didn't do anything wrong, at least not intentionally, and even though I read the paper, I'm not even sure what you did. But I've seen what powerful people will do to get what they want. Little folks, honest folks, get ground up along the way."

He was right, of course. He was always right, it seemed, especially when I thought he was wrong about something that involved me. He had a feel for people, their strengths, weaknesses, and the things that drove them. He'd made a career sorting them out.

"Have they filed that State Bar complaint?"

"Yeah," I said. "It came in this week."

"When is the hearing in the Hausner case? What is it, a dismissal motion?"

"Motion to Dismiss, and no, it's not docketed, yet. Shea claims that his expert is working up a report, and then we'll get to see it. Our guys will examine anything he produces before the case gets back in front of the judge. The State Bar guys will wait to see how that turns out. This could take months."

He shook his head.

"And you're stuck."

"Right now, for sure. But even if I wanted to leave and go into private practice, there's no way. I need to come out of this clean and then win another couple of cases. If I don't, I'll be branded forever by this thing."

"Is that girlfriend of yours alright with this stuff?"

"Yeah, she's solid. Pretty mad that Casey Butler is back in the mix, but I couldn't ask for a better girlfriend."

He nodded and didn't say anything for a moment.

"How long are you on hold? How long can Mac carry you?"

He disassembled his rod and put the lure in the tacklebox.

"We haven't talked about that. I know it's on his mind, but he doesn't have to decide about me until the forensics guys can nail this down. I think he hopes it will all go away because they back me up and corroborate that the bolt came from the Defendant's car."

"What happens with the bar complaint? Do you have a lawyer?"

"That's one bright spot. The prosecutors' association covers the cost of my lawyer. I've already spoken with Gene Cresswell."

"Gene! How is my old pal? I haven't seen him since he went to traffic court with me last year."

I recalled with a chuckle my father's heavy foot and his notion that speed limits were merely recommendations. Gene had represented him as a favor to me.

"He asks me the same questions as Charlotte. 'Why are you still there? When are you leaving?' He's even mentioned my working with him. But he, more than anyone, knows I have to get clear of this mess first."

My father took off his wet shoes and slipped into sandals, done with the river for one day.

"You knew going in it was a job to do for a few years and then you'd move on. You've been working hard, trying cases, chasing bad guys for what, over ten years? It's no life for a fellow with a family."

We were heading into a conversation we'd had on several occasions.

"Twelve years, and I'm still single, remember?"

He leaned toward me, looking out from under those bushy eyebrows.

"That's my point."

He spoke softly, with no trace of lecture or impatience.

"Do you want to stay that way? What's your girlfriend say about that?"

"Pff. You know how that goes. What they say isn't necessarily what they think."

He laughed at that, choking on a sip of beer that he'd inhaled.

"Don't tell your mother I agree with you. But really, where is that going?"

For an old fisherman with no legal training, he could sure narrow the scope of hard questions and cross-examine with the best of them.

"For now, it's good. She has a great job, makes a lot more than I do, and hasn't asked any questions as tough as yours."

"Then what's holding you back?"

Another one.

"I don't know. I guess I've been too busy and too content with the way things have been going to worry about it much."

He took a long sip of his beer, looked across the water and sighed.

"Then you're still thinking about Marshall."

I stared at the river as it eased past us.

He let it go.

"You're a smart fellow. You've worked hard and are damned successful. People like you. But somewhere along the line, you need to figure out what you're going to do with your life. You know that parable, the one I told you that scared the daylights out of me when I was a kid? The one about the master that gave some talents to his servants? Did you ever stay awake in church long enough to hear that one?"

"Remind me."

"It's pretty popular with the clergy. The abridged version is that three servants were given different talents by their master, and a year later he returned to see what they'd done with their gifts. Two had invested and increased their values. But the third guy buried his in a field so he wouldn't lose it. The master was furious and threw him out."

"I recall there being a lot of wailing and gnashing of teeth."

"You remember that part well," he said. "You've got a few talents. Don't bury them in a field. Besides," he continued. "I put a lot of money into braces when you were a kid. Don't ruin those teeth with a lot of gnashing."

We laughed and sipped our beer.

"I know you have my best interests at heart. But right now, being a prosecutor isn't just what I do. It's what I am."

The sun had drifted behind the mountain. A blue haze settled over the valley, and the sounds of evening arose. Frogs, birds, and crickets all sang their tunes of love, loneliness, and prowess. Not so different from us, perhaps.

He turned to me and smiled.

"That's your call. You're the one who's got to find your own path."

I knew that at least some of his concerns for my career came from decisions he'd made, or didn't make, in his own life. We'd covered those over the years, too.

"One last piece of advice and then I'm done."

I braced for it.

"Nothing to do with this life-fulfillment stuff. But we were talking about all the moving parts in your situation a few minutes ago. Mostly the people. It's obvious that you're a step or two behind. You got on top of that trial quick enough. You always do. But there's more you haven't seen or figured out."

He pointed to the surface of the water.

"Look out there. What do you see?"

In the fading light of dusk, the surface of the river looked like a pool of silver, slowly flowing past us. Sporadic splashes broke the silence of the water leaving concentric rings, the brief sign of a fish gobbling smaller prey. The rings drifted downstream with the current.

"If you heard a splash and were about to cast your line, where would you place it?"

This was Fishing 101.

"Cast my lure above the splash, just a few feet upstream."

"Why?"

"Because by the time I've turned around to see where the splash was, the rings have flowed downstream a little and the fish that did it has moved on, probably into the current."

"Right. Cast your line upstream. A fish that's hungry is moving, and since lots of stuff is floating down with the current, he'll go upstream to get at it," he said.

He looked at me with his tired but crystal-clear blue eyes.

"Here's my point, son. You need to figure out how to protect yourself."

I nodded.

"There are things going on that you don't know about. Don't look where you've seen the evidence already. Be smart."

He nodded toward the river.

"Cast your line where the fish are going, not where they've been."

Chapter Twenty-One

Pat Down

The drive back from the river is always a melancholy time for me. Even as a child, it made me sad to leave behind a world of natural beauty, good times with family, and a chance to escape the noise and demands of city life, even if just for a few days or hours. The darkened, two-lane road stretched at least fifty miles before reaching the interstate highway, which became more depressing for its lack of traffic. Everyone, it seemed, was already at home. Reaching my destination meant returning to work, leaving the energy, sun, river, and mountains as a memory to savor until the next time.

Except not for me. Not this time. I would not go to my office or anywhere near it for a while. After years of arriving early, leaving late, visiting crime scenes and police substations, I was consigned to my home, to wait and wonder.

I mused about Tommy Shea. He'd been so confident in the trial but was careless about the photographs. That wasn't like him, even though his case was based on the premise that Hausner was nowhere near the scene of the offense. He'd made no pretrial discovery motions, protecting that alibi.

And yet.

Did he even need any discovery? What if he'd seen all the photographs already? Had Casey Butler shown them to him at the preliminary hearing? Had Dixon? Did Shea just miss the one with the bolt? Is that why Number 17 was such a shock to him?

And Butler . . .

What had he done to prepare for the Motion to Dismiss? Had Shea's expert finished his analysis and report? Will Forensics dissemble it, confirming Hausner's guilt, thereby clearing me? How long, even with an exoneration, before my name won't be associated with scandal and duplicity? How long will I be the punchline of courthouse jokes?

Over and over, I wrestled with these thoughts and images, seeking a key, some revelation that I could use to resolve and end this nightmare. It all seemed just beyond my grasp, as if I were reaching through a wall of fog.

As I approached my home and turned into the drive, I saw the car, backed up against the garage door. It wasn't Charlotte's. The tell-tale silver and blue with distinctive print on the doors made my chest tighten. Once again, sweat ran down my back. Why were the Jefferson County Police at my home?

Two halogen headlight beams lit up my windshield, blinding me as I parked. A stern male voice on a loudspeaker ordered me from the car with hands behind my head. Knowing that any argument was useless, I complied.

"Stand between the vee-hickles and place your hands on the hood of your car," the voice directed.

I obeyed.

"Did Dixon send you?" I said.

If I was going to be harassed in my own driveway by dirty cops, then I was at least going to be insolent.

"Remain still while you are checked for weapons," said the voice.

He was behind me, perhaps twenty feet away. I couldn't see him because of the bright light shining through the darkness. I thought there was a second officer, probably Dixon.

"I'm unarmed, but I guess you won't be taking my word for it."

Two hands grasped my shoulders. Quickly, they ran beneath my arms, across my chest, down my sides and back. They paused, then grasped me firmly on my hips.

"Hold still, you idiot," a female whispered into my ear. "This is the best action I've had in weeks."

She checked my legs, down to my ankles. As she rose, she slapped me on the rear. "Nothing dangerous here, I regret to say."

I leaned forward, my forehead on the hood.

"April, you're going to be the death of me."

She yelled to her companion.

"I got this! He's clean."

Then, she addressed me.

"You, counselor. You can turn around now."

I did and eased down onto the bumper.

"What are you doing, besides taking years off my poor, beleaguered life?"

She stood in front of me, arms crossed, staring, and saying nothing.

"Well?" I said, looking up at her.

"When was the last time you saw your pal, Hausner?"

My adventure at Shea's office must have been passed on to the department. I've read the transcripts of a thousand interrogations, so I was disinclined to answer directly.

"Why? What have you heard?"

She shifted her stance, hands on her hips.

"I'm guessing you don't know?"

"Know what? I've been in the valley all day. As a rule, I haven't been listening to news on the radio lately."

"Did you have a fight with him this morning?"

"April, do you need to give me *Miranda*? Has that punk gotten me charged with assault? Should I be calling Gene Cresswell?"

"Crap."

She turned, walked a few steps away then looked at me again.

"You don't know, do you?"

Once again, it seemed, I was behind everyone else.

"For God's sake, April. Know what?"

"Don't you ever answer your damned cell phone?"

"Not if I can avoid it, and I've never been fond of that thing. But today, I left it at home. I'm not on call. I don't want to talk to reporters, and I most certainly didn't want to talk to anyone today."

She paced, trying to control the conversation while still being cordial.

"Hausner was murdered today. Beaten to death."

Finally, I got it. Hausner was dead and I was a suspect. People saw me shove him, even threaten him, depending on how my words in Shea's lobby were taken.

"Where?"

"The parking garage in Shea's office building. Pretty rough. I'd say someone with a sense of symmetry did it."

I silently cursed. I'd been so stupid, making a public spectacle of myself. I could write the police script: motive and opportunity. My head slipped into my hands.

"Okay, symmetry? Tell me."

She stepped closer and lowered her voice.

"He was found in the passenger seat of his own car. His wrists showed ligature marks, but the restraints were gone by the time his body was discovered. His face had been pounded into the dashboard so many times and with such force that it was unrecognizable. A few teeth had been knocked out. He bled to death right there."

Perfect, I thought. Shortly after I played out my scuffle with Hausner in front of an audience, he turned up dead with injuries just like the ones he'd inflicted on Amanda Fontaine.

"Please, at least tell me he wasn't naked," I said.

She rolled her eyes.

"No, and we're waiting on toxicology to see if you bought him any Tequila Sunrises."

"Who found him?"

"Someone that pulled into the space next to his. The car was locked, so the responding uniforms had to break open the door to see if he might be alive. He'd been dead for an hour or so."

I walked off to the side of the car, out of the glare of the headlights. Standing on the damp grass, looking up at the stars, I wondered if the view of the sky along the Shenandoah was the same, if the sound of the water riffling over the rocks still echoed through the valley, and if I would ever stand on that riverbank again. I turned back toward April with my hands outstretched.

"Alright. What now?"

"I probably shouldn't tell you anymore. You know how this goes. Thanks to your performance in Shea's lobby, Homicide will want to interview you."

I nodded.

"Our conversation," she said, pointing back and forth between us, "cannot screw that up."

She was right. She was already in danger of being reprimanded, or worse, just by meeting with me.

"What about him?"

I motioned to the other officer.

"Did you see his badge and uniform?" she said, cocking her head.

No, of course not. He was in the shadow, behind the headlights.

"My cousin. I needed a male voice just in case you acted up. Not that you ever do that sort of thing, of course."

April was still the sharp cop, but more important right now, she was my friend.

"I'm in enough trouble. I won't be answering any questions," I said. "That's why we have lawyers and *Miranda*, so idiots don't convict themselves."

Like me. What in the world had I been thinking?

She smiled. I never really knew if she liked me as just a prosecutor who gave her credit, or maybe something more. Even over drinks at the Police Rec Center, we'd never gotten personal, but every now and then she'd left a hint. Motive and opportunity? It would have to wait for another day.

"Good. I know you didn't kill that punk. I just wanted to give you a heads up because they've been trying to reach you all day and it looked suspicious—you know, you being gone right after Hausner got whacked. Please do me a favor. Go inside, check your messages and call Mac. Make contact, then get a hold of your pal Cresswell and play this out."

I sighed with resignation. This was not going away anytime soon.

"You got it. Thanks, April. And, by the way, is that the best you can do?"

She looked at me, puzzled.

"That was the weakest pat-down I've ever had."

She waved me off and looked over her shoulder as she walked back to the cruiser.

"The next time I'll put you in cuffs, smart ass."

Chapter Twenty-Two

The Bomber

A few days after April's surprise visit, I was languishing in self-pity when the telephone rang.

"Mr. Duncan, that damn Reuben got hisself in trouble again."

Tony, the courthouse cafeteria manager, was on the line.

"He's in jail, over in Arlington."

Again? But Reuben is harmless.

"What's up, Tony? I'll help him any way I can."

"He's always doin' this. Something stupid. Like, he gets lonely, and he goes to a pay phone and dials 911. Most of the local cops know him and when they show up, he's there grinnin' and wavin'. He just likes the attention. They scold him then drive him home."

Tony snorted in disgust.

"He just loves ridin' in them cruisers."

I stopped myself from laughing but could see Reuben like a kid in a candy store.

"So, what did he do this time? Did someone in Arlington not get the message that Reuben isn't dangerous?"

"Worse 'n that, Mr. Duncan. Worse 'n that. This time, he went into the Metro station and found a security guard. He goes up to the guy and starts talking about bombs and stuff. Next thing you know, he's all locked up and shackled, tossed in jail and charged with a felony."

While Tony paused for breath, I thought through the scenario. The charge was probably Threat to Bomb. Class 4, two to ten.

"When did this happen, Tony?"

"Yesterday. After work. He was down there lookin' for some new place that sells movies."

No doubt.

"I'll call the jail and go see him," I said. "One thing I've got these days is plenty of time."

I was right. Threat to Bomb was the charge and bond was set at fifty thousand dollars. It was relatively high, I learned, because of Reuben's lengthy arrest record. It seems that he has sought to relieve his boredom over the years by saying and doing various things calculated to secure the attention of the local police. Mostly dialing 911, but occasionally offenses, such as Trespassing and one prior conviction of Disorderly Conduct, which was reduced from, not surprisingly, a Threat to Bomb.

The time he'd spent in jail for those offenses was minimal, probably because once he was ensconced in the system, judges and prosecutors realized that he was far from a menace. An irritant, perhaps, but not a hardened criminal.

Still, when a magistrate evaluates the possibility that a recently arrested suspect will either flee or present a danger to the community while awaiting trial, the main criteria for determining the proper bail is the suspect's prior record. So, it was easy to see why Reuben's was set so high. The silver lining was that his preliminary hearing in the General District Court would of necessity be held within twenty-one days of his arrest since he would never be able to post the bond.

Our system requires such a hearing whenever someone is arrested on a felony charge. If he can make bond, the hearing will take place much later, but if he remains incarcerated, the law requires that his preliminary hearing be held in short order. The purpose is to determine probable cause: was there probably a crime, and is the defendant probably the person that did it? If the judge determines the answers to both in the affirmative, the case is referred to the Grand Jury, which considers indictments for the charges brought.

But the preliminary hearing also presents a chance for the prosecutor to sift through the case and determine whether it is really one he can prove, beyond reasonable doubt, a standard far higher than just probable cause.

At this stage, many cases that begin as felonies are resolved as guilty pleas to misdemeanors. The prosecutor has to decide if the case is worthy of bringing upstairs to the Circuit Court. Mac's rule, given to every new prosecutor on Day One, was simple: can you see yourself standing before a jury, asking for a conviction and penitentiary time on the case? If not, keep it downstairs in General District Court, where it can be resolved as a misdemeanor. That's what I was hoping for Reuben's case.

I drove to Arlington to visit him. The jailers didn't know me, of course, and treated me like they would any defense attorney. No casual conversation, no eye contact.

Some of the faces in the waiting area were familiar. Lawyers from several counties around Jefferson recognized me, but none spoke. A nod, perhaps. No more.

I was taken to a room where Reuben was already waiting, wearing a green jump suit. It was several sizes too large, making him appear even smaller and frail.

"I'm real sorry, Bill. Real sorry. Can I go home? I'm real sorry."

He was pale and shaking.

"Reuben, there's no way you can make bail. Even if it gets cut in half, it's too high. Tony would post it if he could."

"Can't you post it for me, Bill?"

"Reuben, I wish I could. But it's all cash up front, fifty big ones, or I have to pay a bondsman ten percent and never get it back."

"How much is that?" he said.

Little that I would say made sense to Reuben, and that was part of the problem. Aside from his own challenges, he was terrified. The novelty of personal attention, this time extended by jailers and fellow inmates, had plainly run its course.

"That would be five thousand dollars, Reuben. And I don't have that lying around." There was no sense in explaining what prosecutors get paid. Five thousand dollars may as well be five million, as far as Reuben was concerned. He had no concept.

"What about that swell girlfriend of yours? I seen her car and them nice clothes she wears. She gotta be rich."

I stifled a laugh.

"And those nice things are why she probably can't afford it, either. Listen, Reuben, this might work out for the best. Stay cool, hold on, and don't cause any trouble. No talk about bombs, no threats in here, okay? I've got an idea that might work out for you, but you have to stay put until your hearing, alright?"

Reuben lowered his head, trying not to cry in front of me.

"Tony said you'd get me out."

The air went out of me. He was like a child. Nothing short of instant escape from this dank jail cell could relieve him.

Defense lawyers must deal with this every day.

He clenched his hands together and bowed his head, beginning to sob. I reached across the table and rested my hand on his.

"We'll take care of this thing, Reuben. But first, you have to tell me what happened. What did you say to the Metro cop?"

He sniffled a bit and sat back in his chair. He bowed his head, embarrassed.

"Tony is so mad at me. He tol' me never to do nothin' like that again. He gonna fire me for sure."

"Hang on, big fella. I talked with Tony. He's worried about you. Mad, yeah. But worried mostly. You just tell me what happened, and I'll take care of Tony."

Reuben stopped crying and started talking.

"I took the Metro down t'Awlinton. I found that new video store, right near the station. They didn't have none of what I was lookin' for, so I got me a hot dog from the guy outside the station. Started to go back home. I was lonely and unhappy, 'cause I could'n watch a movie that night. Didn't wanna call 911. But I seen the Metro cop hanging around inside the station. He came over and said I couldn't eat my hot dog in there no more. Then, I just said it. I'm sorry."

I began to sympathize with my brethren of the defense bar. This was more like dentistry than practicing law. I had to pull the facts out of him.

"Said what, Reuben? Did you get mad and threaten him?"

"No way, Bill. No way. He was plenty big. I just axed him what he would do, you know? What he would do if I had a bomb."

I paused for a moment, considering the elements of the crime for which he was charged. I pressed him once again.

"Reuben, tell me exactly what you said."

"Okay. I said, 'What would you do if I said I had a bomb?'"

"Did you tell him you were going to blow up anything?"

"Huh? Of course not. I didn't have no bomb. I axed what he'd do if I said I had one."

"What happened next?"

"He threw me on the ground and cuffed me. Then, he got on his radio and called for help. Back up, like in the TV shows. They came and emptied my pockets and took off my pants. Stuck me in a cop car and took me here."

I sat back and folded my arms.

"Were there any other people there? You know, Metro passengers?"

He thought for a moment.

"Nope. We was the onliest people in there. It was right in front of the machines, where you pay. I ain't got past the gate yet."

I stood to leave. I reached out and shook his moist, limp hand. He was a child in a grown-up's body, but I needed to treat him like an adult. One with real trouble.

"Reuben, you've given me an idea. Sit tight. You have to stay in here a little longer. I'll go to court with you. We're going to handle this."

He smiled, showing that big grin of his, and clutched my hand.

"Thanks, Bill. Tony said you're the best. I'll work real hard when I get back to the cafeteria and pay you."

"You got it, Reuben. I'll have a bill ready when you get out."

I stood at the door, signaling to a deputy that we were done.

"And do me a favor, Reuben. Please. While you're in here, don't talk about bombs anymore."

He tilted his head, puzzled.

"Why would I do that?"

Chapter Twenty-Three

Friend in Need

The drive back from Arlington gave me time to think. The facts in Reuben's case, presuming they were corroborated by the arresting officer, offered hope. If I presented them to the Assistant Commonwealth's Attorney, we might get a misdemeanor and have Reuben back washing dishes in a couple of weeks. His criminal record might actually help us. My review confirmed that he'd committed similar offenses on a dozen occasions but had yet to do anything violent.

But that conversation would have to wait. The ACA wouldn't be assigned for at least another week.

Reuben's case provided a much-needed distraction, but in the meantime, I continued to wrestle with my own situation.

The questions kept coming.

Why had Casey Butler neglected to tell me the Hausner case was set for a jury trial? Had he let Shea see the entire police file at the preliminary hearing? When did Dixon learn that the 7-Eleven clerk would be a no-show? If he knew it before I picked up the file, why not tell me? Did he try to reach the clerk while I had the file? If so, how? The contact information was in the jacket. Did Dixon have another file? And what was Judge Fairchild doing with this case, since the trial was set for two to three days? He never took cases longer than one day.

Shea had known he was trying the case all along. He'd been ready, his witnesses all lined up, with their stories primed and coordinated.

I called April at CIB as soon as I got home. It was nearly four-thirty in the afternoon, when the detectives' day shifts ended, so she was at her desk, closing out reports.

"I'll keep it short," I said. "Can we meet?"

"Today? Tomorrow? Tell me where."

"Meadowbrook Village. The little coffee shop. Thirty minutes."

"Is that where you lawyer-types get your frou-frou fancy lattes?"

"If that's what it takes to get a cop to talk to us, yes. By the way, keep this to yourself April, okay?"

"You've got my professional curiosity going. Will I have to buy my own coffee?"

"Please. When was the last time a cop paid for his or her own coffee? But I might have to pat you down. Checking for a wire, of course."

"See you in thirty."

***

It was called, simply, The Coffee Shop. It had booths, not open tables, and differed from the usual places in that its primary purpose was to sell bags of coffee beans. One could buy and sample different kinds cheaply and purchase a pound or two of some exotic brand of imported beans to be ground and brewed at home.

It had no Internet service, so the typical crowd that might spend hours hanging around was absent. Customers didn't stay long. I could sit in the back and never be seen or overheard by anyone, thanks to the constant music being played overhead.

I arrived first and instructed the young, tattooed fellow behind the counter to fix my guest whatever she requested and direct her to me. He'd bring it.

April arrived soon after, wearing a gray pantsuit that belied her figure. Always a professional, she tried to look like a detective, plain and understated. A cop.

"Ready for another pat-down? I brought the cuffs, if necessary."

I stood, extending my hand. No social cheek-to-cheek stuff. I liked April, but this was business. Besides, I couldn't risk her occasional flirting getting on Charlotte's bad side.

She sat and spoke immediately.

"I'm presuming you need a favor."

"How did you ever make detective?"

"Feminine wiles," she said.

I smiled.

"Here we are, in a public place, but at a secluded table. Top secret because I can't tell anyone. You've got a lawyer, but you're alone. Call it a wild guess."

"I can tell you this, April. No one is telling me about Hausner's killing. Gene is wired into more people in Homicide than I am, and he's not getting anything. I can't ask Mac, of course."

"What about the Bar complaint? Where's that stand?"

"That's sort of drifting. I have no illusions that those guys down in Richmond are going to let this go, but I think they're waiting to see what the investigation turns up.

"Compared to murder, I guess so. Do you think such a report exists? Or even an expert?"

"Oh, I'm sure Shea might have found someone to say anything he wants. But now that Hausner's dead, who's going to pay for it? Without a client to benefit, why pursue it? And if he was bluffing, now he's off the hook."

"How about the Bar? Would those guys pay for it?"

I hadn't thought of that.

"There may have been some discussions," I said. "The truth is, I'm not really worried about it. I'm as certain as I am sitting here with you that the bolt came from poor Mrs. Hausner's Bonneville. My only fear all along has been that some guy in a white lab coat would swear otherwise. But our forensic guys should be able to back me up."

The tattooed barista brought April a concoction topped with whipped cream and flecks of cinnamon, accompanied by a spoon.

"Thanks, Gus," I said.

Turning to April, I smiled.

"I won't even ask what that is, and you may need to swear me to secrecy. What if CIB got wind of it?"

She just grinned.

"I think they'd be glad I'm only having one of these fancy drinks and aren't chasing women."

"Do the guys still say that?"

"Not as much, at least not so I hear it," she said, taking a sip. "Maybe just Dixon, for all I know. If I don't come across, that's their excuse. But c'mon. You've got me in suspense. What's up?"

I paused. Merely asking this favor, if it ever came out, might be enough to ruin any credibility either of us had with our cohorts.

"I wouldn't ask this if I didn't think some things were odd. Seriously odd. I need to know who's been talking to whom."

April cocked her head slightly and looked at me as she slowly stirred her drink.

"Bill, I can't go into case files or any investigation records. You know that. We're friends, but that's just plain out of bounds."

"No, no, I'm not looking for that. Something simpler, but possibly illuminating," I said. "Phone bills."

She leaned back.

"Elaborate."

"When I had my own personal cell phone, I'd get a statement. It told me what I owed, and ID'd each call from the previous month, both incoming and outgoing. It showed the date, time and exact length of every one of them."

"What do you expect to find?"

"I just want to see if certain people were talking to each other. Dixon to Shea, Shea to Butler. I'm not looking for wire taps or anything a search warrant would get. Just those connections. If I know who's linked up, I might figure out what's going on."

She sat still, staring at me. Neither one of us spoke for a while.

"You think Dixon sabotaged the case?"

"Nothing would surprise me right now. He pulled you after you put it all together. It's obvious now that Butler wasn't working it, so Dixon should have known that. Still, he never said a word to Mac, me, or anyone else, so far as I can tell."

"Why would Dixon undermine a solid case against a guy like Hausner? He's a prick, but he's a cop first."

"I don't know, and that's why I want to see some cell phone bills. He wouldn't have done anything on his own like this. There must have been another reason. Bribe, blackmail, whatever."

"Have you looked at Butler? He's carrying some pretty heavy baggage."

"So, you've read my mind. I need to see records dating from the day of Hausner's arrest until now. Dixon's and Butler's, for starters. They use County issued phones, so there's no 'reasonable expectation of privacy,' no Fourth Amendment issue."

She went quiet again. A couple of sips later, she sighed.

"I know someone at the government building. He's got access to all County invoices. Let me see what I can do. The bills are issued by the phone company, delivered to his office. People with the phones don't pay and in fact, they never even see them. A search warrant shouldn't be necessary."

"April, I know I'm asking a lot."

"Damn right you are. If this gets out, will you find me a job somewhere?"

"It won't get out, unless your friend tells someone. I don't expect ever to use the bills as evidence. This will just tell me who's in touch with who, not what they said. But if it connects certain people and explains what's going on, you'll be on the short list for captain."

"Let me think about it. This makes me feel oily. As much as I can't stand Dixon, it ought to be Internal Affairs that checks him out," she said. "But I guess this is about more than him."

I nodded.

"It's about why a serious felony got mishandled and that calls for decent police work. Give me a couple of days to think this through. I'll see if my conscience can be manipulated," she said.

I finished my coffee and leaned forward to whisper and close out the subject.

"April, you're a solid cop. If you can't do it, I know it's not because you're scared. But think about it, please. And if the answer is 'no,' I'll understand."

Easing back, I offered my last appeal, weakly disguised as humor.

"Just promise you'll visit me when I'm in the joint."

She laughed, almost blowing the latte out her nose.

"You are such a jerk. I'll bring you cigarettes. They still trade those things in there like money, right?"

Chapter Twenty-Four

Peeling Away the Layers

Charlotte came over the next night, with dinner and a bottle of wine. I opened the door to a vision of delight.

"I'm in love," I said, as she entered.

I took the bag and followed her upstairs to the main level.

"A good-looking lawyer that not only makes house calls but brings food and drink. What a babe. What a catch."

"It's just the novelty of the thing, really," she said.

She put her purse on the island and reached into the cabinet for two wine glasses.

"I mean, come on. How often does a girl get a chance to dine with a media figure, a hot shot lawyer, and a murderer, all in one sitting?"

"Keep your eyes open," I said. "I hear he's dangerous."

"Not as dangerous as I am."

She laughed, tipping a glass in my direction, her other hand perfectly placed on her hip.

I couldn't resist her. Before she could open the wine, I swept her up, embracing her slender waist and lifted her feet off the floor. I snuggled against her neck, kissing her, and spinning her around the kitchen.

"I confess. I throw myself on the mercy of the cook."

"So, you want to do some role playing, do you?" She purred. "That's taking it to a new level. Do I get to sentence you?"

"Absolutely. Show no mercy."

Here, in the midst of my life's greatest upheaval, I was wrapped in the warmth and comforting love of a sweet, beautiful woman.

Somehow, I will find a way to make all this work out.

***

After dinner, I cleaned and put away the dishes, leaving Charlotte to pore over the papers I'd assembled. My home office, such as it was, consisted of little more than a bookshelf adjacent to the dining room table, a place to stuff case files, along with assorted folders, copies of legal opinions, and notes relating to upcoming trials. That night, however, the only thing on the table was a collection of notes I had sketched out, along with Dixon's original police file. I had held on to it after the trial.

I'd written down all the people who'd had their hands on the case. Beneath their names were the points that concerned me and required further analysis and possible investigation.

She reached for my notes.

"I see you have Detective Dixon at the top of your list," Charlotte said, sipping coffee. There were no after-dinner liqueurs this night. She insisted on digging into the case with a clear mind, ramped up in full lawyer mode.

"I've never liked him. Maybe that's what bothers me," I said. "He's lazy, cuts corners and never misses a chance to promote himself."

"Didn't he yank the Hausner case away from April Winston? I thought that was so he could take credit for the big win."

"That's what I thought, too. And with all those calls to Amanda's father he noted early on in his file, it sure seemed like he was pulling the usual late career routine, setting himself up for his next position."

I shook my head. "I don't see the old man hiring him now."

"Okay," Charlotte said.

She looked up and sighed.

"He's on the list. Think it through. Why would he undermine the prosecution, or the prosecutor? And what did he do to hurt the case?"

I paced behind her.

"That 7-Eleven clerk. I'd like to know when Dixon knew that guy . . . what's his name? Whitacre? I'd like to know when he knew he was gone. If it was well before the trial, why didn't he speak up or try to get him back here in time? If it was at the last minute, why hadn't he been keeping up with the witnesses?"

"What else?" she said.

She tapped her pencil on the table, as impatient as I felt.

"We know he's not exactly energized, I said. That probably answers half the questions. But what else? What's he getting out of this? A pay-off? From who? Did Hausner have that kind of money? Who's the go-between? Shea would never dirty his hands with something so obvious."

"What did Hausner do, anyway? For a living, I mean."

I sat down across from her.

"I don't know. Something to do with the military, I think, but he was a civilian. Probably employed by one of those defense contractors over near the base. I'll find out."

"So, right now," she said, "Dixon might be a dead end, but we'll keep looking at him. Maybe see if there's a way Hausner paid him off or was going to deliver something else in the future. Next?"

"Tommy Shea."

"What do you suspect him of doing?"

"And still doing. Something isn't right. He's brash, loud, confident. Smooth, too, when the need arises, but he was pretty evasive when I went to his office."

"The day Hausner was killed?"

"Yeah. First of all, back on the first day of the trial, he was very surprised I had the case. Casey Butler hadn't told him. Of course, Casey didn't let me in on it until pretty late in the game, too. Butler's next, by the way."

"Okay, why is it important that Shea thought Butler was trying the case?"

"If Butler was going in the tank on this thing, Shea wanted him there. Once Butler knew he wasn't trying Hausner, it would have been standard procedure to let the other side know. We need to make sure that any last-minute stuff—motions, discovery responses, anything— goes to the right person so we don't miss any deadlines. If Butler didn't tell Shea, that's a red flag."

Charlotte thought about that for a moment.

"But there was no discovery in the case. Shea was protecting that alibi, remember?"

"Right. We need to find out whether Casey made any calls to Shea."

"Why is that important?" she said.

She turned toward me with a quizzical look on her face.

I took the pencil and tapped it on her notes.

"Because unless they were discussing a plea, which we now know they probably weren't, there wasn't any reason for either of them to talk to the other."

"And what if Butler *had* told Shea you had the case?"

"Then why would Shea pretend not to know when I met with him in the cafeteria before the trial?"

She looked across the room and out the window into the darkness. I was distracted, staring at her profile, the sheen of her hair and the curve of her neck.

Enough of this case. Let's enjoy the rest of the evening.

I reached for her hand and she pulled it away.

"For the sake of argument, if Butler was going to tank it, like lose the case on purpose," she said, "then Shea would know and expect him to try it. But if Shea was in the dark about who would prosecute his client, would that still point back to Butler?"

"And maybe Dixon, too."

She shook her head.

"Couldn't Butler have just gotten cold feet? Did he bail out and stick you with the case because he just got scared? If so, maybe that's why he didn't even have the nerve to tell Shea. The way I see it, if Shea was behind it, it might be broader than just Butler. That is, if Shea was up to anything at all."

"So, what's your theory?"

"Let's look at Casey Butler for a moment. You've known him for years. Why would he put you in harm's way?"

"Beats me. Pencil in a possible pay-off? I wouldn't have thought so, except that when Mac gave him the case for the post-trial motion, he nearly folded the first day. No forensics on the bolt and no work on the response brief yet. He acted like he almost wanted Shea's Motion to Dismiss to be granted."

Charlotte rolled her eyes.

"Okay, but why?"

I was stumped. It seemed like the only answer that made sense was that Casey was being bribed or someone had him over a barrel. More women problems? It was certainly possible that he'd put himself in a bind again. But where was the connection?

"He'd begged for decent cases," I said. "But if he was going to tank this one for a bribe, he needed to stay in it, or ruin it so bad that no one, not even me, could save it."

"How about this?" she said. "Your rep with the judges is that you come into court prepared. Well prepared. If the case failed with you at the helm, it would give Butler cover. The fact that he'd given you a weak hand to play would never be known outside of you two."

"And anyone else in the office I bitched to about it."

"If you even did. But if the case had enough problems that losing was likely, it would be on you, not him."

I pondered that for a moment.

"There's one problem with that, Charlotte," I said. "Dixon, Butler, and Shea never knew about the bolt. If they had, and wanted the case to go down, I wouldn't have found the picture of it. That thing would have disappeared."

Charlotte stared at me.

"No," I said. "I don't think Casey, or Dixon and Shea for that matter, knew anything about that photo."

"So, we're back to self-protection. He was saving his own skin. But from what?"

"Something else I have to dig into."

She jotted her notes and stared at them.

"That's a short list," she said. "Anyone else come to mind?"

"One more," I said. "Wally."

She picked up her cup, staring at me over the brim.

"He can be a jerk, okay. But seriously, a Chief Judge on the take to free a violent criminal?"

"I know, I know," I said. "It's a stretch. But why did he keep out those pictures of Amanda's injuries? Why did he grant Shea's motion and let Hausner out on bond, without even letting our office know? And Gene told me that according to his info, Wally may be sending his bailiff to testify at my bar hearing."

"Oh, Bill, come on. I've never heard of a judge doing that. Have you?"

"Never. By law, a judge can't testify about what goes on in a case where he's presided, but nothing says a bailiff—who's got a front row seat for everything in the courtroom—can't. Wally's just sticking it to me on this one."

Charlotte had been jotting notes throughout our conversation. She kept writing for a few more minutes.

"Well," she said. "As for the refusal to postpone the trial, you know how fixated he is on moving the docket. That's nothing new. And those pictures of the victim? If there was even a slender chance of reversible error . . . I mean, what do you think? Fairchild always protects himself. That's nothing new."

I had to agree, grudgingly.

"Yeah," I said. "You're probably right."

"And the big surprise ending you put on? If Shea wasn't successful with his motion, you knew he'd appeal."

She smiled.

"I think Judge Fairchild . . . Wally . . . I think he's just angry at you for putting him on the spot. He could just be afraid of being reversed."

She put down her cup.

"I think we have some work to do, my handsome lawyer."

She stacked the sheets of paper and organized them.

"Where do I start?"

I hadn't told Charlotte that April might be a source for phone records. I couldn't take a chance of exposing her, whether through a text, email, or phone call that was intercepted or just carelessly made. Once I knew who Dixon and Butler had been calling while this case was headed for trial, I'd have a better grip on my predicament. And then I'd settle some scores.

***

The next day I called my old office mate at the courthouse.

"Kent Raker."

"Kent, it's Bill."

"The Invisible Man. How the hell are you? Where've you been?"

"Layin' low. I never appreciated how troublesome celebrity could be."

"I'll say. We haven't had this kind of media attention since those murder-for-hire cases. But you're not just calling to be social, right?"

I cleared my throat. The last thing I wanted was to get Kent in trouble or seem desperate.

"Kent, I need a favor. I wouldn't ask, but I can't think of anyone else that can help on this one."

"As I recall, that's just about the way Casey Butler started a conversation with you a couple of weeks ago."

He never missed a beat.

"Thanks. I know now what I should have said, but I'm hoping you don't say it to me."

He laughed, his smoker's rattle echoing into the telephone.

"Let's hear it."

"This goes back to your Army JAG officer days. Isn't there a standard form that tracks every soldier's military history? Where he served, when, what rank. That kind of thing."

"DD-214. Yep, it lines up every soldier's entire career."

"Is there any way you can pull Jason Hausner's?"

Kent was silent for a moment.

"Probably," he said. "It's public record but usually takes about a month to get. What are you looking for?"

"I have no idea. But we don't know anything about that guy's background, and something isn't adding up."

"How so?"

"Figure this. Service overseas in wartime, honorable discharge, at least according to Shea, and he winds up committing a sex crime, tries to kill a girl he doesn't even know, and then winds up dead in almost identical fashion. I need to dig into this."

"Got it. Anything else?"

"Yeah, just one thing," I said. "What do you hear from Butler these days?"

Chapter Twenty-Five

Pen Pal

I became convinced that Dixon was the key. His motive and method remained unclear, even though I suspected he hoped for a position with GSI, General Fontaine's company, sometime in the near future. But how could he ever hope to achieve that if we failed to convict Hausner, especially if shoddy police work were to blame?

On a whim, and little more than curiosity, I took a drive to the Livingston Correctional facility.

Prisons weren't new to me. Each one is different, but some characteristics remain the same. They are imposing and fortress-like, but inside they're loud and cold, and smell of sweaty, tired, hopeless people.

A series of concentric barriers provide multiple levels of security, the better to minimize any chances of escape and instill a sense of futility. After a rudimentary identity check, during which my wallet and cell phone were held for security purposes, I was led to a small office. Various citations and photographs of state officials decorated the walls. Two prison guards shared the room when they weren't roaming the corridors and grounds, and I figured it was wired for audio as well as visual observation. Even lawyers are suspect when it comes to smuggling weapons, drugs and other contraband.

The guards brought Glen Evans into the room, as I'd requested. He'd been given no warning of my arrival, despite the call I'd made in advance about this visit, and he appeared understandably wary. The prosecutor responsible for his imprisonment in this human warehouse was alone in the room with him. It occurred to me that he'd probably fantasized about such a moment over the past few years.

"Glen, I'm Bill Duncan."

I stood and offered my hand.

"I know who you are."

He sat, ignoring my gesture. Then he turned to the escorting guard.

"This won't take long. Don't go far. *The Simpsons* is on soon, and I ain't missin' it for this shit."

I'd expected him to be reluctant to meet with me. There would be limited opportunity to get his attention and, I hoped, cooperation. The direct approach seemed the only one available.

"I know this takes you by surprise and I know we aren't exactly old friends. I won't waste your time trying to get past all those trials."

He lit a cigarette and looked away.

"I'm not here about your charges, or to threaten to bring any more. You know, of course, that there's no statute of limitations in Virginia for felonies. You wrote hundreds of checks for which you were never prosecuted."

I paused a moment, letting that sink in.

"I don't care about any of them."

That got his attention. He drew a long puff and turned toward me, blowing smoke.

"Go on. At least this is better'n *The Young and the Restless*. So far."

I made a mental note to inform family and friends who shared their taste in television shows with state prisoners.

"Alright, cards on the table. You know the drill with *Miranda*. If there's custodial interrogation, you've got to have the rights read to you if we're going to use anything you say against you. I don't think there's any question about the custodial situation here." –

I waved my hand at the surroundings.

"So, although I have some questions, it's really not an interrogation so there won't be any waiver forms, initials, or anything like that. All the same, I want you to know that nothing you tell me today will be mentioned in any court—anywhere or at any time."

Evans was a confidence man. He looked for the angle in everything he saw. That was how he made his living when he was free, and that's why he was in prison. He rolled a dwindling cigarette between his fingers and blew smoke my way.

"I'm guessing you ain't here to offer no assistance in cuttin' down my time," he said.

"That's right."

"Well, I'm a pretty busy guy these days, what with watching TV, reading comic books, and counting how many bars are on my cell door and all."

He stood up to leave.

"I ain't got time for idle chit-chat. I think I'll be leaving, now."

So much for the social approach.

"Glen, I need to talk to you about Detective Dixon. If you have nothing to say to me, well, that's fine. I'm out of here. You can go back to the block, do whatever. How about one minute?"

"Clock's running on that sumbitch," he said.

As soon as he sat back down, I quickly recounted Evans' testimony from a pre-trial hearing. He'd denied making the broad confession that Dixon claimed, a statement that resulted in his multiple convictions. He made the same denial in his pre-sentence report. Finally, I told him that a recent case had caused me to question Dixon's credibility.

"You drove all the way down here from Jefferson just to ask me if I think Dixon's a liar?"

He had a way with words. The essence of direct.

"A little more than that," I said. "I didn't expect that you'd say otherwise. I just want to hear how it went, and exactly what you admitted to doing and why."

187

Evans leaned back in the vinyl chair and put his feet on the edge of the desk. He seemed to enjoy the diversion from a typical day and the opportunity to talk to someone besides his immediate neighbors about the low-down cop that put him in this predicament.

"This is a game ain't none of us in here started out plannin' on playin'. One day, you're just in it. Especially when you're doin' dope. I mean, I wasn't insane or nothin'. You seen my report. Here."

He reached into his shirt pocket and handed me a photograph of him holding a young girl of about two years of age. His daughter, I guessed.

"I was doing Dilaudid when that was taken. I just went lookin' for a high when everybody else was lookin' for work."

He took back the picture and stared at it. Shaking his head, he returned it to his pocket.

"I got busted some, got tagged, went to jail. I was sure in the game then. But I never hurt nobody, never fought a cop. I went along. Hell, Dixon even said I did, at that hearing my lawyer put on, trying to get my so-called confession kicked out. Wasn't no trouble to nobody. That's part of the game. When they got you, don't give them no reason to beat your ass. They look out for you a little."

There was a culture among people like Evans. They lived their lives on the shoulder of life's roadway, close enough to see, smell, and feel what working stiffs endured each day. But they couldn't muster the stamina or discipline to take part.

"Here," he said. "Here's how it went down."

He shifted in his chair, putting both feet on the floor, and leaned toward me, pointing with his cigarette.

"I'm sitting in a room, cuffs on. Half high. He puts a pile of checks on the table in front of me, then starts showin' me photos. Real nice black and white glossies, eight-by-tens. There I am, in all my handsome glory, in line at a bunch of banks, fixin' to cash checks. He pulls out one of them. I take a look at it. He asks me, 'you write that one?' and I, of course, says 'yeah,' like a real genius."

So far this was almost exactly how Dixon had testified in the suppression hearing. In wondering if my trip was wasted, I struggled to fathom what subtleties might exist in the mind of a career criminal and what he thought was unfair about his case.

"Then he picks up all of 'em and says, 'I guess you done the rest of these, too.' Right about then, I get to thinkin'."

He laughed.

"It's about time, I know. You're right. But remember, I was all gooned-out high. I kind of thumb through those checks, sort of surprised there's so many. So's I ask him, 'What's this worth?' I mean, I'm startin' to figure the time on this stack of paper. I'm a convict with back-up time, and these forgeries go for up to ten years apiece. I gotta get a deal."

He turned away from me, looked out the single window in the room and shook his head.

"He says, 'Well, you know we got you on film. You got prints all over these things and we can ID the handwriting. What do you think it's worth?' Right away, I know I'm in a spot. See, he don't need my statement, not if he's got all that. But there ain't nobody in that room but me and him. Even in my buzz, I'm beginnin' to see that he thinks he has a problem bringin' these things to court and he needs my confession. So's I tell him, 'I ain't admittin' to nothin' but that one check unless I get a deal.'"

He stopped and pulled out the picture of the little girl again, staring at it.

"Then he asks me, 'What kind of deal?' so I tells him I gotta have a cap on the time and it has to run concurrent with the back-up time I'm gonna get revoked on. You know I done been convicted four, maybe five times before and I got suspended time hangin' over me."

He ground his cigarette into an ashtray and lit another.

"That was the last I ever saw of him until he came back and hit me with warrants on all them charges. One for each bank. What was it, ten of 'em?"

"Twelve. What did he say about your deal?"

"Not a damn thing. I was a little curious, you might say, so I asks him what was goin' on, you know? He said, 'Maybe we'll work something out later, after you get a lawyer.' Shit. Work something out. You remember coming to me with an offer?"

He leaned back and put his feet on the edge of the desk again.

Of course not. Why should we? There were witnesses, photographs, and his confession. There was no reason to do anything but await the defendant's guilty plea or take the cases to trial for what promised to be easy convictions.

He dragged on the cigarette.

"You ever wonder how tough it might have been to convict my ass if Dixon didn't testify about my so-called 'confession'? I'll tell you."

He put his feet back on the floor and pulled his chair toward me.

"You had nice little tellers, them girls what could identify their initials on the checks they'd cashed. But none of them would have remembered the exact transactions. You had photographs, but all that showed was me in the bank. I wasn't doin' nothin' but waitin'. You had the account holders, and ain't none of 'em had ever laid an eye on me. And fingerprints? C'mon. How many people you think handled them checks? Stop right there: you see any reasonable doubt in them cases so far?"

He was right, of course. He'd spent enough time in courtrooms to know the elements of each offense in his repertory. He knew we were short-handed on his charges, barring a clear confession.

"Dixon, he took a short cut. He knew the only person who'd contest his word was me, a convicted felon, and him a decorated cop."

He puffed on the cigarette.

"Ain't they all decorated?"

"Let me get this straight," I said. "You and your lawyer knew all this when we went to trial?"

"Yep."

"But Dixon had a *Miranda* waiver form at the suppression hearing. You initialed all the rights, then signed the waiver, didn't you?"

He laughed and shook his head.

"My God, you're slow. You sure you went to law school? What was it, correspondence courses? Somethin' off a matchbook cover? Take this one step at a time. He ain't got my confession, but he's going to say he does. So, since he ain't got my confession, he ain't got no waiver form, neither. You think a handwritin' expert gonna recognize a checkmark in a box? Maybe they can work up somethin' on a signature, but you gotta remember, I wasn't writin' my own name on any checks, and I was tryin' to make it look like different people done it."

He eased back and spread his arms.

"Like I said, without my confession, you guys didn't have diddly-do-da-day."

They didn't teach this lesson in law school. The criminal freely admitted committing the crime, but his sense of honor on the field of play was offended by a detective who cheated.

The pattern Evans described was suspiciously similar. Dixon knew he had the right guy, but the case was definitely thin in some spots. He smoothed over the rough edges merely by lying under oath, testifying that the suspect had confessed to multiple crimes that Dixon knew he'd committed.

How many rough edges had he sanded down in the Hausner case? Was I one of them? Did Ronald Whitacre even exist? Had Amanda's things really been found in a dumpster near Hausners' apartment? Everything Dixon had to do with this case, all of it, was now immersed in doubt.

"You seem surprised."

Evans said it again when I didn't respond.

"Now what?"

What indeed.

***

The drive back from Livingston was peaceful. For good reasons, the Commonwealth locates these institutions far away from any populated areas. I drove many miles, through farms and forests, without seeing another human being or a passing car. It seemed a shame to use this pastoral setting to cloak a place of such desperation.

I called Charlotte once I reached the interstate and had a good signal. I needed to plan my next steps. A theory began to come together.

"Do you have time?" I said.

"I'm still at the office. Let me close the door."

"I'll fill you in later about the meeting I had today, but I'm thinking that Dixon is willing to cheat. As best I know so far, he does it to convict defendants, not acquit them. If he was worried that Hausner was going to walk, he might have looked to balance the scales on his own, maybe with a little help."

I heard her chair rock back.

"How does that connect him with Hausner's killing?"

192

"There are stories, and we prosecutors have heard them for years. Rogue cops looking the other way when some of the local hoodlums got crossways with each other. Street justice."

"Jefferson isn't New York or Chicago."

"Oh, I'm serious. The running joke is that medals are handed out, not arrest warrants, when one of those guys cancels out another. But it gets worse."

Charlotte was a sharp lawyer, but sitting in her sleek, tenth-floor office, drafting corporate transactional documents, she'd never seen the dark, violent underside of the scales of justice.

"At our end, we hear rumors. Hints of police involvement. A cursory investigation of the murder of a local PCP dealer, for example, might end in a case being closed. 'All leads exhausted.' That's supposed to mean that unknown criminal elements, familiar with the recently departed, were probably responsible for his untimely end. No leads, no suspects. Those cases might have been preceded by a failed prosecution or C.I. who mysteriously disappeared. No one gets too worried about dead criminals."

I paused as a tractor trailer passed me.

"You might say that a couple of us have doubts as to the accuracy of those final reports."

"Where does that leave us now, with Hausner?"

"I wonder. Could Dixon have gotten a call from that ex-cop in the lobby, the one working security? Somehow, someone got word to somebody that Hausner was in the building."

"Why?"

"My meeting with Shea was unscheduled," I said. "That makes it impossible for anyone to have planned to frame me in advance. But once I scuffled with Hausner, it opened up a good opportunity. Better than 'all leads exhausted,' that's for sure."

She was quiet for a moment.

"Yeah, I think we have to keep looking at Dixon."

"Something else still nags me about Judge Fairchild, too. Denying my continuance wasn't outside his routine. He'll do anything to force trials to a settlement. But what was he doing on a three-day jury, anyway? That was unusual. And how did Shea know what judge we had before the docket was posted?"

"Do you think the judge had someone call Shea in advance? How else could he have known?"

I mulled over her question. It was standard for a judge to assign himself to a case when he'd heard several pre-trial motions and had a familiarity with it, but there hadn't been any hearings with Hausner.

"The first time that case was in front of a Circuit Court judge was the day of trial," I said. "Do I think Shea got to Fairchild? I'd say it's preposterous, except for the continuance denial, exclusion of the photographs of Amanda, the post-trial release of Hausner. It's crazy, but it just looks bad. Too bad to be coincidental."

I pause for a second to avoid a truck.

"Go on," said Charlotte.

"So, yeah, at a minimum, I think Wally put in a call to Shea. Or he had someone do it. Maybe all that stuff we've heard over the years is true about Shea getting favors because he's on the state judicial review committee."

"But what about the bolt?" she said. "When the whole thing blew up during closing arguments? The judge could have declared a mistrial, or something, right?"

I drove in silence for a while.

"No. I'm convinced that I'm the only one who saw what was in that photograph. The judge had to rule on the spot, and since the exhibit was already in evidence, without objection, and we were wrapping up the trial, I don't think he saw any other way to go."

I thought for a moment.

"Maybe he thought the jury would acquit, since Shea had beaten up Amanda so bad on cross. But he sure found a way the next morning, turning Hausner loose."

She was quick to respond.

"No, I just don't see Fairchild being in on it. Not saying it's impossible, but it's a big stretch," she said.

"Don't forget what I told you about his bailiff. His warning the morning of the trial's second day. Tuck's an old courthouse guy, but he's never come down to my office like that during a trial. I have to think Wally was sending me a message."

Charlotte wasn't buying it.

"And what would that message be? 'Go easy on the defendant?' I worked up there for a year. I don't see Judge Fairchild doing something like that. He can be an imperious jerk, but I never saw a hint of corruption. He wanted you to speed it up, like he always does."

"I know, I know," I said. "It doesn't seem to make sense, except that the rest of it doesn't either, so there has to be an explanation, a connection somehow. Shea's bar association status isn't enough to rate this kind of treatment. It has to be something more, something bigger. Was he paying off Wally? Blackmailing him? If so, about what? Everyone already knows about him and Nancy, his court clerk."

"First of all," she said, "remember that we're on an open cell line. Better put a lid on that stuff for now. I think you need to focus on Dixon, but take a hard look at Butler, too. His lack of preparation. Intentional? Careless? Could he and Dixon have undermined the case?"

That didn't work for me, either.

"That seems to go against all of Dixon's interests. I know he's willing to skew the evidence to convict a perp. And here, he might have had a good job lined up at GSI if we got a conviction."

If all of this was tied up together, it was quite a plan. It had been designed carefully with a purpose of not only shrouding its perpetrators but offering up a substitute.

Me.

"Charlotte, some things are clear," I said. "Dixon recognized some critical facts. Hausner was the culprit, but the case had some holes. Not only was the star witness drunk beyond description, the defendant had a clean background and a good lawyer. Whitacre? The 7-Eleven clerk might not even exist. My calls to the base in Georgia got nowhere. Throw in Butler, who didn't prep at all, and no one connecting the bolt from the Bonneville at the crime scene, until I did the night before trial, and I can understand why he saw an acquittal on the horizon. For all I know, he could have hatched a plan to kill Hausner even before the trial, anticipating an acquittal. Tying up all the loose ends on a criminal he was convinced was guilty."

Charlotte whistled.

"Well, he *was* guilty."

We both went quiet.

"Quite a plan, don't you think?" she said.

"Think about it. Dixon, or somebody working with him, must have been tipped off about Hausner being in Shea's office on the day I went there. Or maybe someone was following him, waiting for a chance to get him alone. The underground parking garage provided a prime opportunity."

"And your public showdown with Hausner just gave them cover," she said.

"Exactly."

They were good, whoever they were. Probably not a speck of evidence left behind, and the only chance I had to unravel this plot might lie in those phone records April had pulled for me, and the calls Dixon made on the morning Hausner was murdered.

Chapter Twenty-Six

Old Friends

Kent Raker called soon after I got home.

"You sure run around a lot for a guy with no job," he said. "I have something I think you'll find good reading. Meet me at the Holiday Inn for happy hour?"

He was waiting for me when I arrived, two beers already on the table. He passed me a thin envelope. He'd gotten Hausner's DD-214.

"These things are pretty sparse. Where a guy served, ranks, promotions, time frame, transfers and the like. But his form is an odd one. Not so much what's in it, but what's not."

"Okay, Kent. You're the Army guy. What's it mean?"

"Not sure. But it looks to me like he got promoted pretty quick while serving in Iraq, so he must have been good at whatever it was that he was doing. Front-line unit from what I can figure and doing intelligence work after the regime collapsed. He re-upped at one point, which means he had at least two years to go, but then, all of a sudden he's discharged only four months into it."

"Wounded? Trouble? What happened?"

"That's the kicker. There's no indication of anything. Suddenly, he's sent back stateside, honorably discharged."

I'd read countless police reports, wading and sifting through the cop jargon figuring out what really happened, but military reports might as well be written in a foreign language, at least as far as I could tell. Be that as it may, as I looked over Hausner's DD-214, it did seem that a component was missing. Something wasn't right.

"Is there any way to get behind this thing? How can we find out what happened to Hausner during that last tour?"

Kent looked at me for a moment.

"I think there's something here for you."

He ordered another drink.

"This is on your tab, right? I forgot my wallet at the office."

He laughed. Some things never changed.

"Good thing I'm suspended with pay. You can cover me the next time. I'll call first to remind you to bring it."

"So, Hausner was doing intelligence work over there. We know that much. Think back. What would those guys be chasing? They had to be separating the friendlies from the uglies. Our guys were planted in those dirt-hole villages, surrounded by pockets of bad guys with shoulder mounted rocket launchers all around them. At least that's what it looked like on CNN. There had to be some dangerous wheelin' and dealin' goin' on over there."

"Like what our Narcotics Squad does every day, only a hundred times worse."

"Exactly," Kent said.

He tapped his empty glass on the table.

"And what was he doing when he got back over here? He was still connected to the Defense Department, right? Or, maybe hooked up with some kind of civilian defense contractor?"

I'd been blind. There was a whole world of possible suspects and conspirators I hadn't even considered.

"Crap," I said. "How the hell do I dig into that?"

"Your lucky day, my friend."

Kent beamed. He was enjoying this. He was one of my best friends, but he was taking morbid glee in peeling away the layers of my skin as he unveiled what he'd learned.

I put down my glass and stared at him.

"Kent, I appreciate the drama but quit screwing with me."

His crooked smile broke wide open.

"Your pal has learned—through unimpeachable but utterly anonymous and inadmissible sources—that once Hausner got back on his feet after his last tour of duty, he became a free agent. He worked for himself but then he hooked up with the black ops guys he knew from his days in the desert. The word is, his official service was translation-type material. De-coding stuff, intercepting transmissions and the like, ferreting out possible terrorist plans."

"The 'word?' Come on, Kent. What word is that?"

"Right. I took the liberty of doing some hunting around for you. I still run a tab at the officers' club over at the base."

He grinned.

"Do you forget to bring your wallet there, too?"

"Hey, it works for me. Anyway, it's all smoke, but there's *lots* of smoke in this case."

"Enlighten me," I said.

"There's at least a little fire burning down in there. Sifting through all the BS, it sounds like Hausner got pretty deep into some of that A-rab stuff. Digging for intel, when he was on active duty, leveraging what he had—you know, food, shoes, maybe even some medicine. He took a liking to a couple of women that were good sources for us. Who's ambushing who, and whatnot. One thing led to another, and they wound up getting stoned."

He hoisted his empty glass.

"And I don't mean they were smokin' weed."

That bit of news didn't go down well with me.

"So, Hausner pushed and pulled to get info on who was al-Queda or whatever, and the women he was using wound up dead?"

"As I said, none of this is documented but that's the talk running through all the winks and nods over at the Officers' Club."

I waved for another round.

"It seems like Hausner pissed off people everywhere."

Kent nodded.

"Yeah, that's right, but one of them had a public spat with him a few minutes before he was murdered, right?"

"That's how Homicide sees it."

I sighed. He stopped smiling and looked at me, leaning over the table.

"We're not supposed to think, let alone talk like this," he said, keeping his voice low. "But that bastard deserved killing. If it was you, I'm not losing any sleep over it."

I looked back at him, and then around the room. We were surrounded by courthouse denizens, most wearing suits with ties loosened, easing into the evening after a day spent wrestling with the law and each other. They might be worried about tomorrow's cases, but none of them were facing murder charges.

"I don't know if I ought to be flattered or insulted. Me, a white shirt and tie-wearing sissy lawyer, killing a combat vet with my bare hands? Really?"

"No weapons, huh? You really are a stud."

Kent was incorrigible.

"What do you think?"

That same sideways grin spread across his face.

"And I'd had such high hopes for you."

"Let's get back to what he was doing here. Not the suspicious stuff, which is truly interesting, but for now it's all speculation. What was his legit business?"

"Like I said, he was doing something with defense contractors, security stuff. Who knows what those guys do?"

"Here's the rub," I said. "If he's into de-coding and translating, isn't that more Homeland Security than DOD? What's the connection to the Army?"

"Point made, but there are lots of agencies that need insight into Iraqi-Sunni-Wahabi-whatever information. I don't think that's how he was making his money."

This was well beyond a local attempted rape case. But I had gotten nowhere on my own, so I was at Kent's mercy.

"Let me guess. Smuggling."

"Bingo. My sources . . . okay, officers' club drunks, would only go so far, and I'm guessing that I was hearing some Pentagon gossip. Whatever Hausner was doing, it was lucrative. Dope, money, valuable artifacts, who knows? Let's just say there were lots of questions about his revenue stream."

I pondered this for a moment.

Hausner was a bad actor. That was easily established by what he did to Amanda. This other stuff confirmed that he was an outlaw. But scheming and smuggling are in different time zones from rape and murder, especially if he'd never met the girl before that night.

I had to tie up another loose end.

"I think I need to speak with Amanda Fontaine again."

Kent nodded.

"Okay, but can we get one more round first?"

Chapter Twenty-Seven

A Date with Amanda

She suggested we meet at the local mall. I agreed, figuring that someone would be watching me regardless of the location. The more public
the place, the better for both of us.

The mall had one of those ubiquitous food courts where about
twenty restaurant counters surround an open area filled with small tables and chairs. The aroma of barbecue, pizza, hamburgers, Chinese,
and everything else capable of being fried, broiled, or baked filled the
air. Even so, it was the noise that overwhelmed me.

We sat near the center. She nibbled at a salad, like every girl who's
trying to convince herself she's dieting. She looked better than she had
during the trial. Her complexion reflected time outdoors and she'd
changed her hair color slightly. Auburn, with mild streaks of blonde.

"So, what do you do with yourself when you're not testifying?" I
said.

"Funny. I hope I never go into that building again."

"I'm beginning to feel the same way."

I smiled back at her.

"If I do, the next time I'll probably be a defendant, not a lawyer."

She stopped, just as she was about to eat a piece of lettuce.

"Oh, no. So, all that stuff is true? You, like, didn't do the evidence
right or something?"

I glanced around instinctively, checking for familiar faces, and took
a moment to collect my thoughts. Amanda understood so little of the
morass of trouble that engulfed me. I didn't know how much I should
try to explain, or if I even could.

"Well, not exactly. The evidence thing is between the state bar and me. If the complaint holds up, they'll suspend my license to practice law. I won't go to jail for that, but I won't have a job either."

She went back to munching, looking at me and nodding.

"Well, I guess that's bad, but not as bad as jail. Right?"

Her face was open, trying to show sympathy. Maybe she really cared. After all, she had sent me flowers the day following the verdict.

"In a way. But there's another problem, too, of course. There are some people who think I killed our friend Jason Hausner."

"Yeah, I like heard something about that, and stuff. I said, 'no way, Mr. Duncan, he's like, a lawyer. Those guys don't go around killing people.'"

She frowned and shook her head.

"No offense, right?"

I laughed aloud, gagging for a second on my coffee.

"Amanda, I hope you're on the jury rolls," I said.

I had to wipe my eyes with a napkin.

"I'm going to need eleven more like you."

She wrinkled her brow and shrugged.

"Whatever."

I had tried to think of the best way to approach this conversation. If she knew Hausner before that night at the NCO club but hadn't told me, she might continue to deny it. I had to read her in the way that lawyers do in cross-examination—pose the question so that I got the answer I was seeking, regardless of what the witness said.

"How often did you go to the NCO club before that night?"

"Um, not a lot. Maybe a couple times a month. But around Christmas, I didn't go at all for a long time. Come the spring, maybe more."

"What was so attractive about it? I mean, there are better bars nearby."

"Well . . ."

She bowed her head, shaking her hair and then lifted her face, smiling, but she was looking past me.

"The guys, right? Just the guys. They buy the drinks, you know, and I wasn't twenty-one. I couldn't get served in the regular bars."

She giggled.

"So, not only could we drink there; it was always free. They were glad to see us and paid for everything."

Another angle that I'd missed seemed obvious now. Amanda was barely out of high school at the time and would have been carded at most places.

"Amanda, when I was preparing you for the trial, I had to ask you some questions that were difficult."

I leaned forward and met her eyes, keeping my voice low but steady.

"I need to do that again. Just answer me yes or no, okay?"

She put down her fork and stared at the table.

"Don't make me tell that story again, please."

She pleaded her case quietly.

"Please, Mr. Duncan."

"Nothing like that, Amanda. Simple questions that won't go beyond this table. I promise."

I tried to get her eyes to meet mine again, but she wouldn't open them. She began to cry.

"Mr. Duncan," she said. "I can't . . . I can't . . . please. That was the worst . . ."

Her words drifted away, lost in her quiet sobs. Her shoulders shook and tears ran down her face. I handed her a napkin, which she pressed against her eyes.

"Amanda, I'd say I understand, but of course I don't. I never will. But I won't hurt you. Please trust me."

She nodded, but kept her face down, embarrassed to be weeping in public.

"Don't worry, Amanda. These people just think I'm breaking up with you."

She laughed, sniffling, then took another napkin to wipe her face and blow her nose.

"Okay, what?"

"Amanda, I just want to know a little more so that I can protect myself. I did my best for you. Can you help me, please?"

The tears were still flowing, but she nodded.

"Before that night, did you ever leave the NCO club with any of those guys?"

She squeezed her eyes shut and shook her head.

"No, never."

"Did you ever date any of the soldiers you met there?"

She laughed and rolled her reddened eyes toward the ceiling.

"God, no. Daddy would have killed me."

She blew her nose again.

"He might have run me over with *his* car."

"A career Army guy like him?"

"Absolutely! He was so mad that I'd gone to the NCO club that night. I never told him I went there all the time. He always told us to watch out for the soldiers. 'I know those guys,' he'd say. 'They're *animals!*' "

"He didn't know you were going to the base? That's hard to believe."

"Oh, he knew that. But he thought we were just eating and going to the movies. My friends and me."

She wiped her nose again.

"We'd go to the NCO club, and they'd let us right in. The only place they checked IDs was at the front gate."

I could envision the scene: three or four eighteen to twenty-year old girls, walking through the door of the NCO club. They could expect red carpet treatment from the young enlisted men, confined to the base and not knowing any females within a hundred miles.

"Had you met Hausner before that night?"

"I'd seen him there, but never talked to him. Never danced with him before that night. He was good, though. I gotta say."

"One last thing. Hausner. Where was he from?"

She looked at me, puzzled.

"How would I know?"

I had my answer.

Chapter Twenty-Eight

What Could Go Wrong?

The drive into Arlington was more difficult than I'd anticipated. This is what defense attorneys do every day—fight traffic and search for parking spaces within remote walking distance of the courthouse. Living and working in Jefferson had protected me from this drudgery—that, and a reserved indoor parking spot beneath the courthouse.

Reuben's case was on the 9:30 General District Criminal docket. Arlington County mixes its felony preliminary hearings with misdemeanor trials because three-quarters of all the serious charges are reduced, or "broken down," to lesser ones and dispatched at that level. If a prosecutor wants to proceed on a charge as a felony, then following the prelim it's sent upstairs to the Circuit Court, where a Grand Jury will consider the case at a later date. After an indictment is certified there, a trial is scheduled.

When I walked in at nine, at least a dozen lawyers were waiting at the front of the courtroom for the Assistant CA in charge of the docket. That day it was Dorothy Metcalf. She went by Dottie, and I'd met her at a state conference of prosecutors a few years earlier. She joined a few of us from the Jefferson office for drinks after a session but took offense at Mac's routine joke that experience in the Arlington CA's office was tantamount to being a defense attorney in Jefferson.

When it was my turn, I spoke to her by name and offered my hand. She declined it, busy as she was with her docket in one hand and Styrofoam cup of coffee in the other.

"Who d'ya got?"

"Reuben Lewis. Prelim for Threat to Bomb."

She set her coffee on the table and flipped several pages, searching for notes she'd prepared before coming to the courtroom. Her eyebrows furrowed, and she shook her head when she found Reuben on her list.

"This guy's a bad actor," she said. "I'm putting it on."

That meant that she intended to take it upstairs as a felony.

Since we hadn't discussed the case at all between us, I was somewhat surprised. One never turns down an opportunity to listen to the opposition. We prosecutors don't know what they might say. Mac was fond of pointing out that we learn a lot more with our mouths shut and ears open. Maybe he was right about Arlington prosecutors.

"Dottie . . ."

"Ms. Metcalf."

Chastened, I tried again.

"Ms. Metcalf. Have you looked closely at Lewis's record? He's almost 60. He's mentally disabled. There was no bomb. In fact, if you check it out, I suspect you'll see there was no threat."

She glared at me.

"You Jefferson guys think you can come in here and just Cadillac around like you own the place. This guy has a record a mile long. I'm putting him away."

I tried to remember how the good lawyers I knew handled moments like this, times when I had probably done the same thing she was doing. I felt the heat rise inside my collar but sensed that arguing would be futile. Begging was unappealing and would probably be unsuccessful, too. It left little alternative.

"That's fine, Ms. Metcalf. For now, our offer is Disorderly Conduct, time served."

She rolled her eyes.

"I'm wasting time here. Judge Graham is coming on in a moment. They'll bring Lewis up in about an hour and we'll put it on as soon as we're done with the misdemeanor docket."

Orpheus J. Graham. I recalled him from when he'd been in private practice. The Big O, we called him. He was smart, deliberate but creative, and had a quirky sense of humor. He occasionally said the funniest things one heard in a courthouse, but rarely broke a smile.

I sat in the back of the courtroom and waited. Most of the defense lawyers were out in the lobby, talking about their cases and the latest courthouse gossip. I saw how several of them looked at me when I stood in line for Metcalf, however, and heard muffled whispers. I'm not one of them, at least not yet, and I had no desire to field inevitable questions about the Hausner case, the Bar complaint, or which judges were carrying on with their law clerks.

Anticipating the worst—having to conduct a preliminary hearing in Reuben's case—I had done my research and prepared. I doubted that Metcalf had performed more than the rudimentary sketching out of the elements of the crime and fed the expected questions to the lone policeman, likely to be her only witness.

Most prosecutors would do the same. The standard of proof at a preliminary hearing is low. Probable cause is all the state must demonstrate to send a case to the Grand Jury. As the judges put it, *was there probably a crime and is the defendant probably the one who did it?*

Reuben's case was finally called and I moved to the front of the courtroom.

"Mr. Duncan, this is a surprise. Have you a new line of work or just discovered your conscience?"

The judge truly enjoyed being on stage.

"Good morning, your honor. It's been a while. I suppose I could ask you the same thing," I said, smiling. "But I'm just doing my *pro bono* duty while on sabbatical."

He chuckled, but true to form did not smile.

"Sabbatical. I like that. May I use it?"

"Absolutely, judge."

His clerk passed him a file jacket as Reuben was escorted by a deputy into the courtroom from a side door.

"*Commonwealth v. Lewis*," he announced. "Is the Commonwealth ready to proceed?"

"Ready to go, your honor," said Metcalf.

"Call your first witness."

She turned and beckoned to a chubby fellow wearing a Metro Police uniform. I knew from my own experience with that department that while they were well-versed in subway security they rarely testified in court.

"Officer, please state your name and occupation."

"Eric Calloway. Metropolitan Transit Police Department."

"And on September 22nd of this year, were you on duty, wearing a uniform and displaying a badge of authority?"

He looked at her, then at the judge, then back at her.

"Yes."

"Did anything unusual happen that day?"

He nodded.

"I'll say."

Metcalf looked at him and he stared back. Both of them were obviously expecting the other to say something more.

"Is there more to this, Ms. Metcalf?" the judge said.

"Yes, your honor. Knowing Mr. Duncan's . . . expertise in these matters, I am trying to avoid objectionable leading questions."

"Well, Mr. Duncan hasn't said anything yet, and at this rate he won't need to," he said. "Please continue."

It was an interesting development. Moments ago, Dottie was ensuring that I knew she was the one running the courtroom, but all the while she was uncertain of herself around me, who she seemed to perceive as a more seasoned trial lawyer.

"Officer Calloway, did there come a time when you made contact with the defendant in this case, Reuben Lewis?"

"Uh, yes."

"Please tell us what happened."

"I was in the Clarendon Metro station. I had situated myself in the vicinity of the open area between the ticket machines and the turnstiles. Keeping an eye on things, as it were."

He paused for a moment, allowing his nervous breathing to catch up with his words.

"I seen Mr. Lewis," he said, slowly pointing at Reuben. "That's him, over there. Sittin' next to his counsel. I seen him walkin' around, actin' s'picious and all."

"Objection, your honor."

I rose from my chair.

"I know this is only a preliminary hearing, but 'suspicious' is a conclusory description, and is thus far based on nothing but Mr. Lewis 'walking around.' The officer's testimony is, at least so far, without foundation."

Judge Graham turned to the prosecutor.

"Ms. Metcalf? The experienced lawyer has made his first objection. What say you?"

"Judge, as an officer, well-trained at the Academy, he is capable of offering his professional . . ."

"Sustained."

There was no jury, of course, and the judge wouldn't be misled by a young policeman's use of a descriptive word. But the officer and prosecutor, having yet to make headway into the meat of the case, had been interrupted and warned that I was not about to let them walk over us and shove this case up to the Grand Jury without a struggle. Their minimal preparation was apparent.

"Officer Calloway, please tell us what Mr. Lewis did and said, without any adjectives," said Metcalf.

"Uh, okay. He walked up to me and made a bomb threat, as it were."

"Thank you. And did this all occur in Arlington County?"

"Uh-huh."

Beaming, she turned to the judge.

"That's our case, your honor."

The judge's eyebrows arched. He seemed to think for a moment, then turned toward me.

"Cross-examine, counselor?"

"Thank you, your honor."

I made a point of standing slowly and moved to the podium between my table and the prosecutor's. I looked at the officer for a moment before I spoke.

"Officer Calloway, I just have a few questions for you. Thank you for your patience."

He was tense, leaning forward in his chair, his hands fidgeting. He glanced at the prosecutor. I guessed that he'd never been cross-examined.

"Did you know Mr. Lewis before September 22nd?"

"No. Never seen him before that day."

"So, it would be fair to say that his manner of walking and talking were unfamiliar to you."

He hesitated and looked at Metcalf, seemingly for direction. She, of course, offered no assistance.

"Yes."

"And since you didn't know him, you would have no idea about his level of mental capacity."

His face took on the appearance of someone chewing a lemon. He turned to Metcalf again, his eyes pleading for help, then back at me.

"Could you repeat the question?"

"You didn't know how smart he was, or not, did you?"

"No."

"Were you afraid of him when he first approached you?"

"No."

"In fact, he appeared harmless."

"I guess."

He glanced at the judge.

"Yes."

"So other than his statement, there was nothing scary about him."

"No. I mean, right."

"Now, Officer Calloway, please try to remember his exact words. What did he say to you in making this bomb threat?"

Calloway's face wrinkled and his teeth clenched.

"Uh, he said, as best I can recall, that he wanted to know what I would do, in so many words, about him having a bomb. I might not remember his exact words."

I looked down at my notes. Picking up the file, I made a show of flipping the papers before focusing on one in particular. I'd read the original police report and had a copy.

"Could he have said, Officer, 'What would you do if I said I have a bomb?"

"Yeah. That's it. That's just what he said."

There was no point in chasing the words any further. It would get no better and might get worse, if he realized the impact of his admission.

"Just a few more questions, Officer, if you don't mind. When you subdued him and placed the handcuffs on Mr. Lewis, you removed his trousers, did you not?"

"Yes."

"And why?"

"For my safety, sir."

"In case he was hiding explosives beneath them?"

"Yes."

"And you found no explosives, did you?"

"No."

"And you found no weapons, either."

"No."

"In fact, you found nothing in there but his briefs, correct?"

Calloway lowered his head, embarrassed at the question.

"Uh, yeah."

"How crowded was the terminal at that time?"

"Not very."

"In fact, Officer, aside from you and Mr. Lewis, there were no others in the area between the ticket machines and the turnstiles, were there?"

Again, he looked in vain at the prosecutor for help.

"Not that I can remember."

"So, no one else heard the exchange between you and Mr. Lewis."

"Exchange? If you mean what we were sayin' to each other?"

"Correct. What you were saying to each other."

"No. Nobody nearby."

"Thank you, Officer Calloway."

I turned to the judge.

"Nothing more, your honor."

"Thank you, Mr. Duncan," he said. "Ms. Metcalf, redirect?"

"Yes, your honor. Officer Calloway, were you in fear for your safety when the defendant spoke to you?"

He straightened himself, lifting his chin.

"I'm trained to put that aside, ma'am, and do my job. We see a lot of crazy stuff on the Metro, even though I feared the worst right then, as it were."

She sighed.

"Thank you. No further questions. The prosecution rests, your honor."

Judge Graham sat quietly for a moment, reviewing his notes. Finally, he turned to the prosecutor.

"Ms. Metcalf, I presume you wish to save argument for rebuttal?"

"Yes, your honor."

"Mr. Duncan?"

I returned to the podium and brought Volume 4 of the Virginia Code with me.

"Your honor, if I may direct the court's attention to Code Section 18.2-83. The elements of this crime require a showing that the person charged must make or communicate to another a 'threat to bomb, burn, destroy or in any manner damage' something. A place of assembly, a building, or a structure."

I waited, watching the judge. When he raised his eyebrows, I continued.

"'Or, he must convey a false communication, as to 'the existence of any peril of bombing, burning, destruction or damage to any such place of assembly, building, other structure, or any means of transportation.'"

I closed the book slowly, staring at Orpheus and held his eyes.

"Your honor, I know that this is only a preliminary hearing, and the standard of proof is low. But for felony probable cause to be shown, there must be at least some evidence of a crime before we determine who probably committed it. The officer's candid admission was that Mr. Lewis asked him, 'What would you do *if* I said I had a bomb?' He *never* said he had one. He *never* threatened to explode one. He *never* articulated, in fact, any threat at all."

I took a moment to gather my thoughts.

"Granted, the subject matter of Mr. Lewis' statement is serious. But in the words of the Supreme Court of Virginia, the term 'threat' is defined as 'an avowed present determination or intent to injure.' That's from *Powell v. Commonwealth*. Nothing like that has been shown here today."

I waited a moment, letting that sink in. It is extremely rare that a judge denies a prosecutor's effort to send a case to the Grand Jury. But Graham was the kind that would stray from the beaten path when given the opportunity to consider a well-prepared theory.

I went on.

"Another case makes it even more plain that Mr. Lewis' statement is not what the statute anticipates. 'Only an individual who maliciously makes and communicates any threat prohibited by the statute will be punished.' *Perkins v. Commonwealth*."

I paused once more.

"Malice? Your honor, Mr. Lewis certainly did not exercise good judgment that afternoon, and we're most assuredly fortunate that Officer Calloway was on the job."

I looked over toward him, nodding.

"But malice? No crime occurred. Not even 'probably.' The Commonwealth's case has fallen woefully short."

I sat.

The judge looked at me for a moment, then turned to the prosecutor.

"Ms. Metcalf, he makes a good point about the charge. Please respond and focus your argument on the issue of whether an actual threat was made."

She picked up her sheaf of paper, none of which held the answer to the judge's question and took the podium.

"Your honor, the Commonwealth has a motion. We move to amend the charge to Section 18.2-415, Disorderly Conduct."

"Well, that's that," said the judge. "Mr. Duncan? That's a Class One Misdemeanor. Any objection?"

I turned to Reuben and whispered to him.

"This is just what we want. If the judge asks, tell him you're okay with it."

Reuben nodded nervously.

"No objection, your honor," I said.

"Alright, Ms. Metcalf. I've made the amendment. This Court now has complete jurisdiction over the matter and can make a final disposition or set it for trial. Is there a plea?"

"Yes, your honor," I said.

I stood.

"Not guilty."

Metcalf slammed her hand on the table and turned to me, snarling.

"You asked for Disorderly. Now you're spinning me!"

"No spin at all, Ms. Metcalf," I said. "I offered that two hours ago and you turned it down, as shown by your attempt to take this case to the Grand Jury. We reached no agreement."

"Counselors," said the judge. "You will address the Court and not each other. I'm not sitting here for decoration, despite occasional appearances to the contrary. If there is not going to be a guilty plea to this charge, we need to set it for trial."

"Pardon me, your honor, but if I may be heard," I said. "Mr. Lewis has been incarcerated for three weeks. I'll defer to the Commonwealth's view of its own case, of course, but unless there are more witnesses and more evidence likely to be presented than what we heard today, Mr. Lewis is willing to submit the case to you on the merits right now for a finding. Can we truly justify waiting another month or more just so we can repeat what you just heard? I realize that this was a preliminary hearing, but the simple truth is, your honor, the case won't change over the next few weeks. You've just seen what the trial would be. Testimony was under oath. Now that the charge is a misdemeanor, you have jurisdiction to make a finding."

The beginnings of a smile crossed his lips.

"Ms. Metcalf, does the Commonwealth have any more witnesses?" said the judge.

She turned and spoke to Calloway. He shook his head.

"No, your honor."

"And would there be any further evidence than what we've seen and heard today?"

"No, your honor," she said.

I could practically hear her sigh across the room.

"Then please address the Court on the subject of Disorderly Conduct. Closing summations?"

Dottie was unprepared for this, but gamely stood firm.

"Your honor, as we've all heard and said so many times, you can't yell 'fire!' in a crowded theater. You just can't engage in talk, using incendiary words that provoke someone else, even terrifying them. This is disorderly conduct. Officer Calloway was provoked."

The judge nodded at her, then turned to me.

"Mr. Duncan?"

I reopened Volume 4.

"Your honor, Section 18.2-415 makes it a crime to do something, and I quote, 'with the intent to cause public inconvenience, annoyance or alarm.' It goes on to prohibit 'conduct having a direct tendency to cause acts of violence by the person or persons at whom, individually, such conduct is directed.'"

I glanced at Dottie, who wouldn't even look back at me.

"Here, in this case, there was no crowd. The only 'public' was Officer Calloway. He testified that, other than Mr. Lewis's words, there was nothing intimidating about him. The simple question, 'What would you do *if* I said I had a bomb?' is a far cry from 'I have a bomb,' or 'I'm going to blow up this terminal.'"

I closed the book and set it on the table.

"The officer testified that there was no sign of danger and therefore there could be no tendency to cause violence before the question was asked as well as after. There was no one in the terminal but the two of them, him and Mr. Lewis. The only person inconvenienced, annoyed or alarmed was Mr. Lewis."

The judge and I looked at each other. He then looked at Reuben with a raised eyebrow, then back at me.

"We ask for a dismissal of the charge and the immediate release of Mr. Lewis."

Metcalf stood up to argue in rebuttal.

"No need, Ms. Metcalf," said the judge, waving her to remain seated. "You've done all you can with this one. Mr. Lewis, please stand."

Reuben stood up, eyes wide open, staring at me.

"Mr. Lewis, how long have you been in jail?"

"Twen . . . twenty days, judge."

"Was that long enough to think about what got you in there?"

"Uh-huh, your judge, your honor."

Reuben was shaking.

"Well, I find you not guilty. You're free to go."

Reuben looked at me in seeming shock and turned back to the judge.

"Judge, can I ax you a question?"

Orpheus looked from me to the prosecutor and back to Reuben.

"I'm looking forward to this," he said.

I cringed, not knowing what might come of it, but gestured to Reuben, letting him speak. After all, he'd been acquitted. Barring another threat to bomb, what could go wrong?

"Them twenty days," Reuben said. "Can I save 'em for next time?"

The judge couldn't hold back any longer. He struggled, but finally gave in to a giggle that became a rolling laughter. He took off his glasses and rubbed his eyes. Trying to speak, he was unable to get past the first word for several tries.

"Mr. Lewis, thank you," he said. "You'd better talk to Mr. Duncan about that. Sweet Jesus, court is in recess."

He stood and headed for the door, still laughing, and looked across the bench at us.

"I'd do this for free some days," he said, before disappearing into his chambers.

***

Flush with victory, Reuben and I left the courthouse. He asked for bus fare, but I insisted on taking him home. As much as I had previously wondered how my brethren of the defense bar could stand spending their days minimizing the impact of the law on their misbegotten and most certainly guilt-ridden clients, I reveled in the aftermath of Reuben's trial. It had been fun, more than I'd had in a courtroom in a very long time.

Without a doubt, Reuben had misbehaved. But he hadn't acted feloniously, not even criminally. He was a troubled soul, and courthouses chew up people like him. Perhaps this was the secret to being able to stomach thieves, drunks, and pimps every day. Viewed as someone's son or daughter, ground up in the gears of the criminal justice system, even if due to their own devices, anyone with a heart would search for a way to lessen the just weight of their punishment.

We drove out of town, putting the Arlington County courthouse and Dottie Metcalf safely behind us for the time being.

"Wish I had a dog," Reuben said. "Had one, when I's a kid."

I knew little of his background, only that Tony had employed him for years in various restaurants and cafeterias.

"Where was that, Reuben?"

"Over 'n Murl'n."

"Maryland?" I said. "Not too far away, then. Whereabouts?"

He paused, staring out the window. We were out of the business district and passing through a leafy neighborhood. Neat houses with front yard flower gardens lined the avenue. Sunlight speckled through the trees and into the car, washing over Reuben's expressionless face.

"Not sure," he said. "Some place out'n th' country. Lots of grass. That's where me an' my dog played."

The memory appeared to be deep-rooted but vague.

"Do you have brothers and sisters?"

"Uh-huh. Couple. Least I think so. I mem'ber a sister, older'n me. An' a brother."

I waited for the next installment, but it didn't come. Curiosity led me to open another door.

"Reuben, how did you come to live in Virginia?"

He sat quietly, still looking out the window. We passed a school bus stop where mothers stood, awaiting their children. Reuben looked at them and then down at his upturned hands, as if searching for something.

"Got lef'."

I'd gone too far. Trying to engage Reuben in what might pass for an adult conversation had awakened long-buried and painful memories. But since I'd opened a wound, I had to tend to it.

"By who, Reuben?" I said. "Who left you?"

Silence. His lips seemed to move slightly, as if he were trying to find words he couldn't remember. He turned his face away so that I couldn't see what I soon realized were tears.

"My folks. They drove me to a place where I learned to do stuff. Work with tools an' all. After a coupl'a weeks, I got on a bus and wen' back home."

His voice failed for a moment, his mouth trying to form words that refused to come. A long moment passed before he tried again.

"No . . . nobody there."

It was my turn to be silent. Being rejected by impatient courthouse regulars and facing rudeness by fellow Metro riders were daily staples for Reuben. But the recollection of how he was pushed from his own home, and having his childhood abruptly ended, still made his throat tighten so he couldn't even speak.

Surely this can't be all there is to his tale.

"Reuben, did you wait for them, or come back later? Maybe they just didn't know you were coming home."

He just stared at the houses we passed. I turned off the boulevard and onto the highway.

"Nope. There was people there, but my fambly was gone."

"Gone?"

"Didn't live there no more."

The fluttering happiness I'd felt a few moments earlier slipped away like a fading sunset. Reuben's own family had abandoned him. He was intellectually crippled but not oblivious, knowing not only that he was limited in his abilities but that he'd been cast aside. People like Tony, or even I, became his closest, and maybe his only friends, because we actually gave him a smile, a word of greeting, or even a brief moment of our busy lives.

The whole story was unimaginable to me. My father once told of how people rid themselves of unwanted pets in his youth. A troublesome dog or cat would be driven out into the countryside, miles from home, then released to make its way in the wild, likely to starve or be killed by other animals. Reuben's family had given him no less of a dispatch.

"You must have been pretty mad at them, I guess."

That was all I could manage to say.

He bowed his head again.

"Nah. I was lotta trouble. A real handful, like Tony says."

He looked at me, smiling, his eyes moist.

"But I'd sure like to see 'em now. Maybe they got a dog."

Even in his pain, Reuben had found forgiveness for those who had betrayed and abandoned him. I wondered how he found the charity in his heart to do it. I wondered how they could live with the memory of what they'd done to their own child and brother.

We drove the rest of the way in silence.

Chapter Twenty-Nine

Homework

My mobile phone rang as we pulled into the parking lot of Reuben's apartment.

"Hey, Duncan."

It was April Winston.

"I got some stuff you need to see. Where are you?"

"Avalon Apartments. You?"

"Boy, you're sinking fast. Did the Sandersons kick you out?"

"Not yet. I'm dropping off a friend."

"A 'friend.' Right. I seem to recall serving warrants on some strippers down there a while back. Are you that lonely?"

"Do you remember their apartment number?"

"I'll look it up. How soon can you get to that coffee place of yours?"

"Twenty minutes."

I pulled alongside the curb adjacent to the entrance to the building. Before Reuben opened the door, I reached over and shook his hand.

"My first client, Reuben. That's you."

He beamed.

"Maybe we can work together s'more," he said. "I'll talk to Tony in the mornin'."

He was grinning from ear to ear.

"You do that, Reuben," I said. "You do that."

***

April brought me the first set of phone bills, which must have been at least four hundred pages. She had segregated each number's calls and I found the ones I wanted without much trouble. April Winston was a gem.

"I pulled a bunch so no one would suspect who I was checking," April said. "It wasn't hard getting the bills at all. But if I'd asked for just a few it's a guarantee that the word would get back to the people we're looking at."

Her caution was well-justified. One never knew who had a friend among the county staff. Relatives, co-workers and the like; there was always somebody who knew somebody. And since Casey Butler's calls were involved, there was at least a fifty-fifty chance that an old girl-friend or two were in the mix.

Dixon had the most. I had my own list of numbers I wanted to know if he'd called, and over the course of time between Hausner's arrest and his murder he'd made hundreds. It would take a while to cross-check them all. Charlotte, I knew, would help. Besides, I couldn't risk asking April to review the numbers herself. She needed to be insulated in case the homicide detectives, bar investigators, or anyone else asked her the wrong questions. The last thing I needed was her knowing what I'd found and having to reveal it to someone else, when that someone might be involved in the case or even investigating me.

I knew I could trust Charlotte. She was safely clear of all the char-acters and conflicts, so that evening I gave her Dixon's list and the numbers of people I wanted to see if he'd called, and when, and maybe even how long the calls had lasted.

I examined Casey Butler's calls myself. He'd contacted Amanda Fontaine just before the preliminary hearing. I figured that would have been when he got her version of the crime, just prior to her testimony. He'd also called Shea's office in the days that followed. There were no incoming calls from Shea, so either Butler initiated them, or he was using his cell to return calls Shea had made on the CA office land line.

Why had Butler called Shea—to discuss a plea deal?

Our case was either good enough to try, putting the risk of a jury verdict and sentence on Shea and Hausner, or Butler thought it was weak, and he was offering something less than the original charges. That didn't seem likely, given Amanda's ID of Hausner. Besides, it had been my case. He'd have talked to me about any plea discussions.

But what if Shea was calling Butler?

The Titmouse's plan was to decline discovery and hide the alibi he'd use at trial. Their story was simple: Hausner was having late night waffles with his Army pals but if we didn't know the time and place or the names of the witnesses in advance, there was nothing we could have done to investigate and refute the story. So, why would Shea want to talk with Butler before the trial?

"Only one thing makes sense," I said to Charlotte after a couple hours of sifting through the billing records. "Butler must have been telling Shea what was in the file. In other words, what Shea would have gotten had he filed a routine discovery motion. But a formal discovery request would have meant he'd have to give notice of any alibi in advance."

"And you think Shea just talked Butler into it?" she said.

"If Butler was that stupid, I'll pull his lungs out through his nostrils, in front of his family, too. Let's hope it was just the Titmouse sandbagging Casey."

"Could he have offered something to Butler?" she said.

I just shrugged.

"I don't know. It doesn't feel right, but I just don't know."

I stretched and walked around the room.

"What have you found? Anything?"

"Not much here," Charlotte said. "I've combed through Dixon's calls. It looks like he called the CA's office a few times, but that could have been about other cases, not just this one."

"How often did he call Amanda's home number?"

"Twice. Once before, and once after the prelim. Nothing after that."

"What about Amanda's cell?"

"Nothing. But is that unusual? Once the case is turned over to the prosecution, wouldn't you be the main contact? After he got her lined up to testify at the prelim, and maybe told her the trial date, why else would he call her?"

She had a point.

"Yeah, probably."

I lay down Butler's records and put my hands behind my head.

"But Butler thought they were going to plead. There wouldn't be much need for her to call him or me—if he'd done that."

"But what about Dixon?"

"I had him pegged for sucking up to the father, not just calling Amanda," I said. "He's about to hit twenty-five years on the job, and the general is a big wig at some defense contractor company. Neither crime nor war are going out of business anytime soon. He was looking for a soft place to land. At least that was my sense of it."

"How do you figure?"

"That's what his file shows me. He checked in with the old man several times and made notes of it. He called Amanda's father more often than he called her."

Charlotte raised her eyebrows and pursed her lips.

"Maybe so, but I guess he wasn't calling him at home. We don't have the general's personal numbers."

I slapped my forehead.

"I'll get them for you."

"What do you mean?"

I laughed.

"During all of this recent turbulence, no one asked me for Dixon's file. I still have it. The general's mobile and office numbers are in there."

"What?"

She slapped the table.

"Aren't you in enough trouble?"

"What else can they do?" I said. "Besides, all the photographs are in the court's evidence locker. What's left are just his investigation notes. And April Winston's, of course."

I went to the bookshelf where I'd left it the night before trial.

"Here. Four, five calls to the general. Here are his numbers."

She slowly shook her head.

"What an idiot."

"Yeah, for a guy whose reputation is mired in laziness, he sure was putting out for the victim's father. Unless, of course, he was trying to convince the old man that his company needed the keen eyes and skills of a soon-to-be-retiring detective."

"Yeah, that's probably it," she said.

I watched her stack the Dixon phone bills neatly on the table.

"Anything else you can see?"

Charlotte bit her lip and shook her head.

"Not at the moment. There are a few others I can't identify that he called a lot, but I guess they doesn't necessarily mean anything. What do you want me to do about them?"

"Try to look them up. Maybe Google them?"

"Ten-four, Boss. Tonight?"

"How late can you stay?"

"All night, if I have to . . ."

She smiled, easing back in her chair.

I grinned, pushing away from the table. "Then I think we've done enough for now."

***

When I awoke in the darkness and reached for Charlotte, I found only the cool sheets where she'd been as I fell asleep. Peering at the clock, I saw it was 2:30, so it seemed unlikely that she'd gone to her gym or office already.

I went to the closet for my robe, but it was gone. I pulled on a pair of sweatpants instead. As I opened the door, I saw light down the hall. I came upon Charlotte at the table, with phone bills, Dixon's file, and her laptop opened in front of her. She was wearing my robe.

"Okay, Sherlock, come back to bed."

"Jesus!"

She jumped up from her chair.

"You startled me."

Her hair was a rumpled mess. I supposed I'd had something to do with that. She pulled the robe tightly around herself.

"How long have you been out here?"

"I don't know. An hour? You got me thinking. Who else might Dixon have been calling that we haven't considered? Not just Shea. Maybe the 7-Eleven guy?"

"Hmm. You're right. I meant to ask you about him."

I shook my head, wondering what else I'd missed.

"Where did you find his number?"

She smiled.

"I looked in Dixon's file. He called that guy right before the grand jury met to indict Hausner. Term Day is the next day, right? So, he should have called again to let him know the trial date. But he didn't, at least not from his cell phone."

"Could be. I don't remember any notes about a later conversation with him. Did you see one at all?"

"No. What do you think?"

It made no sense to me.

"If the 7-Eleven clerk got transferred," she said. "And Dixon knew he wasn't going to be in town for the trial, don't you think he'd have called you or Butler and said so?"

"Dixon's lack of enthusiasm for follow-through is notorious."

"Yes, but you'd think he would have put something in the file."

She tapped her pencil on the table.

"I'll figure it out."

"Then do it tomorrow," I said.

I took her hand and heading back to my room. Moonlight shone through the French doors that led to the balcony, so I left the lights off. I took the robe from her and draped it over a chair.

"How did I get so lucky?" I whispered, holding her close. "But I can't tell which room you work better—the kitchen, the dining room, or this one."

"Ask me that again in about an hour . . ."

She purred and tugged at the waistband of my sweats.

I surrendered peacefully but was distracted by the thought of Casey Butler's calls to Tommy Shea after the preliminary hearing. An explanation was due. And maybe some punishment, but for now, all of that could wait.

Chapter Thirty

Center of Attention

Gene had called me at home. The investigation was confirmed, he said, and I was a "person of interest" in the Jason Hausner murder. I was the only one, from what little I could gather. He summoned me for another meeting.

Sitting in his firm's lobby, I considered the comfortable chairs, oriental rugs, and the various publications on the table, from *Sports Illustrated* to the *Virginia Quarterly*—all comforts we take for granted as normal and expected, but thoroughly unimaginable to a prison inmate. I wondered how many of his clients had sat in one of the same chairs, counting the days until they would leave these things behind for years upon years.

So, this is how they feel.

Whenever I heard the muted sound of the telephone ringing I listened to the receptionist, with her trace of a British accent, answering with precise diction. Calls and messages were moved accordingly, each related to someone's life, prospects of freedom or incarceration. Yet the cool, comfortable and sterile atmosphere of the room reflected none of the pressures felt by the lawyers or clients involved. It seemed that Gene had imposed this climate on his office. It spoke to control and, as a result, the confidence he demanded of his clients.

"He's ready for you now."

I was deep in thought and followed the voice into Gene's office. After a quick hello, he got right to it.

"The state covers all legal fees associated with the bar complaint, but if you get charged with a felony, you're on your own."

I shuddered to think what his fee might be. I had some modest savings and a retirement account with the County, but I could only access that by ceasing my employment.

"I have a sense of what you're thinking," he said. "Let me lay it out for you. For a case like this, the retainer would be in the range of fifty thousand. That's it, start to finish. By finish, I mean acquittal or sentencing. An appeal would require an additional retainer."

After a moment I recovered my breath.

"Gene, I . . ."

He held up his hand.

"Hold on. There is a silver lining. We have an overlap here, to some extent, so the longer I can work this under the notion that I'm defending you against the State Bar, the more prep work I can do toward any criminal charges that might—*might*—come down. So, if—and I stress the word, *if*—you get charged in the Hausner murder, I can probably cut the fee down to thirty."

Still it was a staggering figure. But it was far better than the original and was something my retirement account could handle.

"Thanks, Gene. I know you have bills and a staff to pay."

"Well, that's really it. At thirty, I'm just covering the overhead. Cases like this take months to prepare and try, and unless I miss my mark, we'll be taking this one to trial."

"I guess there's another silver lining," I said. "If we lose, retirement won't be a concern of mine, will it?"

He gave me a tight-lipped smile.

"That's good. A sense of humor will keep you sane over the next couple of months, one way or the other. Now to business. As you know, the CA's office is not exactly an open book when it comes to sharing information or evidence, and that's *after* there's been an indictment. While the investigation is ongoing, they won't tell me a damned thing."

"Can't blame them," I said. "Why let the suspect tune in to the investigation?"

"Exactly. So, we can sit still and wait or do some work to keep you from getting indicted. The golden rule in criminal work, Bill, is this: if you don't get charged, you don't get convicted."

If you don't get charged, you don't get convicted.

Since we prosecutors rarely got involved in cases until after an arrest or indictment had been made, this was a new concept to me. The science of criminal defense, I was learning, was more than just opposing the chess moves of the prosecution. Gene's notion of a good defense began before charges were even brought. Thirty thousand dollars, I thought, was starting to seem quite reasonable.

"You have a plan, I presume?"

"The beginning of one, yes. It may take some developing and could require a few twists and turns. That's how cases go. One possibility is to seek a Special Grand Jury. Those have subpoena power and can actually investigate the case, instead of just sitting there listening to the police."

"Jefferson County hasn't had a Special Grand Jury in years."

"I know. But when was the last time one of its prosecutors was up on murder charges?"

I closed my eyes.

"What else?"

"There are two ways to get the police off your back: convince them that you didn't do it, or that someone else did."

He paused.

"By the way, there's a special prosecutor involved now. Mac asked for one and the Circuit Court made the appointment this morning."

I hadn't expected that.

"I think they're going to skip the arrest warrant and preliminary hearing stage and take it straight to a Grand Jury. You know how those work. Just a detective, telling them what the police think happened, spoon-feeding the jurors enough to indict."

I knew it well.

"But in this case," he said, "if the circumstantial evidence isn't enough for them to return an indictment and you're not charged, it would look like the CA's office covered for you. With an outside prosecutor handling it, either way it goes, it's cleaner."

"Not surprised then that Mac set it up that way. But a prosecutor has very little to do with the actual Grand Jury proceeding."

"True, but when the panel has questions about the law, that's the only person they can ask. Plus, remember that the prosecutor can choose the witnesses that will testify. Anyway, the Circuit Court judges picked someone from over in Arlington. Do you know Dottie Metcalf?"

I sighed and tried not to smirk.

"We've met."

Gene sat upright.

"Wait a minute. Is she the one you spanked last week in that preliminary hearing for the cafeteria guy?"

I nodded.

"Really."

He leaned back in his chair, put a hand over his eyes and exhaled.

"I may need to revisit that fee. You're not making this any easier, my friend. How about staying out of trouble for just a little while?"

I started to say, *but it seemed like such a good idea at the time.*

"Anyway, they like you so far because of that episode in Shea's lobby just moments before Hausner met his unfortunate demise. But beyond that they have little else. Nothing, I'd say. If there was physical evidence, like your blood, scraps of clothing that match, or fingerprints, they'd have arrested you already. I'd be talking about whether it was self-defense."

"Self-defense?"

"You couldn't possibly have known Hausner would be at Shea's office that day. If you and he crossed paths in the garage after that little scrape, it just might be that you two picked up where you left off, and you got the better of him."

"But . . ."

"You have to know, Bill, that this is what they're thinking is what happened that day. But trying to convince the detectives and Metcalf that you acted in self-defense, without any witnesses, won't keep you from getting charged. Self-defense would be an issue for trial. For now, just hide behind me and talk to no one about this. Are we clear?"

I was sweating. This was a conversation Gene had probably been through a hundred times. My fellow prosecutors and I saw defendants paraded through the courthouse, exit the courtroom side doors in hand-cuffs, and disappear into the jail several floors below, but we never saw this side of their lives. Once we convicted them, they didn't come to mind again, one way or the other.

We rarely considered the power and the force of the law rolling on, sweeping over them like a relentless incoming tide, grinding and driving them into our system of penal retribution, as they paid the price for their crimes. The fear and helplessness they felt as they slid down the path toward personal annihilation was unknown to us as we moved on to the next case.

I sensed what Reuben Lewis must have felt as he sat in the Arlington Jail. I wore a better suit, and most assuredly had a better lawyer, but we were the same in other respects.

"Gene, I've been thinking. Shouldn't we do our own press conference? Hausner must've done a dozen of them. Everybody with a television or radio must think I'm guilty. Shouldn't we get my side out there? And Rita Mohr over at the *Post* has left messages for me, offering to do an interview. She's always given us fair coverage."

He put the file down on his desk.

"Bill, you've seen a few of those things, I presume?"

I nodded.

"Think of other cases, where the defendants put on those shows. Who does the talking?"

"The lawyers."

"Right. Do you remember any of those defendants getting acquitted? Have you ever lost a trial because of a defendant's press conference?"

No, of course not.

I didn't need to say it.

"Why get up there and bluster, stake out our position, when we might learn something later on that will change everything? Why take the risk that some reporter will ask a question that we don't want to answer, and then look like we're hiding something? Think about it. Those things are just free commercials for the lawyers."

I felt like a rookie. Once again, I was thinking like a client and not a lawyer.

He stared at me.

"There will be plenty of time for talking to the press after we get clear of this case."

I sank back into my chair like a chastened student.

"And what do you want me to do?"

"First, keep writing down everything you can remember. Finish that memo and get it to me right away. I need to know everything you know. If someone else had a reason to kill Hausner, we need to chase that down. If you have a receipt for a burger you ate at the same time he was getting his head beaten in, get it to me. If you flirted with a waitress, we need to know now so we can lock down her testimony."

I nodded.

"Where were you, by the way, right after the run-in at Shea's office?"

"Driving. I took off for the valley. It took about two hours."

"That's not much help. Did you see anyone between here and when you got there? Buy gas? Anything that can prove where you were?"

"I stopped at a general store. It was late afternoon by then. I'm sure the proprietor would remember it, but I doubt we could fix the time."

Gene pondered that for a moment.

"I need to talk to him. Name and number, okay?"

"Got it."

"Now, listen. You're a trial lawyer. One of the best in this town. But you're in the middle of this thing and your judgment is skewed. Don't try to out-think the cops and get cute. Despite *Miranda*, you know full well that most criminals get nailed because they can't keep their mouths shut. They're not confessing. They're trying to explain their cases away and they just get deeper and deeper in trouble. Right now, it's all circumstantial evidence. No eyewitnesses and no statements from you. What's the jury instruction say about those cases?"

"I think it goes something like 'the prosecution must eliminate every reasonable hypothesis of innocence.' I've only heard that line repeated in closing arguments about, oh, I don't know, a thousand times."

"Well now it's your ally. They won't charge you unless they can get past that. Dottie Metcalf will push the homicide guys to nail everything down. But presuming they do, their case can't get any better than it is now, unless you give them something they don't have, or they find out something we don't know."

I nodded.

"Got it."

"I think we're done for today, Bill. Get out of here. Grab that girl-friend of yours and get out of town if you can. Go fishing, for all I care. Just don't talk to anybody about this case."

I couldn't bring myself to tell him about the phone records April had given me, at least not yet, or about Charlotte's help. I knew it would irritate him, but I had to know what those numbers showed. If anything panned out, I thought, I'd put it in the memo.

I stood up and extended my hand.

"I trust you, Gene. That's why I'm here. I can't stop worrying, but I know I couldn't be in better hands."

"Hold off on that judgment until we're further down the road. Oh, and one more thing."

"Should I sit down again?"

"No. Just an update. I heard from a guy at the country club that Wally was a few martinis into a rant the other night. He was talking about the bar complaint and seemed pretty annoyed with you."

"What did he say?"

"I don't know if it's a direct quote, but according to my source, I gather he said something like, 'That arrogant punk Duncan brought this on himself. He should have *nolle prossed* the case when he knew that the 7-Eleven clerk wasn't gonna show.' I guess you really fouled up his afternoon plans."

I shrugged.

" 'Arrogant punk?' He's got me there."

But how did he know which witness wasn't going to be in court? I didn't identify him when I asked for a continuance.

I left Gene's office not knowing if I should feel confidence or despair.

Chapter Thirty-One

Dial April for Information

There just isn't enough time. When each day brings more calls from police, more witnesses, more lab reports and more cases, it's a wonder we ever have the time to prepare and win any trials at all.

That changed fast, of course, and I was left alone, at home, in an endless desert of time. All around me, it seemed, bedlam, anxiety, motion, and fury loomed. I was powerless to grab hold of anything to slow the thundering legal process closing around me, darkening any hope for my career or even personal freedom.

For once, I had plenty of time. I just had little idea what to do with it.

I continued to review the phone bills. I built on what Charlotte had begun and constructed a series of lists, spreadsheets, and diagrams based on names, corresponding numbers, and dates. Land line calls only appeared when they were dialed to or from the cell phones, so any analysis would miss some exchanges. Tracing Dixon's calls, I found several to the Fontaine home early in the investigation. He'd made many to the CA office, and a few to unknown blocked numbers. None to Whitacre, the 7-Eleven clerk, after the grand jury indicted Hausner. I found a few between Dixon's cell and Casey Butler's direct line. I made a note to ask Kent to check on how many other cases those two had together. There were also the calls registered between Butler's cell and Shea's office.

My frame of mind darkened as I calculated what they must have discussed. More and more, I became convinced that Butler had run his mouth and told Shea about the evidence in the Hausner case, thereby eliminating the defense's need for a discovery motion. If that's what happened, Shea got what he wanted without the formality of a motion and order, and thanks to Butler, he withheld the alibi.

The invoices covered through the month of September, two weeks before the Hausner trial. I called April again.

"I thought you didn't love me anymore," she said. "I come across for you and you forget my number. You don't call; you don't write."

She made me work for it.

"You know better than that. But as we're on an unsecure line, I'll be brief."

"Please."

"Don't beg. It's unseemly, even for you. But seriously, I need another favor."

"I knew it. A lawyer's booty call."

"A what? Oh, never mind. But I do need to ask for more of the same as last time, only brought up to date. Is that doable?"

"I'll see. So far, so good. But I'm not fixing any parking tickets for you."

"Over and out."

April was good. There was no telling whether anyone was listening, but if so, nothing of substance was betrayed.

***

She called a few days later.

"Hey, counselor. Got time for coffee with your favorite cop?"

"Do I have a choice?"

"You have the right to remain silent, but that's as far as it goes. Regular place?"

"One hour?"

"See you there."

***

My study of the numbers and the calendar had yielded mixed results. It was apparent that there had been contact between some of the parties, but other than Butler's contacts with Shea, nothing stood out. Nothing, that is, except the unknown numbers Dixon called, and on occasion, those from which he was on the receiving end. It could have been the same source or several. I couldn't tell from the bills.

She arrived carrying a raincoat over her arm.

"Nothing for me?" I said.

She slid into the booth.

"You bumpkin," she said, laughing. "I figure if someone is watching you, I don't want to be seen handing you anything. You're the star of the show at CIB these days."

My head dropped. I had friends at the Criminal Investigation Bureau, or at least I thought I did. Were they all now scrambling, like bees in a hive, each of them trying to be the hero, the one that cracked the case against me and made a reputation?

"Who's driving the bus?"

"Hard to say, since I'm not involved directly, but Dixon looks to be in the middle of it. That broad from Arlington, Metcalf, has been swinging her fat ass around, demanding this, demanding that. Kind of shook up the place."

"There's a surprise."

"Bill, you got to understand. On the one hand, those that know you don't like this case. It doesn't really add up. No offense, but you're nobody's idea of a killer."

"For now, I'll take it."

"But the evidence shows motive and opportunity. Can't get past that. And the timing. Boy, if only you'd gotten on that elevator before Hausner stepped into the lobby."

"Timing. I've always had the knack."

"Then, there's the guys that just take orders. She's pushing for them to examine every square inch of the garage and Hausner's car. She's got them checking security cameras all around the place, outside the garage, across the street, wherever. She hopes you might show up on video somewhere. Maybe have blood on your hands, throwing away a weapon, be seen with somebody. Anything."

"They can look a long time. It won't matter."

"Then, there's the crowd that says if you whacked Hausner, more power to you. They want to shake your hand and buy a round."

"Those are the ones we probably need to worry about."

"Anyway, when I go, I'm leaving my raincoat on this seat. I'd like it back, but there will be a present for you wrapped in it."

"You're the best, April."

"I took the liberty of running down some of these on my own and I found the IDs on a couple of the unknowns that kept repeating. I think you'll be interested."

"Whose?"

"Just check them out and be careful about who sees this stuff. You and Gene, I understand. Nobody else. I don't know what these people are up to, and I'm fairly sure you don't, either."

April puzzled me, carefully dancing around something she couldn't bring herself to explain. Inside information from the investigation, I thought. Or perhaps a warning.

"Just look. That's all I'm saying."

She was always smarter than I thought.

"One of these days, we'll have to drink something stronger than coffee, counselor."

"What do they serve over at the Police Rec Center these days?"

"Ha. That would be something. But I tell you what. You get past this, and I'll make sure you drink for free over there all year."

"If I get past this, they won't be able to keep enough in stock."

I waited a few minutes after she left, then picked up the raincoat. Outside the coffee shop, I glanced around and, seeing no one, opened the trunk of my car and put the coat inside my gym bag, where I buried it beneath some damp clothes and shoes.

Chapter Thirty-Two

What Goes Around

I'd decided that I needed more military background information, but now that I was a homicide suspect, going to the courthouse to meet Kent was out of the question. The usual local bars weren't a good idea, either.

His direct line made for an easy call. I gave it a shot late in the day when he was likely to be out of court, around five o'clock.

"Kent. It's your favorite killer."

"You don't sound like my ex-wife."

"Unless she's taken a serious turn for the worse, she doesn't look like me, either."

"It's cocktail hour. Is there a coincidence here?"

"None. Completely intentional. How about that dump out on Route 40?"

"I thought we were banned from that place."

"You were banned, Kent. But the staff is all new, so you should be in the clear. Can you be there around six o'clock?"

"Do they still have free food during happy hour?"

"Does it matter? You know I'll end up paying."

"See you at six."

***

Mosby's Grill, so named because the Civil War hero was rumored to have camped nearby, was a dark, worn out joint, but a safe place to rendezvous. The floors remained sticky no matter how often the staff mopped them. The smell of stale beer and cigarettes was embedded in the paneling, even though smoking had been outlawed long ago. The seats and tables were wooden, and their nicks and scrapes revealed several layers of old paint. But the beer was always cold, fried chicken wings and barbecue were hot, and anyone in a coat and tie was viewed with suspicion if not outright hostility.

The main room was long and narrow, allowing one to sit at the bar and face a mirror or take a seat at one of the small tables that lined the opposite side, each of which had two chairs. I took one in the farthest corner and sat with my back to the wall.

Kent arrived, knowing enough to shed his tie and roll up his sleeves. He is the type who can be comfortable in any bar in the world, especially if the tab is someone else's. I'd already ordered his first beer, which was waiting for him on the table.

"You're no killer," he said. "You're way too thoughtful."

"That's my routine. As you might imagine, I fooled Hausner into complacency by buying him a friendly brew."

"So, I should be careful walking to my car tonight?"

I can't imagine a law office in this state, or anywhere else for that matter, where colleagues could joke like this with each other. But Kent always put me at ease, and, whenever we parted I was usually exhausted from laughing.

"I'm going up to Jersey for the Miss Bayonne pageant this weekend. Did I tell you about the talent competition?"

"Yes, Kent. Once or twice."

"It's nothing but class. Like royalty."

This went on until we were into our second round. I passed him an envelope.

"I need another DD-214. Can you get it?"

"I should. They're public records and I don't think the DOD ever purges them. Anything you can tell me?"

"Not yet. And I shouldn't tell you, anyway. But I've got some ideas. Some connections that might add up later. You'll be just about the first to know."

He drained his glass and signaled to the bartender for another round.

"You haven't asked me about Metcalf's investigation."

I shook my head.

"No, and I won't. She's just doing her job, and if you're ever asked whether you spoke to me about the investigation it would go bad for you, Mac, and everybody. Let her run out the string."

"The only thing I can tell you is this. They're looking at a Grand Jury. Straight indictment."

Gene was right. That meant no arrest on a warrant, but it also signaled that there would be no preliminary hearing, when my lawyer would have the chance to probe the evidence and test the witnesses long before the trial. A straight indictment was a strategy to be used when the prosecution was certain of its case and wanted the defense to see the witnesses at trial for the first time. I'd be entitled to pre-trial discovery, but that would only reveal the physical exhibits the Commonwealth intended to use as evidence. Nothing that would reveal case strategy or theory, identity of witnesses or what they'd be expected to say.

"Straight indictment," I said. "Smart move. She'll give up getting a test run at the prelim, but circumstantial evidence cases don't get better by showing them to the other side. I'm somewhat surprised at Dottie."

"Don't be. That was Homicide's idea."

"How much is Mac doing on this thing?"

"Almost nothing. He asked the Circuit Court to appoint a prosecutor from outside the county for the obvious reason. But he's the elected top dog. He makes her tell him everything. It's her case to run, but it's his county."

"Mac will play it fair. I can't complain. At least not about that."

"Plenty of other stuff, right? Butler marks it down for a guilty plea, then you get surprised by a three-day trial, convict the bad guy, and find yourself neck deep in it."

"It may be deeper than that, Kent. It might be well over my head. This train was rolling before I even knew it was on the tracks."

"You know, the second-best way to get out of this thing is to find the real killer."

"Yeah, Gene and I talked about that. I have some ideas, but right now I'm drawing a blank on evidence."

Kent cocked his head and looked at me.

"How well do you know Dixon?"

I grimaced.

"He cuts corners. I don't trust him. But a killer? He's too lazy."

"Well, besides you, who else benefitted from Hausner's death? If Wally had dumped the case on Shea's motion to dismiss, and the brass took a close look at the investigation, who would they blame?"

I thought about it.

"Well, Dixon lost track of the 7-Eleven witness, so the victim's clothes and purse never got into evidence. He never connected Hausner to the wife's car, the Bonneville. April Winston did that, but too late for DNA testing. Never ran the clothes, either. If he'd looked at the photos and spotted the bolt, we could have matched it up cleanly, putting it out front during the trial, instead of sitting on it until rebuttal. Yeah. I see what you mean. Dixon had plenty of motive to keep that motion to dismiss from ever getting heard in court."

Kent leaned across the table and whispered.

"And if you keep digging, who do you think is next to get whacked?"

My chest tightened and I felt that cold sweat again. If Homicide was certain of me for the Hausner murder, and I got taken out before a trial, the case would be closed, and no one would ever search for Hausner's real killer.

I slumped into my seat.

"You see, right?"

Without thinking, I looked around the bar for familiar faces.

"Just to be safe, you could come up to Bayonne with me."

I had to laugh.

"And what? Stay?"

"No, but seriously. Get with Gene. I hear he's petitioning for a Special Grand Jury. If he can get Dottie to agree, it seems to me that you must clear yourself without fingering Dixon or anyone else. In the meantime, stay low. Maybe get out of town."

It made sense. If the case against me collapsed, then my demise would do the real killer no good. The investigation would go on. But that also meant that Dixon had every reason to make me look guilty, then eliminate me and close the case.

My own predicament, of course, dominated my thoughts. But after a moment, I considered Kent.

"You've gone beyond the call of duty, Kent. You're taking a chance even meeting with me, let alone pulling DD-214s."

He looked past me and shrugged.

"Do you remember the trouble I got into a couple of years ago? That dope rip-off murder case?"

"When that detective didn't tell you about a witness's prior statements and the judge blamed you?"

"That's the one. Every TV station, the *Post*, everyone knew my name. I'd probably tried three hundred juries, all straight up, but all they heard was 'Kenton Raker, crooked prosecutor.' It didn't help that the judge fined me personally. Sanctions, he called it. Twenty-five percent of my salary."

I had forgotten that episode. I'd paid for more than a few rounds, back then, trying to ease his embarrassment and humiliation. He'd nearly left the office in disgrace, but there was nowhere for him to go.

"That was always a bullshit deal, Kent. Even the Bar Counsel left that one alone. No knowledge, no intent, nada."

He waved me off, as if dismissing a losing argument.

"I guess what I'm telling you is this, Bill. The lawyers on the other side knew what happened, and the rest of the judges knew what happened. I eventually tried that case and got convictions on both defendants. It was just the judge's play, showing everyone who's the boss. You remember."

I did. The biggest ego in the courthouse, a building that was full of them.

Leaning across the table he spoke through gritted teeth.

"Fucking Wally."

Judge Fairchild had been under consideration for the Court of Appeals at the time and had used Kent to promote himself.

"Anyway, I remember you didn't hide from me like some of the others. You never looked the other way when I wanted to grab lunch or a beer, and you lent me enough that I could pay the fine without losing my house. The night before closing arguments in that case, you worked with me to nail it down. If I can get a couple more DD-214s, or anything else you need, I will. Count on it."

I tapped my empty glass against his.

"One more round, then we're out of here," I said. "I've got home-work to do."

"And I've got to pack for Bayonne."

Chapter Thirty-Three

Room with a View

I spent Thursday evening poring over phone bills, outlining connections, and noting the timelines. Calls to the unknown number, or numbers, were significant enough that serving a subpoena on the telephone company might become necessary to determine who it was. Gene would do that if I was indicted. The additional records April gave me would have to wait until after the weekend, so I left them hidden in the trunk of my car. All the other papers and records, spread from one end of the dining room table to the other, would remain in place until Sunday evening when I returned.

***

Charlotte arrived at eight o'clock Friday morning, right on schedule. She had suggested a weekend out of town, something we both needed. A large coffee was waiting for me in the console cup holder. I put my bag in her trunk and we were on the road.

I rarely took off a day from work, and almost never a Friday because that's when sentencing hearings are held. Defendants who have pled or been found guilty have the right to request a pre-sentence investigation and report. A probation officer spends a month preparing it, interviewing the defendant, his family, employer if he has one, and the victim. It is the last chance for a criminal to avoid, or at least minimize, his punishment. In Virginia, a judge can reduce the sentence handed down by a jury but may not increase it. When it comes to guilty pleas or verdicts in nonjury trials, the sentence is completely within the judge's discretion, restricted only by statutory limits.

On those days, when I was in court, I argued to respect the judgments of juries, to remember victims' injuries and sometimes just to give judges support for making hard decisions in the face of beseeching defendants and their weeping families.

"Every now and then," a judge once told me, "I need you to be the bad guy."

They wanted supporting cover when it was necessary to hand out a heavy sentence. We understood.

But on this Friday, I sat in a convertible BMW, drinking a four-dollar coffee next to a pretty woman who was taking me to the country for the weekend. There would be hiking, good food, a little wine, and if my good fortune held, a lot of romance.

"What's our destination?"

"A little place I found," Charlotte said, "and I think you'll like it. Views of the mountains, can't see another house, and no cell phone reception."

"Can I stay?"

"As long as you like," she said, smiling at me from behind sunglasses. "But I'm leaving Sunday afternoon."

It seems almost immoral to leave town during morning rush hour. We drove west, passing miles of eastbound commuters on their way to work. The sun seemed to shine brighter, the sky was bluer, and the road was more inviting on a day like this. Tonight, those commuters would be on our side of the highway, heading home, but we'd be long removed from this road and deep in the mountains, far from the conflicts and strains of recent weeks.

"You need time away from the case. I know you're doing what you can, and you can't sit still while you think there's anything at all you *can* do to, well, do anything," she said. "But you need to trust Gene."

She turned and smiled.

"And we're going to have a good time."

"I just can't shake it," I said.

"Dixon? What Kent told you?"

"Yeah. One thing that occurred to me last night is that you might be in danger just by being around me."

She looked straight ahead for a moment, considering that possibility.

"I see it like this," she said, measuring her words. "Dixon's the guy—and whoever is working with him. If you didn't kill Hausner, then he's the one with the most to lose, and therefore the best motive. What a shoddy investigation. He never ID'd the right car. Detective Winston did that, but it was months later, and there wasn't even an attempt to get DNA evidence out of it. He also lost track of the 7-Eleven witness, blowing the chain of custody, so the victim's purse and clothes couldn't come into evidence. And he never checked out the wife."

We drove in silence for a few moments, the wind blowing over us the only sound.

"But, get this," Charlotte said. "Until you're convicted, or at least indicted, it's an open case. All they've got on you is circumstantial. They've got you with motive and in the same building around the time of the murder. If you're suddenly out of the picture, and without more of a case, the investigation continues. Dixon needs you around long enough to convince everyone that you did it. In other words, he needs you to be alive and safe for a little while longer. There's just not enough, yet."

She took a different view than Kent, and I hoped she was correct.

"Maybe you're right," I said. "Dixon has got to be involved. He's the guy."

She looked over at me, smiling.

"So, don't worry so much. Take the weekend off."

Her point was dissimilar to what Kent had surmised, but somehow Charlotte's version of it gave me hope. Her confidence and theory were tantalizing. And yet, I wasn't completely convinced. Gene was still trying to persuade the prosecutor to hold a Special Grand Jury just for my case, but if he was unsuccessful, then a week from Monday, Dixon would be sitting before seven people in the Grand Jury room, testifying as to why the police believed I killed Jason Hausner. The next day, I'd be in court setting a trial date.

I couldn't get past the puzzle I was trying to solve before a jail cell door would close on me. All the same, I rationalized that a couple of days away from the phone numbers, photographs and the constant fretting and worrying would be good for Charlotte and me. I'd leaned heavily on her but offered little back. If there was any hope that I could survive this investigation, I wanted a life with her that was founded on more than Chinese food, case files, and sleepovers.

We left the highway and wound our way through a series of small towns, gliding along country roads and up the side of the foothills into the Blue Ridge Mountains. The cottage she'd rented appeared capable of housing an entire family. The deck offered a broad view of the valley below, the great room was centered around a massive fireplace, and the kitchen might have been designed for a restaurant. A jacuzzi sat on one end of the deck.

"Help me bring in these groceries and I'll fix us some lunch."

We unloaded her car.

"Then it's time for some exploring," she said.

"Exploring?"

"The brochure says there's a trail nearby, leading to a waterfall and some great views."

"How about I wait here and guard the jacuzzi?" I said.

She peered over her sunglasses.

"Not a chance, buster. I'm planning a fine dinner and I want you good and hungry."

Her prediction was correct. The walk was worth the trouble. About two hours and four miles of hills later, we were back at the cottage. The beer and wine were well-chilled by then.

We reclined on the deck, drinks in hand. From our vantage point, we looked down on the nearest town, miles away. Birds flew below. The loudest sounds came from the crickets in the surrounding woods. I spent most days immersed in people and constant noise. Here, with Charlotte, and in the quiet of the mountains, I seemed to have all I could ever want or need. The allure of courthouse drama faded.

I napped and awoke as the sun set over the valley. Charlotte was preparing dinner. My role, as usual, was to slice a vegetable or two, keep the wine glasses full and stay out of the way, except for kissing the chef on cue.

Neither of us wanted to talk about the case anymore, but it was on both our minds and the conversation lagged. When dinner was ready, we lit candles and turned off the lights. The sunset had passed but a resilient streak of crimson lined the sky above the mountain. By then I was so far removed from the fears, which had been smothering me for weeks, that it was difficult to understand how a world like the one we'd left behind could exist.

After dinner, we moved out to the deck with a second bottle of wine and a candle.

"If I get clear of this stuff, I don't know that I want to go back," I said.

"Just stay up here and think deep thoughts, right?"

"What's it pay?"

"Not as much as this place costs."

Is it still what I am, not just what I do?

As I mused, Charlotte's eyes reflected the candlelight, beacons shining at me in the quiet darkness.

"I mean leave the CA's office. Maybe it's time. Time to take the long view. Do what it seems like everyone except Mac and Kent have been telling me for a while now."

"White collar defense? Government contract litigation?" she said. "I watched them all from the clerk's desk. Believe me, you can handle those guys. The paper is intensive but when it's time to show up and try a case, you'll be fine."

I took her glass and refilled it, then my own. I felt the wine's warm, relaxing embrace. My thoughts came in random waves but always with the same message.

I am tired of the fight.

How can I face another judge or jury with the fearless confidence I need, and for which I have studied and prepared throughout my career?

"Maybe it's just time for something different," I said.

Charlotte put down her glass and leaned toward me.

"Bill, you didn't do anything wrong. You took a tough case and worked it like a pro. You always do. You won. You whipped Tommy Shea, and not too many prosecutors can say that. Forensics will back you up, I know it. All this will go away. Then, you can use it as a springboard to a better place."

"A springboard."

"Sure. Can you imagine ever having this much publicity again? It looks bad now, but when it all clears up, you'll be exonerated. In retrospect, it will be great for you."

I wanted to believe her, but I shook my head.

"It's hard to see that from here."

"Have confidence."

"Why?"

"Because it's true. Think about it. Every time you ever lost a case, you learned something. You never let the same thing happen again. You prepare to exhaustion. That's why the judges respect you. Remember, I worked in chambers for a year. I heard it."

I stood up and walked to the railing. The orange sky had turned black. Only the distant lights of the town below and our single candle breached the darkness.

"Maybe you're right. It's just hard to imagine too many people knocking on my door right now, not when I'm under the gun with the Bar and facing a Grand Jury indictment in a little over a week."

She stood up and came to my side.

"Look at it this way: in about ten days, you'll know a lot more. If they think it's a winnable case, you'll be indicted. But all the signals seem to be indicating that what they've got is the same circumstantial evidence they've had since Day One. If it was any better than that, they'd have arrested you by now. If they don't indict, you're in the clear. My money is on that one. Have a little faith."

I put my arms around her, pressing her into my chest, my hand stroking her hair.

"I'd like to think that. Dixon's history and all those calls between him and the blocked numbers bother me. If Shea had a photo of the bolt the night after the trial and got it to his own expert, it must have come from him. It just seems like . . ."

"Bill . . ."

"Charlotte, it's not a matter of truth, it's about evidence. If a straight indictment comes down, it's got to be because they have something I don't know about."

"Enough."

She cut me off and pulled away.

I could barely see her in the darkness, as she walked to the far end of the deck and the jacuzzi. She lifted the straps of her sundress from her shoulders and allowed it to drop to her feet. Shedding the rest, she stepped into the water and turned to me.

"Blow out the candle and bring my glass."

Chapter Thirty-Four

Where There's Smoke

Sunday evening came too soon, of course. The long, luxurious weekend that had stretched out before us just two days before had raced to its conclusion, one savored moment at a time. The quiet and beautiful desolation of the mountains defied the danger awaiting me in Jefferson but that respite soon became a passing memory in the distance.

We spoke sparingly on the ride home. For me, each mile brought us nearer to the source of my distress. Charlotte understood and held my hand as she drove.

It was also a time for reflection. The previous days had been blissfully restful. Aside from the daily hikes along scenic trails, we did little but relax, eat, drink, and make love. Charlotte had been silent then as well, and our lack of conversation only added to the intensity of her passion. Perhaps that's how the women of convicts about to begin prison sentences bid farewell to their men. Whatever the reason, Charlotte expressed herself with a vigor I had not known previously.

When we arrived at my home, I removed my bag and invited her to stay. There was much work to do and we had often shared the effort.

She demurred and smiled at me from behind the wheel.

"Not tonight, Bill."

"Last chance. I won't beg but so often," I said. "Like, every day."

"I know. But I can't."

I leaned into her window, lingering to extend our days of solace just a little longer. She closed her eyes and I kissed her.

"Goodbye, Bill."

And she was off.

I opened the door and climbed the stairs, missing her already. The scent of her hair, the touch of her fingertips. I wanted them again and again.

It was difficult to accept that I had enjoyed most of three days without the intrusion of the sharp-edged world in which we both lived and worked.

Whatever I do, whatever I can, if I get out of this mess, I want to be with her and have more days like these. Thousands of them. All of them.

This was another moment when I thought it was all too good to be true, but then a happy realization would shine through.

No, it isn't. It's real, and this could go on forever.

I tossed the contents of my bag into the laundry bin and ambled into the kitchen to start a pot of coffee. It would serve me well as I resumed the analysis of phone records and other documents on the dining room table, figuring out what Casey Butler might have told Tommy Shea and what plot Detective Dixon had concocted to cover his negligence.

As I waited for it to brew, I stepped outside onto the deck and watched the last flickers of sunlight disappear behind the trees, reflecting on the water. The platform in the lake listed silently, slowly drifting back and forth. For a moment, I considered swimming out to it, putting off the effort that awaited me in the next room. Anything, I suppose, to relive the memories of each luscious moment with Charlotte.

I resisted the temptation, wandered into the dining room, and nearly dropped the mug of fresh coffee.

Gone.

Every scrap of paper I'd left behind on Friday morning was gone. I searched frantically, trying to convince myself that I had put them away somewhere secure. Somehow, they had to be here, just beyond my view. I knew better, but still couldn't believe the unblemished void that lay before me.

All gone—every last file, document, photograph, note, and paper-clip.

Who?

I turned to the shelves for Dixon's case file and found only empty space. That was missing as well. My eyes raced around the room, searching for what else might have been taken. The silverware was intact. The one crystal bowl I owned remained in place. Nothing was amiss.

Whoever knew I would be gone for the weekend and that the records were here had been watching and probably listening to my phone calls. Dixon must have remembered that I had the investigation binder. Did he know about the phone records before he got here? If not, April's assistance might remain unknown. But it was only a matter of time before he tracked down the source of the bills and how they got to me. If he'd known that I had them beforehand, April might have been compromised. Either way, she was in danger.

Or was April the intruder?

Had she been caught helping me?

Had she flipped and told Dixon?

The coffee shop was out. My telephones were no longer an option. I thought of the Chinese restaurant nearby, the one Charlotte and I seemed to keep in business. No one would have thought to monitor that telephone—at least I hoped.

I grabbed my keys to drive there and call April. We could meet somewhere safe and I'd warn her or find out if she had been turned by Dixon. One way or the other, I'd be a step closer to the truth.

I raced down the steps and out the front door. I slammed it behind me and bolted for my car. A voice boomed before I could get into it.

"Don't move, Duncan. You're surrounded."

I stiffened, slowly raising my hands.

"Dixon?" I said. "I know, Dixon. I know."

"Shut up and put your hands behind your back."

A hood went over my head, my hands were cuffed behind me, and I was pulled into a waiting car.

"I'd say 'let's see the warrant' but I suspect this isn't really an arrest, is it?"

No one answered me or spoke a word as the car backed out of my driveway. I was wedged between two men. At least I thought they were men.

***

The turns, circles, back-ups, and changes of speed left me without any sense of direction. The drive took at least an hour, perhaps longer.

We finally turned off a paved road, drove for a few minutes on gravel, and stopped. I was pulled out of the car. Someone took me, still hooded, by one arm and led me through deep grass and into a forest.

If I were going to kill someone, this is the sort of place I'd do it.

Witnesses and evidence would be in short supply here. We continued for several minutes through underbrush and around trees. Branches scraped against my face through the hood. We finally reached what seemed to be a clearing. If I was to die here, I figured my body wouldn't be found for a long time.

I heard people speaking quietly, their footsteps treading on leaves and fallen branches, and could make out only one phrase spoken clearly.

"He'll be here in a minute."

The hands released me, but I remained cuffed, hooded and standing. Listening as well as I could, I heard nothing but low voices and the rustling of leaves in the light breeze. There were no sounds of even distant traffic. We were far from any beaten path, it seemed.

"Okay, listen up," said a voice.

Orders were issued, sending men in different directions to secure and guard the area. Try as I might, I recognized none of the voices. I smelled cigar smoke.

"Mr. Duncan," a man said.

The speaker was nearby, perhaps an arm's length away.

"It appears that you've been quite busy."

I said nothing in response. Mindful of criminals that talk their way into prison, I tried to exercise my right, if not ability, to remain silent.

"You have caused me a great deal of concern."

"Just an overworked, underpaid civil servant," I said.

So much for my right to silence.

"And you know, as an officer of the court, I am duty-bound to inform you that on top of whatever penalty is imposed for abduction, it can only be exacerbated by smoking on county property, if that's where we are."

If I were to die here, at least it would be with a modicum of defiance. I imagined their response. *Remember that lawyer we whacked last fall? At least he was cool to the end.*

I expected the hood to be removed but it stayed in place, preserving their anonymity and my uncertainty.

"Even when you're off-duty, you're working hard," he said.

The voice was deep and raspy.

"And you're a smart ass."

"As you say."

I could tell he was the one puffing on a cigar, blowing smoke at me.

"All that effort has made this little meeting necessary," he said.

"And this is how you'll silence me? You, Dixon, and his cohorts? Not very professional."

He puffed again.

"Mr. Duncan, you've done a lot of work, but the sum total of it hasn't cleared you. Worse, it has put someone close to you in grave danger."

Of course. They'd watched my home and listened to my calls. They knew about Charlotte.

"In fact," he said, "if your friend knows as much as you, she may be in even more danger."

He walked around me.

"It makes me wonder. Do I need to speak with her?"

What have I done?

I sank to my knees into the wet grass, as if pulled down by an anchor.

What was I thinking, letting Charlotte get involved in this? If they were willing to kill Hausner, frame and now likely kill me, why wouldn't they erase her as well?

I struggled to breathe.

"Why are you telling me this? You're going to kill me anyway. Are you amused in some despicable way?"

I heard him pace back and forth in the grass.

"Not exactly. We might be a little more professional than you think. Listen to me now and listen closely. I'll not repeat myself."

I bowed my head, nodding.

Anything, if it will save Charlotte. And if I live through this, I'll find these people, Dixon and his gang. I'll find them.

"Your lawyer has filed a motion for a Special Grand Jury, and the hearing is to be this coming Friday. He seeks to put forth all of the evidence you've amassed and somehow convince a panel that a web of conspiracy exists, falsely portraying you as the cause of the late Mr. Hausner's demise."

He puffed again.

"Tell him to stop and remove it from the docket."

I listened for more, but heard only the leaves rustling above us, and no other voices.

"Why?"

"Let the regular Grand Jury proceed. As you know all too well, it meets one week from tomorrow, on Monday."

Dixon would tell the jurors his theory of the case and summarize the evidence. The defense would have no opportunity to speak to them, and only four of the seven needed to agree to hand down an indictment. It was practically automatic.

"And just get indicted? You must be confident of a conviction at trial. What do you have? Who's going to lie for you? You may as well tell me. There's nothing I can do to stop you."

Dead silence.

"That's it," he said.

I was befuddled.

"And . . . and if I do, you'll leave Charlotte alone?"

"I must stress to you the importance of following my directions," he said. "Do nothing. Stay away from the courthouse. Avoid anyone associated with the case. By that, I mean everyone. Your fellow prose-cutors. The police. The media."

Another pause.

"And no coffee shops. Do you understand?"

So much for my clandestine meetings with April.

"And you'll leave Charlotte alone?"

He seemed to sigh with exasperation.

"Will I need to speak with your friend?"

I sat back on my heels, shaking, whether from fear or a tidal wave of adrenaline. I'd been on the wrong end of jury verdicts. I'd had cases wither in my hands as witnesses forgot critical evidence or just lost interest. But never had I known such utter frustration.

"And if I don't?"

"Do you have any choice, Mr. Duncan?"

No one spoke. I heard the others, quietly moving away, stepping on twigs and grass.

"Do you?"

I didn't need to respond. He knew.

Someone stepped behind me and uncuffed my wrists. I leaned forward, resting my hands in the grass. The sound of footsteps moving away drifted until I was left in silence.

The hood was secured by a drawstring. After a few moments, I untied and removed it, only to see that they had left me on the shore of my lake, on the opposite side from the carriage house. My kitchen light shone across the lawn and reflected on the water.

I threw the hood to the ground and walked home with one thought in mind.

Enough. I will find them.

***

By the time I was home again, it was well past midnight. The Chinese restaurant was closed, April was no doubt asleep, and I didn't trust my phone to be secure. I wanted to reach her, however, and could think of only one way without doing it directly.

I dialed Charlotte, hoping she could return to the carriage house. A written note, a whisper outside—somehow, I would get a message to April through her. The call went directly to voice mail, however, and I hung up. If she were awake, she'd see my number and call me. I couldn't get to anyone, I reasoned, without the police following me.

And then I remembered.

How could I have forgotten?

The last installment of phone bills April had given me was still hidden in the trunk of my car, tucked into a gym bag and buried under clothes.

I took a grocery bag from the kitchen, went outside, opened the trunk and found it still wrapped in April's raincoat, stuffed beneath gym clothes and equipment. Leaning over, rooting through it all, I tried to block any view of the envelope and slipped it into the bag.

I returned to the kitchen and tore it open. Hundreds of pages spilled out, some invoices marked, tabbed and highlighted. April had secured the unknown numbers.

It was too much to digest that night, but I had a lot of thinking to do and decisions to make. I poured out the pot of cold coffee and brewed another.

It would be a long night. There would be no sleep.

Chapter Thirty-Five

Grand Jury

A week passed. Monday. Grand jury. It seemed like a trial date to me. I slept little the night before and I gave up on sleep at four thirty, fixed coffee and sat outside, looking at the lake.

Dawn came. I watched as the sun lit up the lake, rising over the house and shining on the trees, their reflection stretching across the water. The early morning breeze drifted over the surface, rocking the platform, the sound of ripples slapping against it and echoing up to where I stood.

It seemed that despite my efforts, the monolith that comprises our legal system was about to engulf me. The indictment would be handed down later in the day and tomorrow a trial date would be set. At some point during the next eight weeks, I would sit before a jury of Jefferson County citizens with the rest of my life in their hands. How many more opportunities would I have to drink coffee at sunrise, overlooking my lake? Would I ever swim to the platform with Charlotte again, and savor her affection and the general sweetness of life?

I showered and dressed. Gene and I had arranged to meet at his office to await word from the courthouse. I hadn't told him about the previous Sunday night's adventure or my fears for Charlotte. When he and I last spoke he was puzzled and irritated at me for calling off his negotiations with Dottie Metcalf to empanel a Special Grand Jury, as well as his pending motion before the Court to force one, as this was the leverage he had held over her and was ready to use for my benefit.

He was already in his lobby when I opened the door, primed to meet me.

"Don't sit down," he said. "We're leaving."

"It's not even ten o'clock," I said. "The Grand Jury hasn't started yet."

"Mac called and wants to see us right away."

Gene offered nothing more. He'd recovered from my upsetting his well-designed strategy. He was a pro, responding to the change in direction with cool detachment, putting aside any personal consideration and looking ahead to what promised to be a hard-fought trial. We walked across the street to the courthouse in silence.

The deputies working the main doors saw us coming and waved us past the lines awaiting passage through the metal detectors. We both carried county bar cards that exempted us from the tedious examination, but still appreciated the deference.

As we entered the Commonwealth Attorney's suite, the receptionist sent us back to Mac's office immediately. The hall was silent, as all the prosecutors had departed to their assigned courtrooms for the days' trials. The blinds in his office were open and sunlight filled the room. He stood, hands on hips, his face drawn tight. Dottie Metcalf sat in a chair against the wall, staring out the window.

"Gentleman," he said. "I think you know Ms. Metcalf from Arlington."

She remained seated. Gene and I nodded in her direction, but neither one of us moved toward her or hinted at any pleasantries.

"There has been a development. I presume you are unaware?"

He looked at us. Trial lawyers to the end, neither of us betrayed surprise but I had no idea what Mac meant.

"Thought so. We received information over the weekend and early this morning. Evidence continues to develop in the Hausner murder investigation."

My heart sank.

What could they have found?

What witness could have surfaced?

What could Dixon have fabricated?

What did all the cloak and dagger business of a few nights ago mean now?

Mac folded his arms and leaned against the window behind his desk.

"Ms. Metcalf and I have discussed the matter and concluded that it is not in the Commonwealth's interest at this time to present a charge against Mr. Duncan to the grand jury. In fact, it is not likely to be presented—ever—but I think you can appreciate that until the case is finally and officially closed, we cannot rule out a future indictment."

The words were clear, in Mac's typical manner, but it was as if they had been delivered in a foreign language. I barely grasped their meaning and couldn't understand how they came to be, especially so suddenly, with no warning.

Gene spoke first.

"May we inquire as to what 'developed' over the past few days?"

Mac and Dottie exchanged glances. I surmised that this decision had not been smoothly concluded, and I suspected it had not been entirely unanimous.

"The investigation continues, but I can tell you this. Certain exculpatory evidence was confirmed."

He stopped and laughed, shaking his head.

"Imagine the irony. Duncan, you've been saved by *Brady* evidence."

The humor was lost on me, and he continued.

"Some of the details discovered at the crime scene on Hausner's body have remained concealed. No one that wasn't an investigator or a perpetrator would have known about them. I got a visit Saturday night

271

at home from a couple of black-suited, sunglasses-in-the-nighttime guys from the National Security Administration. It seems they've been tracking what they call 'chatter,' and some Middle East noise makers are claiming responsibility for Hausner's untimely departure from this life."

What about the hooded drive and trek through the forest?

Had that not been the Jefferson County Police but the NSA?

I glanced at Metcalf. She fidgeted and looked down. This was Mac's show now.

"It seems that someone considered Hausner to have been responsible for the deaths of four young girls while he was in Iraq. That's not a complete surprise, I suppose, given his proclivities. But it appears that his killer, or killers, left a calling card."

I glanced at Gene, then back to Mac.

"Four of Hausner's teeth had been removed and placed in his shirt pocket," he said. "The chatter bragged about it, and the fact that a local lawyer was going to go to prison for what they'd done. I gather they were quite pleased with themselves."

"Four teeth," I said.

"Right. They weren't knocked out against his dashboard as you might have heard. They were pulled out and stuffed in his pocket. I don't know how Forensics knows, but those guys tell me that it happened before he was dead."

"You have to admire the symmetry," Gene said.

"So," Mac said, "you can see that if an indictment were to be handed down, we'd have to turn that information over to you. The teeth, combined with the NSA confirmation of terrorists bragging about killing Hausner, is plainly exculpatory. Put that in the hands of a reasonably competent lawyer—even you, Cresswell, and . . ."

He raised an eyebrow.

"Well, any jury would find reasonable doubt."

Looking over at Metcalf, Mac continued.

"Hell, I got no doubt at all."

Metcalf stood.

"I guess we're done here."

She walked to me and grimly extended a hand.

"No hard feelings?"

"Not on my side," I said.

I accepted her grasp, still processing what I'd just heard from Mac.

"I assume this means you won't be coming back to Arlington any time soon," she said.

I shrugged.

"I don't know, Dottie."

She grimaced when I used her first name.

"You folks treated me so nice over there, I might just make it a habit."

Without even a trace of a smile, she nodded to Mac, picked up her briefcase and left.

"Sit down, gentlemen," Mac said, as soon as she was out of earshot.

He sank into his chair and leaned back.

"I am only slightly less relieved than you are."

"Did she fight you on this, Mac?" Gene asked.

"Like a hellcat. 'Can't rely on the NSA,' she said. 'Anyone can put that stuff out there,' For God's sakes, I told her, of course they can. But still, we had to turn over the information to you and there's not a chance in hell a jury would convict when the story about those teeth came out. But most of all . . ."

He leaned forward and pointed at me.

"Most of all, the story rings true. Bill, you were a logical suspect because there was no one else. Opportunity and motive? Right?"

I nodded.

He continued.

"But the brutal way Hausner was killed never seemed like a one-man job. And the story about the teeth matched what I confirmed yesterday. Hausner got sent home from Iraq because he screwed up over there and got four women, known assets, tortured and killed. I got the same thing from the Pentagon."

I had been delivered. My sense told me not to question the veracity of the story that restored my freedom. Still, something seemed wrong.

"Mac, if the Iraqi women were killed, that was by the other side. Isn't that who the NSA is tracking? Why would they send someone over here to kill Hausner?"

He leaned back in his chair.

"The way I hear it, you can't tell who's playing on what team, and they change all the time. It's not just our guys and their guys going at it. They've got factions, Sunni versus Shia, local chieftains and their enemies, the works. There are also fathers, brothers, and husbands. Don't forget them. Our people are listening in on all of them. I think somebody from whatever dirt hole village Hausner was working finally tracked him down. All that publicity he made for himself, those damned press conferences of his, put him up on a stage for everyone to see. He's the one that kept bragging about his military service over there. This case was all over the news, probably seen around the world. Hell, he was probably on Al Jazeera. He wasn't hard to find. They could just keep tabs on him through his press conferences and follow him until they got him alone."

"The more he was out there, talking about Bill," Gene said, "the more obvious a target he became."

Mac shrugged.

"Seems to be."

Turning toward me, he spread his hands.

"So, when are you coming back? Patty tells me we've got some trials that need covering. Schedule conflicts. You know how that goes."

I had anticipated being in court the following day to set my own trial date. The next two months had been reserved for trying to prove my innocence. Now, instead, it seemed I could be trying cases on behalf of the Commonwealth later in the week.

But no.

"I need to sort out a few things, if that's alright."

Mac smiled.

"Fine. So do I, and the first thing I need to do is find out what the hell happened to the Hausner case between you and Butler."

He set his jaw and shook his head.

"First day back, we talk."

I nodded. We stood, and Mac reached across his desk and shook my hand.

"I want you back, Bill. I need you. I needed you a month ago. Oh, and by the way, here's something you might appreciate."

He handed me a file.

"I've been on those Forensics guys to wrap this up. Came through this morning."

I opened the folder and scanned the contents. A report concluded that Commonwealth's Exhibit Number 17 was the photograph of a bolt consistent with those used to attach undercarriages of Pontiac wheel wells.

"The Titmouse was trying to spin us the whole time," Mac said.

I put on my best poker face.

"I know," I said. "I always knew."

Gene and I left the room. He grabbed my shoulder.

"Let's talk," he said.

We walked down the hall toward my office. Waiting by the door was Detective April Winston.

"I just heard," she said, smiling. "I'll tell the Police Rec Center to stock up."

She reached for my hand and squeezed it.

"Thanks, April," I said. "You remember Gene?"

"Counselor," she said, nodding at him.

"How can I forget the best rookie detective the Department ever had?"

Gene laughed and reached an arm around her shoulder.

"Let me know when you open your bar tab for this guy. I'll meet you over there."

"For sure," she said.

April looked up at me and after a long pause, she released my hand.

Gene and I stepped into my office, neglected for all these weeks.

"This place ought to be quiet enough," I said.

He shut the door and sat in my chair, with his hands folded on the desk. He glanced around, surveying the unopened mail and stacks of binders and files, mementos of trials long past. He shook his head and smiled, recognizing that nothing had changed since his time as an ACA.

"So," he said. "Thoughts?"

A sudden exhaustion crept over me. The roaring storm of adrenaline began to subside, and I sensed how beaten down and bone tired I was.

"I haven't really processed it," I said. "I've anticipated all sorts of things these past couple of months, but I never expected this."

He looked at me, lifting his chin and giving me the laser-like stare I usually saw during his cross-examinations.

"They came to me first," he said.

"Who? The NSA guys?"

I looked at him. He nodded.

"Saturday morning, I got a call and met them at my office. They told me the same story Mac just gave us and asked me what I wanted to do with the information."

I collapsed into one of the chairs I kept for witnesses.

"*They came to you*? What in the world . . .?"

"Someone was returning a favor. I represented one of those NSA guys a while back. A little misunderstanding between him, his girl-friend and, as I recall, his wife."

He shook his head.

"If people ever stop putting themselves in harm's way, I'll be out of work."

That would certainly include me.

"I told them to get it to Mac. I wanted him to know before the grand jury met and figured he'd do just what happened this morning. As I think I've mentioned in the past, it's a whole lot easier not to get convicted if you don't get indicted."

I'd read and re-read the transcript of the trial, researched the cases Tommy Shea had cited in his motion to dismiss, reviewed hundreds of pages of phone records and diagramed countless connections between suspected conspirators. Now, it had all come down to a shadowy report of foreign terrorists bragging about their exploits on the eve of my likely indictment.

"You knew he'd do the right thing."

Gene shrugged.

"It was the right thing, but strategically it was also the smart move. He'd much rather sit on an indictment than be forced to drop a murder case later. Plus, of course, there's no statute of limitations for felonies in this state."

I got out of the chair and paced around the small room.

"And so, that's it? We're done?"

He spread open his hands.

"Looks like it."

I shook my head.

"I still have some homework to do."

He raised an eyebrow.

"All I did was my job." I said. "I out-worked, out-thought and out-fought the Titmouse, and despite Wally's interference, I nailed that monster, Hausner. But thanks to others, I've been put through the wringer. Butler, Dixon, Shea."

I paused, clenching my teeth.

"Whoever. I'm not done with them."

"No, Bill," he said.

He looked down and shook his head.

"Let it go."

He looked at me.

"You're in the clear. Mac will issue a statement, maybe have that press conference you wanted, and you'll look like an absolute hero. You can even call that reporter, Rita Mohr. This all will fade away over time. Leave it be."

I shook my head.

"No, Gene. You're a brilliant lawyer, and more than that, you're my true friend. But you haven't had the sleepless nights, your phone bugged, your home tossed, your life upended."

My voice began to quiver with rage.

He sighed and let his eyes wander around the room.

"Bill, as an old friend of yours and mine once said, 'in our line of work we rarely see people at their best.' This has been a rough stretch for you, but you played it straight and came out of it on top. Look forward, not back. Let it go."

I shook my head.

"No," I said.

I looked at Gene and pointed my thumb over my shoulder.

"Somebody's going to pay."

Chapter Thirty-Six

Where the Fish Have Gone

Despite Gene's best effort and advice, I didn't let it go. Perhaps he was right. Perhaps I should have just left it all alone, and I wouldn't have known what April's final installment of phone records contained. I most assuredly wouldn't have known what a fool I'd been.

She'd gone to some trouble and must have called in some serious favors. She'd not only identified the unknowns for me; she had linked names to numbers, and even color coded some of them. I cross-referenced the calls against my calendar, trying to deny the obvious. I checked the calls and their dates again and again.

Impossible. Inconceivable.

But it was true. There was no doubt. What I'd thought were coincidences were instead the results of careful plans, and what I had thought were favors were acts of betrayal.

After leaving the courthouse that day, I'd worked through another night and finished reviewing the hundreds of pages April had delivered. As dawn arrived, I stepped out on the deck, my back stiff from sitting at the table for hours and was chilled by the early morning breeze. I watched the sunlight peer over the roof and glisten on the lake.

Trust and betrayal, two sides of the same coin, and one that I hadn't imagined could entrap me so easily, now lay before me. A person can be foolish, I suppose, and willingly, too, if the foolishness is appealing enough.

It certainly had been for me.

Maybe it's time to dust off those Puccini arias.

I stood on the deck, considering all that I'd learned in the previous hours, and thought to pour myself a shot. It was five o'clock, but the wrong one. More than a drink, however, I needed to talk to someone. More than bourbon, I needed to pour out the truth I'd discovered, to confess my blindness, to seek direction and hope.

I decided against the drink and picked up my keys.

***

The early fall colors enhanced the drive deep into the Valley. The farther I got from the courthouse, the less real any of the events of the previous months seemed.

I passed Claude's general store, tooting the horn without stopping. Perhaps I'd stop by on the return trip, but for now I had no interest in small talk.

I turned off the highway. The road to the river was muddy from the previous night's light rain, and tracks confirmed that the angler had preceded me to his favorite spot. As I rounded the bend, riding alongside the river, I spotted his truck.

He was standing beside it, nursing a Styrofoam cup of Claude's coffee, assembling the rod, reel, stringer, and lures for the day's pursuit of smallmouth bass. The crisp morning temperature restricted him to casting from the bank, rather than wading in the cold water.

"I thought you might drop in," my father said. "I read about your case in this morning's paper. Cold beer in the cooler, by the way, once you've had enough coffee."

"Thanks," I said. "I tried to call you yesterday afternoon, but Mom said you'd come down here the night before. Since Uncle John's place still doesn't have a telephone, I couldn't reach you. You might speak to your brother about that one day."

281

He nodded.

"No one could reach me. That's why I come down here. I thought you were going to be indicted and didn't want to talk to anyone, especially that reporter. Do you know her?"

I sat on the tailgate of his truck.

"Well, the Grand Jury part worked out alright. And Rita's fine. She just writes about the news. She doesn't make it."

He continued to size up lures for the morning's effort.

"With the water getting colder," he said, "they'll be hitting on the surface."

We sat in silence for a while.

"So, what was the other part that seems to have brought you all the way down here, Son?"

I reached for the words I'd prepared throughout the drive that morning. They weren't stuck in my throat; they were gone, like the morning mist lying low over the river, chased away by the rising sun.

"Charlotte . . ."

My voice was no more than a whisper.

He put down the lures and looked out at the river.

"I figured that might be it. You have a look on your face like somebody stole your insides."

I shook my head slowly.

"I know, Dad. I know. 'What happened?' That's a question I ought to be able to answer, I guess. The short version is, I don't know. The longer version is that she was using me all along."

He threaded the line through the rings of the fishing rod, still facing the river.

"Go on."

"I got my hands on a slew of telephone records—I can't tell you how or from whom—and with a little help I traced who was connected to each other. Charlotte was helping me, at least I thought, to sort it all out. But instead, she was tuning in someone else about everything I found."

I paused.

"I think she was probably slowing me down, too, by hiding information."

He picked up a lure and fastened it to the line.

"I'm sorry, Son. How did you find out?"

"The last bundle of records. She never saw them. My source had traced the unknown numbers to their account holders, and it all came together. That idiot, Casey Butler, had talked to Hausner's lawyer after the preliminary hearing, long before I got the case back. I'd already suspected that, and it explains why Shea never sought discovery. Sandbagged us on the alibi. Butler must have told him everything he knew about the case. Hell, even Dixon was in on it. That lazy fool must have had his ego massaged beyond belief because Shea was calling him directly, between the prelim and the grand jury. I think he had both convinced that Hausner would plead out."

I shook my head in disgust.

"But she even . . ."

I could barely speak the words.

"She even made a call the night I met her."

He moved to the riverbank and cast the line far out into the water, just below a line of rocks.

"What do you think she was doing?"

I paced behind his truck, walking in the damp grass.

"Oh, she was tracking the calls, too, and probably checking for her own number. It was one of the unknowns in most of the records, just like the one she was calling. She'd have made sure I never found out. But I did, eventually. The last bundle of invoices, that's what blew her cover. She was in constant contact, and especially after every time she worked the files at my place. I think she even made calls from my house."

Dad turned away from the water and let his lure float downstream.

"Son, it's been said that 'the heart is deceitful above all things; who can understand it?'"

He always had a ready quote or a wise expression. Something just right for the moment.

"Walt Whitman?" I asked.

"Old Testament. You really ought not sleep in on Sundays. Get to church every now and then. Do you some good."

He reeled in the lure, pointing the rod low and varying the speed to mimic a small fish. "Who was she calling?"

I stepped into the field, away from the river.

How does one measure humiliation, devastation, and heartbreak?

How does one describe the unfathomable?

I turned back toward him.

"The man who killed Jason Hausner."

Chapter Thirty-Seven

Family Ties

I'd thought to make an impression, getting a box of expensive Nicaraguan cigars. I had tried one after a dinner party at Gene's home some time ago. He swore they were better than Cubans. I never imagined anyone could enjoy burning things so absurdly expensive, but it might be a good investment if they could get me some answers.

I drove out to Glenwood, the most exclusive gated community in the region. The entrance, at the end of a secluded winding avenue, framed by old growth trees, was manned by a uniformed guard.

"Good afternoon, Sir," a large man said. "Who might you be visiting today?"

"General Fontaine. I don't have an appointment, but I think he'll see me."

"Name?"

"William Duncan."

He stepped back into his booth and made a call, spoke briefly, and returned.

"Can I see some I.D., please?"

I handed over my driver's license. He looked at the picture and back at me.

"DMV didn't do you no favors, Sir," he said, without smiling. "Have a nice visit."

The elaborate metal gates parted, and I drove into the enclave. Homes were set back far from the road on manicured, partially wooded lots of about ten acres each. Horse barns stood behind some, and the smell of chlorine indicated swimming pools.

I drove until I reached the address I'd taken from Dixon's file before it was stolen from my home. It was one of the larger houses, if such a building could properly be called a house. An estate, perhaps.

It had its own security gate as well. An eight-foot metal fence surrounded the lot and brick pillars bracketed the entrance. A guard awaited, wearing a uniform different from the other one. I saw no badges or labels, but presumed he was employed by Global Solutions International. He directed me to park beside the road and get out of the car.

"Stand still, please. Arms extended."

He waved an electronic wand up, down, and around me.

"The box?"

He inspected the contents.

"Good move," he said, without expression.

He spoke into a shoulder-mounted radio transmitter.

"All clear."

"What?" I said. "No pat down?"

He pointed to the gate, staring at me. Once again, my attempt at levity went unappreciated.

Where do they get these humorless robots?

The walk to the house took me across an expansive lawn with a decorative pond, replete with a fountain. The front door opened as I climbed the front steps.

"Mr. Duncan, how do you do? I'm Tom Fontaine."

He extended his hand, engulfing and holding mine firmly for several seconds.

He was taller than I by several inches and sported cropped white hair. I expected someone distinguished looking, as would befit a retired general and corporate CEO, and he didn't disappoint. I'd gotten only a brief glance at him after Amanda's testimony, when he draped his arm around her and walked out of the courtroom. He resembled a movie star, Lee Marvin, perhaps. Handsome in a rough, coarse way, but offset by a warm manner.

"This has been a long time coming, it seems," he said.

Indeed.

"We spoke briefly several weeks ago," I said. "But I didn't expect to see you again, especially after the trial."

He turned, waving me to follow, walked through a parlor, and led me toward the rear of the home.

"This way. I love the fall, and it's far too nice to sit inside."

We stepped out onto a patio. A tennis court was situated past a swimming pool. We followed a stone path to what he called his gazebo, an open, sheltered area equipped with a fireplace, a wide screen television, and hidden speakers playing soft classical music. Loose curtains hung on the sides. The furniture was far nicer than what I had inside my home. He guided me to a table where two drinks waited for us.

"My wife has a fit if I smoke in the house. So much for being a general, right?" he said, shaking his head. "But I like it out here. I can watch the games and put my feet on the furniture. Have a seat and let's see what you brought."

"It seems you already know," I said, recalling the guard who had called ahead.

He spread his arms, palms up.

"I'm in the business."

Before me was a clear drink, tall and full of ice.

"Vodka and tonic. You like those, as I recall," he said.

His friendly approach notwithstanding, it appeared I would have few surprises for him.

"It will do."

I laid the box in front of him.

"A token."

He opened the lid and beamed.

"Ah, Nicaraguans. And Padrons! My favorite," he said. "Perhaps you've done some homework, too."

I shrugged, pretending I had.

"I'm in business, too."

He pulled a cigar cutter from his pocket and offered it to me. I clipped the tip off one and handed it back, and he did the same. We lit and puffed in silence.

"This is a good one, Mr. Duncan. Good choice."

He rolled the cigar between his thumb and fingers, admiring it.

"How they make 'em for the price, I'll never know."

I winced, knowing the price.

"So, where do we begin?" he said. "I sincerely appreciate the smokes, but you could've mailed them."

He kept a tight smile but stared at me from behind his white, bushy eyebrows.

"I sense a question or two. Isn't that in your nature? As a prosecutor, I mean."

I'd pondered this moment for days, wondering if he even would meet with me. He was either fearless or knew a lot more than I, and probably both. He might not volunteer anything I didn't already know or at least suspect, so the best I was likely to get was clarification. If I played it right, perhaps I'd bluff him into a little more.

"You've heard that I wasn't indicted for the murder of Jason Hausner."

"Yes. Good news it was indeed. I'm quite relieved and happy for you," he said. "Especially since you proved what that man . . . did to my daughter, Amanda."

"Thank you. But were you surprised?"

He puffed again, then resumed rolling the cigar between his fingers. "This is a good smoke."

He said nothing more for a moment. Neither did I.

"Oh, it's always hard to say," he said. "I'm sure you've seen this sort of thing often enough. The papers and news shows get themselves all worked up into a lather, and then it turns out the truth is quite different altogether."

It was my turn to stare.

"Yes, certainly. But you weren't surprised, were you?"

He didn't blink.

"It is my business to be surprised as little as possible."

"Right. Your business. Just what does GSI do, General?"

"Tom, please. May I call you Bill?"

He puffed slowly.

"What do we do? Oh, a little of this, a little of that. We're all veterans, mostly with combat experience. I do some strategic planning and advise DOD on occasion. We also run some training programs for defense contractors and security teams, domestic and abroad."

"Like Blackwater?"

He blew a puff of smoke.

"This really is a good cigar."

I waited.

"You know they're not called that anymore," he said.

"But is GSI like that?"

He puffed again.

"Somewhat. But the reason GSI is in business and successful is that we are like no one else, and no one else can be like us. Now let's leave it at that."

Another silence. I sipped my drink and waited a moment.

"You and Hausner," I said. "You had a history, I believe."

The general turned and looked at me. I'd wanted to keep him eye-to-eye, like when pinning down a witness, but he'd reversed the tables on me. Beneath those eyebrows his pale eyes were aimed back at me, laser-like.

"Your friend Raker pulled my DD-214. I know. And so, you know that Hausner served under me when I was a colonel in Iraq. Is that 'history'?"

"Matching up his DD-214 with yours, it appears that he was under your command when he suddenly got sent stateside and released out of the service," I said, not looking away.

He waved to a man behind us and called for two more drinks.

"And Mr. Duncan likes his vodka tonics dry, Malcolm."

He turned his large frame toward me.

"You were saying?"

"What happened over there, and why was he sent home so early during his last tour?"

The general sighed and looked at his cigar.

"I know you're not wired, and I don't think you're the type that will go running to the press," he said.

He took time to measure his words.

"They're not exactly your friends, are they?"

"You and me, General. What happened?"

He leaned toward me, his face darkening.

"Hausner was a good combat soldier, and when we moved him into ground level intel he seemed to be a natural. He was fearless, focused, and smart. All the things one needs to be good at that job. But he was a ruthless, cruel bastard and he put people in jeopardy. I had to get rid of him."

"Why the early discharge, and why with honor?"

He shook his head.

"I still have heartburn about that. He'd made such a mess that I had to pull him out. He should have been locked up, and for a long time. But if we'd have court martialed him, the reasons would have gotten out eventually and God knows how many more would have been hurt or even killed."

He sank back into his chair. Malcolm delivered the drinks, placing fresh napkins on the table beneath them. The general continued.

"The honorable discharge was a cover. Anything less, that early in his tour, would have raised questions and drawn attention to him."

"And?"

"He'd done his job well, getting close to some friendlies. But you must understand, anyone that ever talked to an American over there was in danger. Eventually, he used that as a weapon with women. They had all sorts of reasons to be scared."

"Women? Sources of intel?"

"He was a master at it. Most of them were completely at our mercy. The economy was wrecked, so they were starving. A little American generosity now and then bought some cooperation. Hausner took it to another level. He'd connive his way into their bedrooms in exchange for food, medicine, and other essentials. The pillow talk led to what guys in what neighborhood were on the wrong side, and, of course, who we might want to enlist on ours."

He paused, looking away.

"All of that might have gone fine but eventually some of them got exposed. Dragged out of their homes one day and stoned to death, but only after being stripped and tortured in front of their families."

He looked down and shook his head. He began to speak again but faltered.

His version of the story fit but it wasn't complete.

"It sounds awful, General, but I'm having a hard time believing Hausner was the only soldier screwing local women."

"Tom, please. And hardly, but that wasn't the worst of it. The way they were discovered was that Hausner started to work for himself. Once his contacts were in place, he tried to smuggle jewelry, artifacts, anything of value that had been hidden during the collapse. He black-mailed his informants. Get him what he wanted, or he'd let slip how they'd cooperated with us. One of them put up an argument, it seems, and he left some marks on her. I don't know if it was her father, husband or someone else who saw them, but that started Hausner's circle of informants to unravel."

He looked down at his cigar and rolled it between his fingers.

"I've had to ask myself a hundred times—could I have saved those women?"

My cigar had gone out. I placed it in the porcelain ash tray between us. I saw that his was out as well.

"So, he really was into smuggling."

He laughed and shook his head.

"Not exactly. He certainly tried, but that was his downfall, like so many others. He was good at some things, and so thought he was a genius in everything. When it came to smuggling, he was an abysmal failure. He got caught almost immediately."

He stopped and re-lit his cigar.

"Dumb son of a bitch."

A light breeze moved the curtains behind us, blowing the smoke up and away. I turned back to him.

"How many girls were there, General?"

"I think you know."

"Four?"

He puffed on the cigar, getting it lit properly again.

"These really are fine smokes, Bill."

Once again, we sat in silence. I slowly worked my way through the second drink. When I'd drained it, I turned back toward him.

"There were a great many people interested in Jason Hausner. Why was it necessary for you to spy on his prosecution here in Jefferson?"

He was back to rolling the cigar, staring at it. I hoped for something more than just another compliment for tobacco farmers.

"A logical question. A trial, conviction and heavy sentence would have been welcomed. But that's not how it looked to be shaping up. It is pure speculation, of course, from my view. I know nothing of these things. But if I were to suggest a theory, it would go something like this."

He leaned toward me, the cigar in his hand pointing at me, like Glen Evans with his cigarette during my prison visit.

"For several weeks, no one knew who had attacked Amanda. When Hausner was finally identified and apprehended, the evidence was strong enough to be convincing that he'd done it. But the case had substantial weaknesses. For example, Amanda was blind drunk. She described a car completely different from what was later seen in the park. Had she left with one man and met another one later on, somewhere else? She couldn't say. There was no blood or DNA evidence taken from the scene or the right car, again because of the time delay and, frankly, shoddy police work."

"Dixon?"

"Absolutely. He knew it was a tough case from the beginning, so when he couldn't close it quickly, he dumped it on that woman detective, Winston. She pulled it together, but then that kiss-ass Dixon plowed back in, trying to cozy up to me, hinting about a job with GSI."

He shook his head in seeming dismay.

"Then there was the prosecutor that covered for you at the preliminary hearing, Butler. Adequate, I understand, but it seemed that after he'd sorted out the problems I just described, he got cold feet. It's my guess that he sensed a loser and bailed out, pawning it off on you. I gather that a miscommunication of sorts led your office to believe that Hausner was going to plead guilty. When Butler realized his error, he ran to you. If you *nolle prossed* it—that's the term, I believe—the case might never be brought again, and Hausner would go free. Given all those factors, anyone who wanted justice for Hausner might not have believed it would come to pass in a courtroom. Your success was a welcome surprise."

He took a deep breath and looked away.

"But as I understand it," I said, "Hausner met his fate at the hands of some Middle East terrorist group."

The tone of my voice made it clear that I didn't buy it.

"Isn't that what you've heard, too?"

He put down the cigar, rose from his chair and walked to the edge of the gazebo, hands in his pockets. No words passed between us for a moment. He turned and looked at me again.

"Yes, and I'm certain that is exactly what happened to the departed Mr. Hausner. Those people are barbarians. But Bill, if I may call you that, which I think I already have . . . Bill, you have no wife or children. You may someday, and I hope that when you do, you think back on this conversation."

I waited for him to continue.

"Can you imagine the savagery that men like Hausner inflict on people, and if so, can you really shove that into a sterile, antiseptic, windowless courtroom and think that real, true justice ever can be secured? Think of it."

His fists trembled with rage.

"A well-trained, professional killer, educated in a gruesome war, beats and attempts to rape a young girl from the suburbs. He then tries to crush her out of existence. And why? Because he hates her? He hates women? No, far from it. He hates the girl's father, the man that ripped away his strength, his power, and his uniform, then sent him home to be a mere civilian."

I held my drink, waiting for him to erupt.

"Tell me, Bill, do you really think your little system, with its fancy Latin words and elegant robes, can really set that record straight? Balance those scales of justice?"

He glared at me, picked up his cigar, puffing once while clenching it in his teeth.

"Of course not. You may as well ask the pigs in the sty which composer they like better, Mozart or Beethoven."

He held my gaze.

"Or Puccini."

His words were bitter and harsh, but his face was sad and pained.

"That aside, General . . . Tom . . . how did those Middle East assassins know that Hausner was going to be in Shea's building on that particular day? Before you answer, you should know that I've seen the phone logs."

I let that stand for a moment, then risked a bluff.

"A call went from Shea's office to a number registered to GSI that morning."

His response was measured and quiet.

"It appears you've answered your own question."

"It was Eckhardt, wasn't it?"

The general smiled and shook his head.

"No, I'm afraid that call originated a little higher in the chain of command."

I edged forward.

"Shea?"

He sat down again and crossed his legs.

"Think about it, Bill. He had much to lose, if he failed to get the case dismissed or at least secure a new trial. And you and I both know he had no evidence that the bolt came from any other vehicle. He'd gambled by passing up pre-trial discovery to hide the alibi from you and lost, thanks to your rather deft handling of the photographs. If his client went to prison, what do you think Hausner's next move would have been?"

He could file an appeal based on the same reasons underlying his motion to dismiss. But since Shea hadn't objected to their introduction at trial, that was likely to fail as well.

"Hausner would get another lawyer and blame Shea," I said. "They'd claim ineffective assistance of counsel and appeal."

"Correct."

We sat in silence again.

"So, Tommy Shea had good reason to see the whole problem go away. But helping to kill his own client?"

"Please, Bill. Shea was loyal to no one but himself, just like his client. What is it you prosecutors call him?"

"The Titmouse."

"Yes, the Titmouse. He was at risk for professional negligence and the blame for a twenty-five-year prison sentence. The damning evidence was right in front of him, and he never even objected. His reputation would never recover. But then again, Hausner was plainly guilty, and he was Shea's client, not his friend. So really, what would be the harm if the fellow were to run afoul of people that were, let's say, as single-minded as he?"

Even the Titmouse.

No wonder he stalled and was evasive with me that day in his office.

"Hausner was never going to rest until he'd hurt that girl's father as much as possible. He was an animal. A rabid animal. He needed to be put down."

The general signaled to Malcolm for another round.

"By someone else, of course," I said. "Terrorists."

I leaned back and considered his words.

"General, the rules of law you hold in such low regard are what separate us from the animals."

He nodded, looked away for a moment, then moved next to me.

"Bill, you may be right. In fact, I'm sure you're correct. But there's a hitch. When a man decides he's entitled to go outside those rules, that he no longer must abide by them, then everyone around him is in danger. If he's going to act like a vicious beast, shouldn't he be treated like one for the sake of the innocents?"

"Who are we talking about now, General?"

He looked away again and chewed his cigar.

I could never fully appreciate the grief and heartache this man had known, seeing his daughter near death, her body desecrated and broken, because Hausner had hunted down his child to inflict vengeance, the sole purpose being to punish her father.

One last matter weighed on me.

"How did you learn about Butler and the problems with the case on our end?"

"I think you know."

He'd confirmed what I suspected. I hesitated before my next question.

"How did you turn Charlotte?"

Another pause. We were on opposite sides of a chasm, separated by the depths of loyalty, betrayal, passion, and revenge.

"Bill, you must understand. She never turned. She was always help-ing me."

Of course.

I thought back to the night of the DUI seminar. She approached me, an attractive and highly paid lawyer in a national corporate firm, pur-porting to be interested in learning about traffic court procedures. I winced with embarrassment as I remembered how she'd laughed at my stories, and eagerly intimated her willingness to meet again.

"Winchester & Ford, and she, have represented GSI since our be-ginning. I needed someone to monitor the case against Hausner. I surely wasn't going to rely on Dixon or Butler."

His pale eyes met mine again. There was a trace of a smile on his lips.

"From the beginning, we knew that case was yours. The rest just fell into place."

My chest tightened and cool sweat ran down my back. The feeling was not unlike the morning after the Hausner verdict, when I sat in Patty's office, wondering how I'd gone from a conquering hero to a scoundrel, and so quickly. Now, I'd descended from an irresistible lover to a dupe.

"Don't think badly of her, Son," he said.

He took another moment to watch me deflate.

"If anyone turned her, it was you. There came a time when I thought she might forget where her true loyalties lay."

I lifted my head and looked at him.

"She grew quite fond of you. I was worried that she was going to break and tell you everything. In fact, she insisted that under no cir-cumstances were you to be indicted," he said. "She was the guiding force at the end. In fact, I expect that once this affair has cooled down, you'll hear from her again. She seemed quite taken with you, the last we spoke."

"When was that?"

"The day after you took that walk in the woods," he said. "I sent her away."

"Where?"

"Costa Rica. I have a place down there."

I rolled my eyes.

"I appreciate your trying to excuse, or smooth over what she did," I said. "But how could she, or you, for that matter, be assured that the NSA would fall for your ruse, the so-called 'chatter' that got me off the hook? You people . . ."

He bowed his head, smiling, then spoke again.

"Tell me, Bill. Have you ever seen NSA credentials?"

I didn't answer.

No, of course not.

"I expect your boss, Mr. McGuire, hasn't either, nor that woman from Arlington."

The complexities of trial practice had sharpened my ability to separate suspicion from fact and theory from truth. But nothing had prepared me for the unimaginable depth and layers of deceit in this case.

We'd all been buffaloed—not only me but Mac and Dottie Metcalf as well.

"What about Gene Cresswell, my lawyer? He's nobody's fool, and he said they called him first."

The smile broadened.

"No, he's not a fool, and yes, they called him first. He's quite a good lawyer. Very good. In fact, he's represented some of my best people when they've gotten into various scrapes. He did and said just what it took to protect you. And now, here you are, in the clear and smoking cigars with the CEO of the world's preeminent international security company. It's time to stop complaining. Put this behind you, Bill, and get on with the rest of your life. Accept the gift."

"I suppose threatening Charlotte, that night in the woods, was just insurance."

He blew a cloud of smoke toward me.

"Who spoke Charlotte's name that night?"

I thought back to the moment when the threat to someone close to me was made. I'd drawn the obvious and likely intended conclusion. But only I had called out her name.

"Then who was it, who was at risk?"

"Who else could it have been, Bill?"

April.

Of course.

I had suspected her of betrayal, but she might be the only one that had been completely truthful to me during this entire sordid affair. The general and I sat a few more minutes before I stood to leave.

"You know, General, I'm not amused. Impressed, yes. But you and your people put me through the tortures of the damned. All I did was try the hell out of a case and get a bad guy convicted of attempting to rape and kill your daughter."

I pointed my cigar at him.

"Your daughter."

I wanted that to sink in.

"And what did I get for it? I was the fall guy for a lawless vigilante execution, and to top it off, I got turned inside out by a beauty who put my heart in a blender, threw the switch, and walked away."

The general just looked at me.

"To put it bluntly, Sir, I ain't happy. And I'm not done with you. You, Dixon, and Butler. Or Charlotte Spencer, for that matter."

He took a final puff and lay the remnant of his cigar in the ashtray. "Son, vengeance may not be as fulfilling as you think," he said.

"I'm going to give it a shot."

He showed no concern for my threat, slowly uncrossing his legs and leaning toward me. "The grudge you carry can be a terrible weight. You think you're going to unload it on someone, but then you'll find the burden is still yours. Don't waste your life chasing it." He sounded confident.

"Besides," he said. "I find that things have a way of working out on their own."

"Like Hausner?"

"It crossed my mind. I think, had he lived, he'd have gone to prison. Right where you sent him. And yet, in death, he's left deep scars on several people. Only time will tell if they are permanent."

I looked at his hands, tanned, rough and strong, then back at his eyes and said nothing.

"You seem pretty certain of yourself, young man," he said. "You apparently perceive that you hold a threat over me. But tell me, now that you know, and you know that I know you know, have you thought about what it will be like, looking over your shoulder each day? You really should be more grateful. It was your decision not to *nolle pros* that case. It was your decision to go forward without an important witness and critical evidence. Most of all, it was your decision to sandbag the Titmouse with the photograph, embarrass him and invite the subsequent investigation and State Bar complaint. No one else can be blamed for that. You should consider this whole turn of events and be thankful."

He was accustomed to controlling every detail, leaving nothing unattended or to chance. No loose ends. Everything tied up nice with a bow.

"Well, I'm not worried, General," I said. "In fact, I think I'm just about the safest fellow in Jefferson County."

He rocked back in his chair, enjoying the moment.

"And why, pray tell, is that?"

"Because you and GSI will ensure it."

He finished his drink, waved off Malcolm, and looked at me.

"I have no need or intention of telling anyone about this calamity," I said. "I did nothing wrong. I was arrogant, perhaps, forceful but ethical. All the same, I don't need to advertise how I was played for a fool. I took the precaution, however, of compiling a narrative of everything I learned about Hausner, GSI, the investigation, and, of course, you. I included the phone records I still had and made a list of the ones that your burglars took from my home, which can be recreated without much trouble, I'm sure."

He didn't blink.

I continued.

"It's all wrapped up together, neatly organized in a package that will be distributed immediately to news services around the nation, should anything unfortunate happen to me."

He cocked his head, thinking for a moment before choosing his words.

"I take you at your word," he said. "But there's not a safe deposit box, lawyer's office, or church sanctuary I can't reach."

I nodded.

"I'm sure you're right, General. But there's only one way to find out, isn't there?"

His face gave way to a thin smile.

"You know we'll start looking today. I'll find it. And when I do, you might begin to worry again. Neither that lawyer, or policewoman friend of yours, will be able to protect you if you try to hurt GSI, Charlotte or me."

I knew that to be true as well, but until they looked behind the bait cooler at Claude Shiflett's General Store I was going to be safe.

Finally, I've cast my line where the fish are going and not where they've been.

"Enjoy the Nicaraguans," I said. "Tom."

He picked up the box.

"I will. In fact, I'm taking them with me tonight . . . to Costa Rica."

I sank back into my chair.

"You're going to Charlotte."

"Yes, I am. We both enjoy Costa Rica and have for quite a long time."

"She's been more than just your lawyer, it appears."

"Oh, yes. Much more."

I considered asking for another vodka and tonic.

"She's quite a woman," he said. "In fact, one day she'll succeed me as CEO of Global Solutions."

The breeze filtered through the curtains, cooling the sweat gathering on my forehead.

What kind of people are they?

Is there no limit to their deceit?

"If Mrs. Fontaine disapproves of cigar smoking in the house," I said, "how will she take to your paramour being GSI's next CEO?"

He could barely speak through his own laughter.

"Paramour, Bill? My dear boy," he said. "Charlotte is my daughter."

I tried to squeeze out a response, but no words came.

"My daughter, Bill. Amanda's big sister."

Chapter Thirty-Eight

Reconciliation

Monday morning at seven o'clock, I was back in the office. Dolly had anticipated my return and several weeks of mail lay on my desk. The flashing light on the telephone warned that countless messages awaited. It must have been full, because a pile of hand-written messages sat on my keyboard, too. It was an annoying habit of Dolly's, placing them so I couldn't use the computer without handling the slips of paper. The only thing I disliked more was how she'd put documents on my chair instead of my in-box.

I sat in that chair, the same one I'd used for a dozen years, staring at the notes and files of untold cases and tried to put aside the emptiness I still felt over Charlotte.

It hadn't taken long for me to reluctantly, and then soon quite willingly, allow myself to fall for her. I knew that the deeper I let my feelings for her take hold, the more vulnerable I would become. When the time finally arrived to acknowledge it, I gladly embraced the risk of pain and loss. *It would never happen*, I told myself. And that was the real beauty of being in love with her. I would hand over my heart, trusting and believing that she would never break it. She had done the same for me, I'd thought.

And yet.

I had a meeting with Mac and Casey in a couple of hours. Gene offered to sit in with me, but I needed to do it alone. The boss insisted on reviewing how the Hausner case was prosecuted, starting with the preliminary hearing, the run-up to trial, and the last-minute hand-off. I expected Mac to demand names, dates, witnesses contacted and when, evidence prepared, and a full explanation for how we failed to have all the trial exhibits lined up and the appearance of a major witness secured. I also expected to flay Butler alive—personally.

I'd deal with Charlotte later.

Butler's cowardice had put me in harm's way and regardless of the exoneration I'd received, thanks to Forensics and the reluctant withdrawal of charges by the State Bar Disciplinary Board, I held him responsible. I'd rescued his career once before, and probably saved his marriage. He repaid the favor by shoving me into the path of an oncoming locomotive. I'd been fooled by his appeal to my sense of duty and, I suppose, my ego.

I'll try any case.

Right.

At about seven-thirty, Butler appeared at my door.

"Bill? Can I come in for a minute?"

"I've got a few."

I nodded toward a chair but didn't get up or offer my hand. This was a day for closure, for tying up my own loose ends. He shut the door and took a seat in front of my desk.

"Should I start packing?" he said.

He laughed nervously and I offered no encouragement.

"Up to Mac," I said.

He stammered, leaning his face into a hand.

"I got sandbagged, Bill. After the prelim, Shea seemed so overwhelmed by the victim's testimony. He hinted about asking for a plea agreement down the line. You know, something like pleading to one count, dropping the other. He told me he had to at least see the trial evidence so he could tell Hausner how hopeless his case was. You can see why I thought they were going to plead out. So, I showed him the file, everything. He knew about the 7-Eleven clerk, what that guy had found, and even Amanda's hospital records."

He stared at the floor. "That included her BAC, of course."

As I'd suspected.

"I was such an idiot. You can't imagine . . . I can't . . . Bill, when I saw it was set for a jury, I just froze."

I didn't say a word.

"It had nothing to do with you, I swear. I just . . . well, I just had to get out of that trial." His voice began to break.

"Shea would have gotten most of the evidence with a standard discovery motion, so I figured it was no big deal. He even asked me if it was okay to speak to Detective Dixon, and I let him."

Unbelievable.

I saw exactly how the Titmouse had seduced him.

"Anyway, a few weeks later, I saw the trial calendar in Patty's office, and it was set for a three-day jury trial. I realized I'd been had. When it turned out I had a schedule conflict, I knew that was my way out. Since you'd had the case originally, it was easy to hand it back."

He tried to look at me, but his eyes just couldn't do it.

"I had no idea, Bill. I just had no idea that it could get you in so much trouble."

As he sat in my office, I couldn't decide whether I despised Butler or pitied him.

Maybe both.

He put his face in his hands, the same way he'd done years before when he pleaded for me to talk Mac out of firing him.

"You gotta believe me, Bill. I just couldn't gear up for that case after turning over the evidence without a demand for Hausner's alibi. He played me. That schedule conflict gave me a way out. I kept the check kiter and gave you Hausner."

It made sense, not that it mattered to me. At least I knew why he'd been asleep at the wheel and done nothing on the case after sending it to the grand jury.

"We'll talk again at nine," I said.

Butler nodded and slipped out of the room.

I sifted through the mail and phone messages. Buried deep in the pile, I saw it. Ronald Whitacre, the 7-Eleven clerk, with a Delaware phone number. I immediately called.

"Whitacre."

"Ronald Whitacre? This is Bill Duncan. Jefferson County Commonwealth's Attorney's office. You called me a couple of weeks ago."

"Yeah! Right! I need to know when that Hausner trial is."

"Mr. Whitacre, I've got a couple of questions. I thought you were in Georgia."

"I was. Then Alabama, and now Dover, Delaware. Just the Air Force's way of screwing with me. I had some training exercises. Now, I'm settled in and want to make sure I get back to testify. Your receptionist told me the case was yours."

"Did you ever speak with Mr. Butler of this office?"

"Butler? No. Just Detective Dixon. He said I might have to come to court, but he'd get back to me if it ever went to trial."

"It did. You were subpoenaed but it seems the papers weren't served before you left."

"Really? Crap. What happened?"

A simple question but with a such long and complicated answer.

"Justice was served. Case closed."

"Wow. That's great. Detective Dixon said the girl was hurt pretty bad. Who was Hausner?"

"Just a local guy. But he's out of commission now."

"How much time did he get?"

"All of it."

"Life?"

"In a way, yeah. He's off the street for good."

"Great. So, you don't need me? I don't have to come back to Virginia?"

"You're welcome to visit, but no, you don't have to come back for this case. Thanks for your cooperation. If people like you don't step up, we can't do our jobs. Good luck in the Air Force, Mr. Whitacre. Thank you for your service to the nation."

So, he really did exist, and Dixon's half-assed case prep had let him slip away. If April had been able to keep the file, she would have hand-carried him to the witness stand, all the way from Alabama or Delaware or wherever he was. His testimony might have been more important than that godforsaken bolt.

As nine o'clock approached, I gathered the few notes I needed to meet with Mac. I cared little for a re-hash of the case of Jason Hausner, but Casey Butler's negligence, if not duplicity, would be the subject of my concise and direct demand for his termination.

Dolly buzzed me.

"There's a cop on the phone, wants to talk to you. She's been calling for a couple of days, but your voice mail is full."

"Detective Winston?"

"No."

"Then it can wait. Take a message. I've got a meeting with Mac in a few moments."

Reuben Lewis met me in the hallway before I could get out the door of my office. His shirt was rumpled and partially untucked, and one shoelace was untied. He grinned like he'd just won a prize. He had a coffee in his hand.

"Hey, Bill! Tony said today's your first day back. I brung you coffee, just the way you like it."

"A little honey, one cream?"

"Yep. I don' forget nothin'."

"Thanks, Reuben. It's good to be back. Are you staying away from Metro cops?"

His face clouded.

"Oh, yeah. I ain't never goin' on no Metro no more, least not in Awlin'ton."

I laughed.

"Good. That's good, Reuben. I don't think I'd have the same luck the next time."

"You need to get a dog, Bill," he said, shifting to his favorite subject. "I could come over and play with him sometimes."

I pictured him as a boy, with the pet of his youth, before he learned life's lessons of disappointment and betrayal.

How long ago has that been? How many people have hurt him over those years?

"Maybe after I return all these phone calls, Reuben."

He nodded and smiled.

"I gotta go. Tony has a new dishwashin' machine and I gotta learn it."

"Don't repair it, Reuben."

He tilted his head and looked puzzled.

"Why would I do that?"

"Never mind."

I watched him depart, measuring his innocence against the steady onslaught of brutality and sorrow this building held. He and I spent most of our waking hours under this same roof, and although our perceptions of what we saw each day were quite different, neither of us were immune from its harshness.

How different our lives have been. But lately, perhaps, maybe not that much after all.

I took the coffee and stopped at Dolly's desk before heading to Mac's office.

"Here's the message from that woman cop," she said.

As she handed me the note, my heart skipped a beat.

"Dolly, that's not a cop. That's her name."

"Well, *sor-ry*. Blame her parents, not me . . . oh, well."

"No, not 'oh, well,'" I said.

I folded the note and shoved it into my pocket.

"There's no call back number."

"I know. She didn't leave one and the screen said 'unavailable.'"

I sighed and walked down the hall to Mac's office.

Why now?

I shook my head. The watchword in our profession is "prepare," but the past several weeks had proved—to me, at least—that I might reduce the chances of being struck by lightning, but if there's a bolt out there with my name on it I may as well just stand still, put a target on my chest and wait for it.

Casey sat meekly in one of the two chairs in front of the desk.

"Come in, Bill. Shut the door," Mac said, waving me inside.

I remained standing and leaned against the bookshelves. I didn't want to sit or look at Casey. He kept glancing over at me, seeking some sign, some semblance of mercy. I said nothing and waited for Mac to speak. He leaned back, arms folded, staring at us.

"Gentlemen, you know the drill," he said. "I've got no interest in excuses, just explanations. What in the hell happened?"

Casey hesitated. I just sipped the coffee and looked down at the cup. He was adrift, trying to navigate between the expected excoriation he'd earned and the professional shame that was certain to come from being fired. Neither seemed avoidable. He nervously bounced his foot against the floor and clenched his hands. He'd been confronted by a challenge and wilted. I pictured him trying to explain all of this to his wife later that day.

"Mr. McGuire," he said. "It was Bill's case, and I covered the prelim. Then . . ."

"Boss," I said, "I don't mean to interrupt, but it's like this."

Casey tensed, turning in his chair to look at me. I had his job, career, and I suppose at least metaphorically, his throat, right in my hands. I had endured weeks of sleepless nights and torment, fearing the worst, and all of it had culminated in public scrutiny, embarrassment, and bitterness.

This is the day it will all end.

I was determined to make this the day when I would bury this episode and reclaim my life. I would balance the scales and take back what was mine.

I put my coffee on the shelf and moved behind Casey.

"Boss, what the Hausner case did was give me a chance to see how some things around here have shaped up," I said.

I looked at him, then at Casey, who seemed to fold into his chair, crumpling like a deflated balloon and bracing for the beating he deserved. His fists, pressing into his knees, were white and shaking.

"Going forward, I recommend that Casey handle financial crimes only. Remember, he took down that check kiter and those are hard cases, with nothing but circumstantial evidence. The Fraud squad needs someone with a steady hand on those things, not a new face every time one comes in the door."

Mac's eyes narrowed and his head tilted back. I'd seen that skeptical look a hundred times, usually at the beginning of a lengthy cross-examination.

"Casey's good with those guys, good with numbers. But you can't work those cases and do sex crimes, too," I said. "The witness prep time with them is just too much and there aren't enough hours in the day to do both."

Mac just looked at me, at Casey, and then back at me.

"That's it?" he said.

"That's it."

He wasn't fooled, but he was ready to get past Hausner, and if I was satisfied, he'd be content, at least for now. We'd talk again one day, over vodka and tonics, the way he and I always did after one of us delivered a big jury verdict.

"Fine," he said. "Are you ready to get going? Patty's screaming at me about the cases she has lined up. No surprise, we've got schedule conflicts and need another hand on some juries."

"I'm back. I'll go see her this afternoon. I've got a pile of stuff on my desk that I'd better check out first before anything in there catches fire."

"Good. Gentlemen, let's get after it. Bill, stay a minute."

Casey was finally breathing.

"Butler, close the door," Mac said, "on your way out."

Casey glanced at us both and then scurried away before Mac changed his mind.

He sighed and shook his head as Butler left.

"How did 'Casey' come out of 'Theodore,' anyway?" he said.

"Short for 'Casanova,'" I said.

I retrieved my coffee from the shelf as Mac lowered his face into his hands.

"And I've been calling him that all this time," he said. "You guys will be the death of me."

I shrugged, tilting a hand back and forth.

"Got to watch that blood pressure, Boss."

He didn't smile.

"You know you could have lost that case," he said, looking up and pointing at me. "You got your Irish up. Believe me, I know how that goes. But when Shea got under your skin and Wally denied your motion to continue, you just put your head down and charged ahead. That missing witness and the dumpster evidence would have clinched a conviction, but you risked an acquittal."

He had me, but I just smiled back.

"I had it covered all the way, Boss. It was never in doubt."

He glared, looking over his half-lenses.

"Going in that morning, you figured Shea to put on an alibi, right?"

I could see where this was headed.

"Yes."

I sighed.

"And you had no idea what it was, right?"

I didn't need to answer.

"You played those photographs well, blowing a fastball past Shea early on, but what would you have done if he'd been more careful and spotted that bolt right off? Or worse, what if Butler had showed it to him? You had no reason to believe he hadn't, at that point, did you?"

I absorbed the lecture in silence.

"He'd have dragged in some half-assed expert on the second day to testify that the bolt came from a Ford or a Chevy. You'd never have covered it. Hell, one of the Simonson brothers would have eaten your lunch on that one. They don't miss anything. Not as flashy as the Titmouse, but nothing gets past them."

"Yeah, but you know those guys. They'd have stretched the trial out five days at least. By then, Wally would have been flogging them instead of me."

Again, the glare.

"But who would have won?" he said.

We just looked at each other until I turned to the window and the courtyard below, where Jason Hausner held his first press conference just a few weeks ago.

"Anyway," he said, waving off the scolding, "you're a lawyer, not a bonehead prize fighter. You should have known better."

"Mac, come on." I leaned toward him, risking a smile. "Aren't you the one always talking about the rules of the Marquess of Queensberry?"

He slammed his palm on the desk.

"That's right, goddammit! And I've told you a thousand times, they don't play by those rules!"

He was exasperated again, his face turning a familiar red, the veins in his neck bulging. "But never mind about that. Keep your head in the game. You're good, very good, but being undisciplined isn't smart."

He was right.

"Lesson learned. Thanks, Boss."

He got up and walked around to the front of his desk and leaned against it, facing me.

"There's one more thing."

His tone changed and voice lowered.

"I've been 'approached,' as the expression goes. The state attorney general is going to run for governor next year. It seems that the talent pool is sufficiently shallow so the party wants me to run for the open AG position."

He looked at me.

"You can see where I'm going with this."

I couldn't. He grinned.

"You, you bull-headed Mick. I want you to run for my office."

I fumbled and nearly dropped my coffee.

"Mac, what? I'm . . ."

"I'll do for you what Butch did for me twenty years ago. Resign, so I can campaign freely, and the Circuit Court judges will appoint a temporary successor, an acting Commonwealth's Attorney. I'll recommend you, and next fall you can run for election as an incumbent. We'll be on the same ticket, if you can imagine that."

I stared at him.

"If that's a poker face," he said, "don't play cards anytime soon. You'll lose your shirt."

I drifted behind his desk and sat in his chair. It might have been there for all of those twenty years, and it creaked with age.

"First," I said, "I think I'll order some new furniture."

"Not so fast. You need to get a few decent trials under your belt, get past this Hausner business, and then campaign as a white knight next year. I've got Patty lining up some trials with the top detectives for you. They'll get good media coverage, and people will recognize your name as the guy that's always winning big cases."

He spread his arms.

"How hard can it be?"

We both laughed, and perhaps too fast and too hard from relief.

I sat there, slowly shaking my head. It had been only a few days since I'd stood in this same office, expecting to be indicted. Instead, I walked out that morning, exonerated and free.

"By the way, nice hit on that Hausner jury. Twenty-five years without photos of the victim in evidence, and you made Wally work for three whole days."

Mac laughed again.

"That might have been the toughest part of the entire trial. Now, get out of here and go see Patty."

Casey was waiting for me in the hallway outside the door of his office.

"I didn't think that was the way you were heading, Bill," he said.

I stopped and looked at him.

"Life is full of surprises, Casey."

He looked as if he hadn't slept in days, anticipating this morning's meeting.

"Sometimes, we surprise even ourselves."

He stared back at me, puzzled. He began to speak but stopped himself. Perhaps he'd understand one day, when he wasn't preoccupied with putting out his own fires. At this point, all he could appreciate was that he'd been spared once again.

Did he see me as weak? Foolish? Confused?

It didn't matter. After the past few months, all I knew was that I had to live in my own skin. The general was right. I'd have found no solace in Casey's destruction.

"Okay. Well, Bill, thanks anyway."

He retreated into his office. Turning back in the doorway, he spoke again.

"I really am sorry, Bill. Who in the world would have seen all this coming?"

I shook my head.

"It damn sure wasn't me."

I walked past the offices, Dolly's desk and across the lobby, then down the stairs to the cafeteria. I cut behind the counters and into the kitchen. Tony was trying to explain to Reuben how to work the new dishwasher. Reuben held a screwdriver and looked like he'd been given a Christmas present. It appeared that parts of the machine lay on the floor.

"Tony," I said. "Can I speak with my client for a moment?"

"Sure. He ain't listen to me no way no how."

I took Reuben aside.

"Have you ever been fishing, Reuben?"

His eyes opened wide and he jumped.

"Really? You mean, me an' you, Bill?"

"Saturday, if you're not too busy. I'll pick you up at eight o'clock, okay?"

"Oh, man, Bill. This'll be fun. Thanks, Bill. Oh, man!"

I put my hand on his shoulder.

"It will be a good time for both of us."

I climbed back up the stairs. There were calls to return and cases to try. But first, I went to my own office, closed the door and pulled out the telephone message Dolly had given me and carefully unfolded it. I resisted looking at it for a moment.

The old man is right.

Who can ever understand the heart?

I placed it in the center of a clear space on my desk, smoothed it out and read the words, first to myself, and then out loud.

I'm so happy you're alright.

—Marshall

Chapter Thirty-Nine

Final Installment

Memorandum

To: Eugene Cresswell

From: William Duncan

Re: Pending Charges; Attorney-Client Privileged Communication

Final Submission

Nice work, but I figured out that NSA nonsense. I was somewhat irritated at you for a few days, once I figured out how you'd played me, but I understand why you kept me in the dark.

"Don't get indicted," you said.

Good advice. I'll keep it in mind.

As Mac likes to say, "How hard can it be?"

There was a time when I had sunk into the darkness of despair. Thanks at least in part to your able assistance, I'm seeing a light of hope.

I learned that Charlotte was briefly married several years ago but kept her ex's name, so I didn't catch the connection with the Fontaine family. I guess you can see why she never took me home to meet her parents. She got back from Costa Rica after a few weeks and finally called, but I haven't spoken with her. It still hurts, and I'm unsure of it all. I have a lingering ache for what we had together. But what was real? Any of it? Like so much of my recent life, I just don't know where the truth lies, and that's something of a hazard in our business.

As for Wally, and how he knew that the 7-Eleven clerk was the missing witness, I figure it was Tommy Shea who told him when he went into chambers the morning after the Hausner verdict to get his client sprung on that motion to dismiss. That would explain the drunken tirade at your country club. No telling what else the little Titmouse said that day.

Mac told me he spoke to you about his proposition. It is intriguing, to say the very least, and an easy call. I'll love the job, and I'd keep the same simple rule that he tells all the new assistants on their first day. "Do the right thing, and don't embarrass the office."

So far, I'm feeling few residual bruises from the *Hausner* case, especially after Rita Mohr's story in *The Washington Post*. She cleaned me up quite well, and the media have forgotten how they branded me a cheating case fixer. In an interesting twist, they're now going after the feds for letting a terrorist cell operate right here in the shadow of the nation's capital.

Heads will roll. I wonder if the general has any concerns about where that story might lead. What do you think, is now a good time for that press conference?

I'm back in the saddle, Gene. This is where I belong. When I stand before a jury, introduce myself, begin an opening statement and point toward the defendant, I am at ease. I am home. That comfortable familiarity is back, like putting on a favorite pair of old gloves for the first time since last winter.

Each day, I know I am on the right side.

But whether it's just what I do or what I am, you'll have to ask me another time.

Then again, maybe I'll say the hell with it all and go fishing.

Maybe I'll just get a dog.

Chapter Forty

As Time Goes By

The mountains were blanketed with clusters of red and yellow, as autumn tightened its grasp on the valley and the river that divides it. Soon, the colors would fade into the grays of winter, and the sound of water coursing over the rocks that have formed the path of the Shenandoah for thousands of years would be the only sign of life until spring.

On this cool morning, the sun shone through the trees bordering the riverbank. Reuben held a fishing rod for the first time. My father equipped him with tackle we hoped would allow a smallmouth bass to catch itself. He stood wearing rubber boots, knee deep in the water, astride a rock shelf upstream from a well-known and favorite spot, where a crevice ran deep enough for fish to gather and feast on smaller prey tumbling through the riffles.

The red and white cork bobbed in the slow current, a tantalizing plastic worm dangling beneath it, a hook buried in its center.

"Just keep an eye on that bobber, Reuben," my father said. "If you can't see the red part, it means a fish is nibbling. Give it a good tug and hook him."

I watched Reuben's intense focus without readying my own rod, savoring the view, the warmth of the sun on my back, and the crisp coffee I'd poured at Claude Shiflett's store earlier that morning.

"Are you fishin' or not?" said my father.

"In a minute, I mean, what's the point of a day off if I've got to hurry?"

"Amateurs."

He grunted.

"Speaking of days off, when are you going back to work?"

I sipped the coffee.

"Last Monday. I had a trial on Wednesday. Just a little two-day jury."

"Dare I ask who the judge was?"

I chuckled.

"Wally assigns the cases and I'm pretty sure he doesn't want to see me for a while."

He threaded a line through his rod.

"Any more thoughts about that phone call from Marshall?"

He'd known Marshall well, and she'd spent many an evening seated next to him in our home, talking about so many things—music, history, and even sports. Still, the sound of her name struck me like cold water poured into my veins.

"That message from her just added confusion to my life," I said, "and I've had enough of that to last me well into the next one. If she calls again, I don't know what I'll do or say."

I finished the coffee.

"But as you know, that's never stopped me in the past."

"Fair enough," he said. "Fair enough. And what about you and Casey Butler? You on speaking terms, yet?"

"Yeah, but there will be a chill at that end of the hall for a while," I said. "He's embarrassed and I'm not much for fake small talk. It will take time."

"But you're past it? All that anger and bile?"

I nodded.

"Life's too short."

He rummaged in his tackle box, seeking the right lure.

We both watched Reuben, waiting intently for some action.

"And Charlotte?" Dad said. "Have you spoken with her?"

I looked out at the river. The sound of its rolling permanence never changed. It was the same when she and I were happy together, or so I'd thought. No matter what turns life may take, the delight of warm affection or the darkness of a night's loneliness, the river courses onward.

"No," I said. "I don't see that happening, at least not anytime soon."

His hands dropped, lowering the rod, and he turned toward me.

"You forgave Butler, but you can't even talk to her? He led you into a briar patch without even a warning. She was trying to make sure that the man who damn near killed her baby sister got what was coming to him. And you can't get past that? I know you're angry about how she did it, but what about the way you felt toward her? Didn't you mean it? Was that all made up?"

"It's not that simple," I said.

"It's never simple when it involves a woman," he snorted. "But what's in your heart? What did you just say? 'Life's too short.'"

I tossed the empty cup into the back of his truck.

"I'll think about it," I said.

"Well, you'd better think fast."

A smile wrinkled across his face. "I'm going to check on Reuben."

The sound of tires on gravel echoed across the field. I turned and watched as a car slowly drove down the hill on the far side of the meadow, approached the river and turned toward us.

"What did you do?" I shouted at him, by then in a sudden whirlwind of emotion.

He waved me off as he waded into the shallow water.

"I got to check on Reuben."

The blue BMW glided to a stop behind the truck. She got out of the car and stood next to it, leaning back against the door, wearing white slacks and a black sweater. Around her neck was a pendant I'd given her. She took off her sunglasses and looked at me, arms folded. I winced at the thought of what conversation must have passed between Charlotte and my father, the two people to whom I'd spoken of everything in the world that mattered most to me.

"I won't even ask how you knew where I was or how to get here," I said. "You're always a step ahead of me, even now."

She smiled and shrugged.

"It's a good day for a drive in the country."

I stuck both hands into my pockets.

"You're not dressed for wading the river," I said, nodding at her shoes.

"I was hoping to catch something better than fish."

I tried to keep my memories of her embrace at bay, of nuzzling my face in her hair, feeling her warmth.

"We'll be here a while. I owe Reuben the whole day."

"I was hoping we might have dinner tomorrow evening."

Again, I resisted the thought of her cooking in my kitchen, the sound of music in our ears and the taste of wine on our lips.

"I don't have much of anything at my place," I said.

She unfolded her arms and dropped her hands.

"I had something different in mind," she said, taking a step toward me. "I'd like to bring you home to meet my family."

I looked over at my father, standing in the river next to Reuben. He offered a brief nod.

It's never simple.

I turned back to Charlotte and opened my arms.

About the Author

Stephen H. Moriarty was born and raised in Virginia, graduating from the University of Virginia and the University of Richmond Law School.

Between college and law school he worked for the Federal Bureau of Investigation, supporting a counter-intelligence squad in the Washington Field Office.

He began the practice of law as a prosecutor in the office of the Fairfax County Commonwealth's Attorney, where he tried all manner of misdemeanors and felonies, providing the inspiration for *Restitution* and some of its characters. He has since represented clients in matters ranging from property rights to fraud and conspiracy.

He has written several short stories that have been published in an annual anthology. He lives in Virginia with his family and spent many hours fishing with his father on the Shenandoah River.

Upcoming New Release

RECKONING AT PARADISE LAKE
A BILL DUNCAN MYSTERY
BOOK 2
BY
STEPHEN H. MORIARTY

Bill Duncan, now the elected Commonwealth's Attorney for Jefferson County, is summoned to a neighboring jurisdiction to investigate and prosecute the attempted murder of a former colleague. The quaint, small-town atmosphere masks a conspiracy of greed, corruption and violence, leading Duncan to question the motives within the local law enforcement and his ability to uncover the truth and bring the guilty to justice.

Duncan's courtroom skills alone are not enough to ferret out the culprits and avoid being the next victim…

For more information
visit: www.SpeakingVolumes.us

 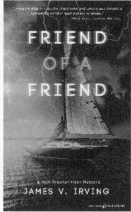 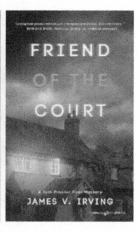

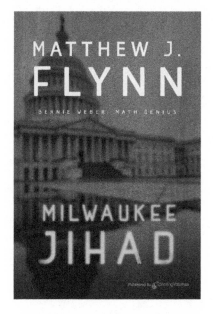